She faked a sm...

She didn't need or w...
this man over again...
sign her contract so she could get out of Brookhollow. "I'll have an offer by Wednesday, but we should go over the preliminary paperwork as soon as possible." She scanned the store for a place to lay out her documents. "The major chain store interested in purchasing–"

Luke turned off the lights and unplugged the strand of multicolored Christmas lights draped across the window.

"Do…you prefer we do this in the dark?" she asked sarcastically.

He put his coat on and wrapped a scarf around his neck. "I have dinner plans."

The familiar scent of his musky cologne made her pulse race. "Tomorrow, then." She stepped out into the frigid air. "I'll come by in the morning." She pulled out a silver monogrammed cardholder. Her hand shook as she handed one of her cards to Luke.

"Your card?"

"It has my cell number on it." Her teeth chattered.

"Victoria, this is Brookhollow." He laughed. "I could stand in the center and call to you, and wherever you are, you'll hear me."

Dear Reader,

Everyone remembers their first love. Despite time, distance and future loves—that first experience of a spark or a connection seems to hold a special place in our hearts even as the memories fade. In this first book of my Brookhollow series, I wanted to write about what happens when that first love is so strong that it can never be replaced and how sometimes all it needs is a second chance.

My favorite romance stories have always been holiday-themed, as I feel that Christmas is the ultimate time to celebrate love and family and heart and home—the essence of this new Heartwarming series. I hope you enjoy losing yourself in this beautiful town as much as I enjoyed creating it.

Warmest wishes to you and your family this holiday season,

Jennifer

Jennifer Snow

The Trouble with Mistletoe

First published in Great Britain 2013
by Mills & Boon, an imprint of Harlequin (UK) Limited,
Eton House, 18-24 Paradise Road, Richmond, Surrey TW9 1SR

© Jennifer Snow 2013

ISBN: 978 0 263 91128 2

33-1213

Harlequin (UK) policy is to use papers that are natural, renewable and recyclable products and made from wood grown in sustainable forests. The logging and manufacturing processes conform to the legal environmental regulations of the country of origin.

Printed and bound in Spain
by Blackprint CPI, Barcelona

JENNIFER SNOW
Jennifer Snow has been writing fairy tales with happy endings from a very young age, always with one goal in mind—to become a part of the Harlequin/Mills & Boon® family. Living in Edmonton, Alberta, with her husband and three-year-old son, she is dedicated to creating lasting, heartfelt romances that readers can share with those they love.

www.JenniferSnowBooks.com

Acknowledgments

Thank you to my family—my beautiful creative mom, hardworking father, encouraging brother, amazing son and supportive husband for everything. I wouldn't be living my dream if it weren't for each of you. Also, thank you a million times to my agent, Stephany Evans, for taking a chance on this story and my talented editor, Victoria Curran, for offering me a home here at the Heartwarming series.

CHAPTER ONE

"PLEASE DON'T HIT, please." Victoria Mason closed her eyes as her tiny rental car slid into the parking space on Main Street. Parallel parking was not a skill she possessed and yet she was relieved to see she'd cleared the other cars. She wrapped her scarf around her neck and reapplied her lipstick. The pink, shimmery gloss did the trick of adding a touch of color to her pale complexion. The two-hour drive on the busy interstate from New York City to Brookhollow, New Jersey, had tested her already frazzled nerves. She prayed the unpleasant road trip, with its bumper-to-bumper traffic and icy road conditions, wasn't a sign of things to come as she stepped out into the cold. The early-December wind whipped through her cashmere winter coat and her breath came in puffs of white clouds as she locked the car. An unnecessary gesture in her small hometown. This wasn't New York. Anyone here for more than two minutes could see Brookhollow at rush hour was the opposite of Manhattan's fast pace and crazy traffic.

The Christmas season was in full swing and all the small mom-and-pop shops lining both sides of the quiet street boasted holiday displays in their storefront windows. Kitty-corner from where she stood, Pearl's Petals showcased a frosty winter wonderland with pale pink and white poinsettias lining the base of the window. The crystal snowflakes hanging from the ceiling glistened against the white scrim backdrop. Next door, the town's secondhand bookstore, Dog-Eared Books, featured a selection of holiday cookbooks and children's stories positioned under a Christmas tree decorated with crayons and book-marks.

From here, she could also see Town Center Square in the distance. The twenty-foot Christmas tree had been put up the day before, as was the tradition for the first weekend in December. On the corner the town's welcome sign was bordered with holly and twinkling white lights. Welcome to Historic Brookhollow, Population 10,810. According to her mother, that number had decreased in recent years. Victoria had certainly been eager to remove herself from the population count. Now here she was, for the first time in three years. Freezing her butt off.

Victoria shivered as she walked the short distance to Legend's Sporting Goods. The quicker she started the acquisition process, the better. Her previous acquisitions had closed without the slightest hiccup, but she suspected this would be different. Why hadn't she declined this one? Being back in her hometown was tough enough. Having to deal with this particular store owner would be torture.

Her gaze fell to the acquisition papers in her hand. Luke Dawson. She hadn't seen or spoken to her ex-fiancé in twelve years. A different agent, a stranger in Brookhollow, may have had an easier time. Leaving town for a career in New York, abandoning the star quarterback and homecoming king two weeks before their wedding, hadn't exactly put her on Brookhollow's favorite people list. She bit her lip. Could she really be successful in a place she'd always considered a roadblock to her ambition?

She had to focus on what mattered: securing this purchase and getting out of Brook-hollow before Christmas. Pausing in front of the store, she checked her reflection in the window, running a hand over her blond, shoulder-length hair. She forced several, slow deep breaths. It had been twelve years, how bad could this reunion be? She reached for the door handle.

"The store is closed for renovations," a deep voice said to her right, several feet above her.

"Oh, well, I have a meeting with—" Victoria turned and took in the man on the ladder she'd walked right past without seeing "—Luke?" She placed a hand over her eyes to shield them from the low, setting sun glaring off the roof of Ginger Snaps, the bakery next door. She could barely make out his face in the blinding light, but the voice was unmistakable. "How long have you just been watching me from up there?"

"Long enough to enjoy that painful parking job." He turned back to his work, placing a string of lights along the roof.

She glanced toward the rental car, parked on a slight angle in the space that now looked much larger than it had when she was trying to park in it. Squaring her shoulders, she moved closer. "Renovations? Didn't you receive the letter from Clarke and Johnston Acquisitions earlier this week?"

"The one claiming you'd be here at noon today?" Luke asked.

Victoria struggled to maintain her composure. This wasn't exactly how she'd pictured this meeting. In truth, she'd had no idea what to expect, but she hated that she'd given him the upper hand by being late. "Traffic was a lot slower than I'd predicted." And she'd left the city three hours later then planned. "Anyway, the letter also stated that my firm will be placing an offer on Legend's within the week."

"I'm not interested in selling the store." The sound of the nail gun reverberating off the awning made her wince.

"Either way, we should still discuss my client's interest in obtaining it."

He ignored her as he continued to work. An older couple she didn't recognize stepped out of the bakery and shot her suspicious looks as they passed.

Victoria shivered as big, wet snowflakes began to fall from the darkening sky. "Do you think we could go inside?" She danced from one foot to the other, her feet chilled in her two-inch leather boots. "I'm kind of in a hurry."

"Well, maybe you should have gotten here earlier." He paused to look at her with a raised eyebrow.

"Luke," she said, tilting her head to the side.

He waved her away. "Go on inside, the door's open. I'll be right with you."

"Fine." She pushed open the door. A small bell chimed as she entered Legend's and looked around. Nothing had changed inside and an unwelcome sense of familiarity washed over her.

The same wooden shelves lined the wall behind the counter, displaying rows of trophies, marking the town's many achievements in baseball, football and soccer. The New York Giant's number-eighteen football jersey that belonged to Mr. Jameson, the previous store owner, still hung on the wall above. The front window was decorated the same way it had been year after year, with red-and-white lights bordering a cardboard cutout of a Santa sleigh driven by the Brookhollow High Cougars mascot and pulled by the football players. Pictures of the various high school teams framed the storefront.

She scanned the photos, and one in the corner—of the 1996 junior boys soccer victory—caught her eye. In the top-row center stood Luke, grinning from ear to ear in his Crimson Cleats uniform, division trophy held high above his head. A knot formed in her stomach as she wondered if the Dawsons had heard of her visit and if she'd run into his family. Despite how close the two families had been in the past, his mother and sisters had been quite clear about how they felt about Victoria ever since the day she left town. Ever since she'd said goodbye to Luke and returned her engagement ring.

She turned away from the photos and moved farther into the store, stepping over boxes of sporting goods. Everything from hockey sticks to baseball gloves littered the floor. Judging by the scattered goods, Luke had run out of room to store his stock. That didn't bode well for the acquisition. More stock and upgrades meant she'd need more money to buy out the store.

Toward the back she paused in front of Mr.

Jameson's personal display of sports memorabilia, an extensive and impressive array of autographed footballs and jerseys. He'd also collected rare baseball trading cards, secured behind glass frames. Victoria ran a finger along the edge of the shelf and a puff of dust rose in the air. She shook her head. These items were worth a lot and they'd meant something to Mr. Jameson. If he knew how Luke was caring for them, he'd be rolling over in his grave.

She moved away from the collection and continued toward the stockroom, giving the swinging door a push.

"Hey."

At the sound of a voice above her head Victoria started and her hand flew to her chest. A boy stood precariously on the top rung of a tall ladder, balancing a large box over his head. "I'm just waiting for…Luke." She watched, horrified, as the kid scurried down.

"He said he'll be back in about ten minutes. Mrs. Norris asked him to hang Christmas lights in her store window." He moved the ladder to the corner of the stockroom.

"Yeah, I saw him stringing lights on the roof."

The boy smiled at that, and she immediately got the joke. Ginger Norris was known for her add-on projects. Left alone, the older woman could find things for Luke to do all evening.

As he picked up a box, Victoria held the door for him and he carried it past her into the store. He set his load down in an aisle and turned to her. "You're Victoria Mason, aren't you?"

She hesitated as she looked at the young man. His face wasn't familiar, but then again he would have been a baby or not yet born, when she'd left Brookhollow. She nodded.

"I heard you were coming to town. Are you home for Christmas?" He opened a box and began stocking a shelf with baseball mitts. Stopping to examine one, he shoved his hand in it, punching the leather a few times with his other hand.

Great, even this kid had heard the rumors. Asking her mother to keep a secret was futile, and gossip in this place spread faster than wildfire. She wondered what people were saying about her. After all this time, she hated that she still cared about the opinions of her former neighbors.

She shook her head. "No, I'm only here for a few days." Her holiday plans never included Brookhollow. Every year she insisted her parents visit her in New York over the Thanksgiving weekend instead. She and her mother shopped, and her father took in a sporting event. Thanksgiving dinner was usually Chinese takeout while watching the replay of the Macy's parade. Regrettably, that was their only real time together each year as her busy travel schedule and last-minute acquisition trips made taking planned holiday time nearly impossible. Christmas was spent on the ski slopes in Vermont with her New York friends, where she could ski and relax on Christmas Day in front of the lodge fireplace, where they always did their Secret Santa gift exchange. It was the only real vacation she took each year.

She made a mental note to confirm her room reservation and spa booking at the resort. She'd been putting it off, unsure if her workload would allow her to take a full week or just a couple of days. She certainly needed it. Sixteen successful acquisitions this year had exhausted her.

The bell above the door chimed as Luke

entered. A snowdrift followed him in and he stomped his boots on the mat near the door. A broad grin spread across his older but still handsome face. The radiance reflecting in his ice-blue eyes drew her in and, for a moment, she forgot why she was here. Her breath caught at the familiar sight that used to make her pulse race. Like it did now.

He moved past her to take a heavy box from the boy. "You can head out now, Steve. The snow is falling hard, and I told your mom I'd send you home before it gets dark."

"Are you sure, Uncle Luke? There's still a lot of boxes out there and the grand reopening is—"

"I'm sure." Luke cut him off with a quick glance in Victoria's direction. "Here's the money for today and I'll see you tomorrow." He handed the boy several bills and his coat and gave him a friendly push out the door. "Call or text me when you get home."

"Okay." The boy nodded, tugging his hat over his head.

Luke pointed a finger. "Don't forget, like last time."

"I won't." Steve zipped his coat as he closed the door behind him. He jogged down the street, past the window, his head bent against the blowing snow.

She did the math. Alisha Dawson, Luke's older sister, had been six months pregnant when Victoria had left town.

Luke coughed.

She turned to face him. "Grand reopening?"

He nodded. "That's right. Next weekend, just in time for the last-minute shoppers," he said, carrying several empty boxes to the back room.

Victoria collided with the swinging door as she followed him. She bit the inside of her cheek. Reopening with more stock for the Christmas season could generate significant profit for the small store. That would complicate a sale and drive the buyout price higher. "Well, hopefully, you won't need to reopen. Play Hard Sports usually pays more than market value for the stores they purchase." It made dealing with their acquisitions a pleasure.

She moved out of Luke's way as he pushed past with more empty boxes.

He placed the broken-down cardboard under one arm. "I told you I'm not selling the store, so if that's all you came for, you can go." Picking up two large garbage bags, he headed for the front. "Right after you get the door for me."

Same old Luke.

She refused to let their personal history distract her or forget her professionalism. Just because they'd been best of friends since the second grade when Luke had stood up for her against bullies in the school yard making fun of her braces and thick glasses. This was business. She pushed the front door open and stepped back to let him pass. But she couldn't let him go without asking, "Why on earth did you buy this store?" She shivered as a gust of wind blew her blond hair across her face.

Luke studied her, his piercing eyes now void of emotion. "It must be worth something. Why else would your company send someone all the way out here to acquire it?"

Victoria's gaze fell to his left hand. No wedding band. The relief she experienced both irritated and confused her.

"Well, we're not actually interested in own-ing *this* store. My company's client ran into complications obtaining a permit to build one of their own locations, with Legend's still doing business nearby."

"Well, I guess they're out of luck. I just bought the place and I plan on keeping it." Luke collected the discarded packing paper, crumpled it and tossed it into a waste basket near the counter.

"I'm surprised that you want to own a run-down sporting goods store." Her eyes narrowed. The Luke she used to know would rather build and remodel the old-fashioned buildings in the downtown core, not own a business in one of them. He'd always had a talent for designing and building things. When they were kids, his derby cars were always the best in the race, and she remembered the lemonade stand he'd made her from the wood left over from building his sister's tree house. The stand had been the summer hotspot for all their friends that year.

"We haven't spoken in a long time. Maybe I'm not the same guy you remember." Pulling a Swiss Army Knife from his jeans pocket, he tore into the remaining cardboard boxes, breaking them down.

Victoria watched him work. She had noticed the changes in him, despite her best efforts. Time had been good to him. He was bigger now, muscular and slightly wider around the waist. No longer the physique of a struggling architectural student. His face showed signs of maturity, but the fine lines around his mouth and eyes only enhanced his gorgeous, blond looks. The temptation to touch the five-o'clock shadow along his jaw was overpowering.

Luke straightened and his gaze met hers. "Besides, this store has a history in the community. That means something to most of us."

Of course. Luke had worked in the store every summer when they were teenagers. Maybe his interest in preserving it made sense. "Okay, well I guess we should get to work." She faked a smile, forcing her professionalism. She didn't need or want to get to know this man over again. What she wanted was for him to sign her contract so she could get out of Brookhollow. "I'll have an offer by Wednesday, but we should go over the preliminary paperwork as soon as possible." She scanned the store for a place to lay out her documents. "The major chain store interested in purchasing Legend's Sporting Goods is—"

Luke turned off the lights and unplugged

the multicolored Christmas strand draped across the window. Only the glow from the pole lamp outside illuminated them.

"Do you prefer we do this in the dark?" she asked sarcastically.

He slid into his coat and wrapped his scarf around his neck. "I have dinner plans." He stood next to the door.

The familiar scent of his musky cologne made her pulse race. She suddenly remembered the nights she'd fallen asleep in his T-shirt, when he'd been away at college, enveloped by that smell. "Tomorrow, then." She opened the door and stepped out into the frigid air. "I'll come by in the morning," she said through the icy burst of wind and snow. Reaching into her purse, she pulled out a silver monogrammed cardholder. She popped it open with a manicured fingernail and slid one of her cards free, handing it to Luke.

"Your card?"

"It has my cell number on it." Her teeth chattered. The sun had almost disappeared and the temperature drop in the last half hour was significant.

"Victoria, this is Brookhollow." He laughed.

"I could stand in the center and call out to you, and wherever you are, you'd hear me."

The rich, deep sound of his laughter wasn't at all the boyish laugh she remembered.

"What?"

"Nothing." Her cheeks flushed and she looked away. "Anyway, let's not test that theory. Use the cell number." But he was right; the card was unnecessary. If he needed to find her, it wouldn't be hard. She shivered again, wishing she'd packed a warmer coat. The pretty white cashmere did nothing for warmth.

Her cell rang in her purse and, tugging off a glove, she dug around in the side compartment until she found it. The office number flashed on the screen. *Shoot.* In her stress over returning to town, she'd forgotten to check in. "Hello?" she answered, turning away from Luke.

"Victoria, it's…" Static scrambled the receptionist's voice.

"Kim…Kim, you're breaking up." She moved a few feet down the street. "Can you hear me?"

"Victoria?"

"Yes, I'm here. Can you hear me?" Silence.

Victoria held her phone up in the air, shook it then brought it back to her ear. "Kim?"

Call failed.

Small-town reception.

She sighed and turned back to Luke who seemed to be hiding a laugh behind his hand.

"What's so funny?" She glared at him. She'd love to know exactly what aspect of this turn of events he found so entertaining. She glanced at her phone again. By now she suspected her   would be full, as well.

Luke cleared his throat and shook his head. "Nothing," he said, looking down the street. "Hey, check out your rental."

She turned and gasped. A large amount of snow had fallen in the short time she'd been in the store.

"I have a snow scraper in my truck. Give me a second, and I'll grab it."

Victoria grabbed his arm to stop him.

His gaze fell to her glove on his sleeve, and she pulled her hand away. "No, that's okay. I have one in the car." She hoped. Rule number one in an acquisition: *Don't indebt yourself to the seller.* She began to walk away, her toes icicles in her two-inch-heel boots.

Luke shrugged, checking his watch. "Suit

yourself," he said as he disappeared around the side of the building.

Victoria's temple throbbed a she stood frozen in place, watching him walk away. This would be the hardest acquisition and opponent she'd ever gone up against.

LUKE RAKED A HAND through his thick, snow-covered hair as he made his way carefully on the slick sidewalk to his truck. Despite the below-freezing temperature, sweat pooled on the back of his shirt beneath his coat. Victoria Mason. He'd known she was coming. Had been expecting her, but certainly hadn't been prepared for the sight of her. Even more beautiful than the photos he'd seen posted on her Facebook page.

She obviously still knew the happenings in the small town she'd abandoned two weeks before their wedding. Enough to know the store was in a transition, during which time it could be vulnerable. He'd never thought she'd be capable of something like this, though. The big city certainly changed people. The girl he remembered may have had a wild side and a stubborn streak, but she'd been kind-hearted and well-meaning. The Victoria he fell in love with would never have considered pulling something like this.

She'd always been interested in the betterment of the community…and of him. If it wasn't for her belief in him, he might never have considered applying to college after having struggled with academics throughout high school. The support and encouragement she'd always offered him made it impossible for him to stay angry with her now. But he didn't understand how she could be back here to buy out his store.

How could she forget the contributions that Legend's made to local organizations each year? Without the sponsorship programs provided by the store, the junior hockey team—the Brookhollow Blades—wouldn't have the funding to compete against bigger-city teams. He wished she'd tried to pull this a year ago when Mr. Jameson had been in charge. Now Luke was forced to deal with his ex-fiancée himself. He prayed he was up for the challenge.

The store's role in his own involvement with sports from a young age was the reason he'd agreed to buy it when Mr. Jameson had asked him about it a month before he'd passed away. Claiming Luke was the closest thing to family he had, because of the bond they'd formed while working in the store and their shared passion for sports, he'd sold him Legend's for next to nothing. Luke hadn't the heart to refuse. He just hoped the business generated some profit in the New Year, otherwise the overhead would cut into his capital.

Climbing into his truck, he turned the key in the ignition. The old engine resisted. "Come on…" he said, closing his eyes and trying again. The engine sputtered to life. If it lasted the winter, he'd consider himself lucky. He hated the idea of parting with the old beast. Good memories were tied to this truck—Victoria close to him as he drove, her hand tucked in his.

After all this time, he'd hoped he wouldn't have reacted to her as he had. He barely thought of her anymore. Okay, that was a lie. He thought of her more often than he cared to admit. Thought of her smile, her laugh, her soft skin…how she'd left him, and how he'd been crazy to just let her go. Frowning, he turned the truck onto the quiet street. He'd been angry and hurt for a long time, but the emotions had turned to a dull longing. He'd fought every urge to contact her, despite the attempts of social media to reconnect them through mutual friends. He always found a reason to be out of town when there was a chance she might be coming in—Rachel Harper's wedding three years ago… her grandmother's funeral two years before that… Now here she was and there would be no avoiding her.

She would be gone before the week was over, but only *if* he gave her what she came for.

CHAPTER TWO

"SINCE WHEN IS Luke Dawson interested in owning an old sporting goods store?" Victoria asked her mother an hour later.

Sheila Mason bent to look through the glass of the oven door. Her light blond hair, streaked with gray, was tied in a loose ponytail at the base of her neck and fell over one shoulder. The rich aroma of her chicken-and-mushroom casserole filled the kitchen. "I don't know, dear." The timer on the oven rang and she hit the off button on the stove.

Victoria paced the kitchen, biting her thumbnail. Her perfect manicure didn't stand a chance of surviving the week.

"Stop biting your nails." Her mother smacked her hand away from her mouth. "Can you hand me the oven mitts?" Opening the oven door, she fanned the blast of escaping heat.

Victoria opened the same kitchen drawer

where the mitts had been for as long as she could remember. Nothing had changed here. From the antique table-and-chair set in the corner that had once belonged to her grandmother, to the lace curtains hanging in the tiny kitchen window, everything looked just as it always had. Even the advent calendar hung in the same spot on the wall near the window, where it had year after year. She remembered how excited she used to be on the first of December when they would fill the tiny squares with chocolate balls and count down the days until Christmas Eve. Despite the absence of children in the house now, her mother still kept up the tradition.

Victoria handed the mitts to her mother. "But I thought you said he was working for an architecture firm? And he usually worked out of town." So many unanswered questions.

"I really don't know. The store does mean a lot to Brookhollow." Her mom shrugged, taking a knife from the block on the counter. "You'll have to ask Luke those questions," she said, cutting into the casserole.

Victoria's stomach growled. "Since when have you become so tight-lipped?" she asked pointedly. Her mother would be the first one to admit she couldn't keep a secret. She prided herself on being a source of information in town, even if that information wasn't always accurate.

"Are you calling me a gossip?" Her mother faked an expression of shock. She set the knife in the sink and rinsed it. "Look, all I know is what I hear around town.... You know Darlene Dawson and I don't talk much anymore."

Victoria sighed. Her ignorance about what was going on locally couldn't be blamed on her mother. She'd done her best to distance herself from the everyday happenings in Brookhollow. Over the years, she'd been successful in convincing herself that she wasn't missing much. She grabbed a fork and sampled the casserole. "Oh, my God, that's good."

Her mother swiped her hand away. "Don't pick. Your aunt and uncle should be here any minute and then we can eat."

Her dad swung open the kitchen door and poked his head inside the kitchen. "Luke's truck just pulled into the cul-de-sac."

"What? You invited Luke? Mom, you can't be serious." Victoria dropped her fork onto the counter and turned toward her father. "And you—how could you not tell me?"

"I had nothing to do with it," he said, quickly escaping the kitchen.

Turning, her mom set the dinner plates onto the counter and said, "Oh, relax. I saw him earlier today, replacing the burned-out bulbs in Ginger's Christmas lights and he said he was looking forward to seeing you again, so I invited him to dinner." Her mother shrugged.

"Mom, he is my ex-fiancé, in case you've forgotten. Not to mention my company is working for the store trying to buy out Legend's." She paced back and forth in the kitchen, frowning. How could her mother have invited him to dinner? How could he *accept* knowing the reason for her visit? And why hadn't he said anything?

"Business is business, honey. I'm sure you two will figure that stuff out. But can't you just put it aside for the evening and have a pleasant dinner with an old friend? I'm sure Luke has long gotten over the fact you left him at the altar." Her mom waved a hand dismissively and busied herself with the pie she was making. "Even if his mother hasn't," she mumbled, rolling out the crust.

"I didn't leave him at the altar." Victoria stopped pacing, wondering how many times they'd had this conversation. Too many. "I called off the wedding two weeks before and, besides, he certainly didn't try to stop me." Memories of those last few weeks before her supposed wedding day were painful to recall. The stress of the preparations—her mother and Luke's mother forcing her to taste wedding cakes and try on dress after dress—even though her heart wasn't in it. The entire time, hidden in her bedside table drawer had been an acceptance letter for an entry-level position with Clarke and Johnson Acquisitions.

When she'd applied the summer before she'd never imagined the big New York firm would accept her application—she'd had only a two-year business diploma. But they had offered her a job and she'd had a month to decide. Keeping the offer to herself and struggling with her conflicting desires had created tension between her and Luke and had made her question her commitment to him. Their ideas about a life together had seemed worlds apart.

She'd chosen the unpaid internship with a dream of a future so different from the one he'd been planning, and left him behind. And he hadn't tried to stop her.

Her mother waved a hand. "You know what I mean. Anyway, it's in the past. At least *I've* learned to keep it there…unlike some people."

Victoria shook her head. Her mother was impossible, and Luke's mother would be furious if she found out. The two women, once best friends, hadn't spoken since the day Victoria left town. According to her mother, she'd let the feud between them die, but Luke's mother still held a grudge. The two avoided each other as much as possible in the small community.

The doorbell rang.

How was she supposed to sit at the same table with him, after everything they'd been through? She was here to do battle with him over a store. And this was supposed to be a pleasant evening? She peered through the glass opening of the kitchen door.

Luke shifted from one foot to the other on the front porch. Wearing clean jeans and his leather jacket, his short hair gelled into a spiky, controlled mess, he'd obviously gone home to shower and change.

She made no move to let him in. Why couldn't he have gotten fat? Or bald? Or both?

"Victoria, go take off your suit jacket and brush your hair, while I get the door." Her mom removed her apron and straightened her sweater.

Victoria held out an arm to block her mother. "I have a better idea. You go get pretty for Luke, and I'll let him in. He may as well get used to seeing me at my worst."

VICTORIA FORKED A LUMP of potatoes and savored the rich, buttery carb combination. No one used butter quite like her mother. If she wasn't careful, she'd pile on a few pounds in her short visit. She pushed a mushroom around her plate, only half listening to the conversations around her. Her father, Uncle Frank and Luke discussed football statistics across the table and her mother and Aunt Linda complained about the new format of the *Brookhollow View,* the local newspaper.

"I can never find the movie listings or my horoscope. They keep shifting things from one section to another," Linda said, shaking her head as she wiped her mouth with her napkin.

"Uh-huh." Sheila nodded in agreement. "And last week the flyer inserts were missing." She turned to Luke. "How's the casserole?" she asked as she poured him another glass of wine.

"Thank you. It's delicious…better than I remember." He smiled and shot Victoria a glance.

She lowered her eyes to her plate. *Just get through this meal.* Her mother's attempt to create a blast from the past was working. From their favorite dinner dishes to the old picture albums of the two of them in junior high and high school she'd produced before dinner, the memories were overpowering as they came rushing back.

The last thing Victoria wanted was to remember. Remember the long summer nights in Brookhollow when they would drive for miles outside of town, cut the engine and lie on the hood of Luke's truck, gazing up at the stars. Or the fall days when they'd walk hand in hand through the leaves in the park and kiss in the shelter of the big oak tree that held their carved initials inside a heart. She'd forced those special moments from her mind years ago, replacing them with new friends, exciting work, brunches and dinners in trendy restaurants.

"So, Victoria, your mom says you still play soccer in the city," her aunt said with a polite smile.

She nodded. "Sort of. I play on the corporate team, just once or twice a year. Usually some sort of charity game against one of our clients."

"Well, with you on the team I'm sure they win every time," her uncle said.

She hesitated, not wanting to disappoint him. Of everyone in her family, her mother's brother, a retired lawyer, was by far the most understanding about her life choices. He'd told her time and again how proud and impressed he was by the success she'd had in the city. "Um...well, we're actually not allowed to win," she confessed with a wry grin.

"Huh?"

"Apparently, it isn't good for business."

Uncle Frank cocked his head. "Well, that must be tough for you with your competitive spirit."

She laughed and admitted, "Yes, it is."

"What about your volunteer work—do you still keep that up?" her aunt asked. She didn't pause for an answer. "You know they still have that Adopt-A-Grandparent program you started years ago at the seniors' complex."

Victoria glanced at her mother. "Yes, Mom mentioned that." The Adopt-A-Grandparent program seemed to be the last thing she'd done that her mom was truly proud of. Victoria had had the idea for a seniors' visitation program when she'd been to see her own grandparents as a teenager. She'd always stay much longer than planned, playing cards or watching movies with some of the other residents without family nearby. The idea of asking other kids from the school to visit along with her had started small, with just a few of her close friends baking cookies to deliver or helping plant flowers in the complex garden, but then it quickly grew into a larger program organized by the school principal.

"You were always up to something…could never sit still for long." Linda chuckled.

"From what I remember, you were quite the handful sometimes, too," Frank teased her.

It was to be expected that her uncle would bring up her long-ago antics. Despite her visits to Brookhollow over the years, she hadn't spent much time with her extended family.

Whenever she came to town for weddings or funerals, she stayed a day or two at most—the only time her busy work schedule would allow. A pang of regret hit her then. She should have tried harder to find the time.

She blushed as her eyes met Luke's. "I don't know what you're talking about."

"I do," her father piped up. "Should I remind you of the time you snuck into the science lab at the school and rescued all those rabbits you thought they were planning to use for experiments?"

Linda, a tenth-grade math teacher at the school, chuckled. "I remember that. The school had agreed to house them overnight while the local pet shop painted the bunny room. It was the only place in town big enough to keep all of them."

Victoria winced as the others laughed. How was she supposed to have known? If the science lab had in fact been planning to use them for experiments, everyone would have praised her good deed. Instead she'd gotten a suspension for breaking the lab window. "I still think Mr. Douglas was up to no good," she said. The twelfth-grade biology teacher had always seemed strange to her.

"Mr. Douglas is a vegetarian. He'd never hurt a fly." Her aunt shook her head and wiped a tear out of the corner of her eye.

"I think my favorite was when you and Rachel tied yourselves to that big maple tree in the park, to save it from being cut down," remembered Uncle Frank.

"That would have worked…if it had been the right tree," she mumbled.

Another fit of laughter erupted around her.

Her mom stood and collected the empty dinner plates.

"Mom, sit. Let me clean up," she offered, her chest tight. *Please, let this be the only family dinner on this trip*. All this talk about her childhood antics was taking its toll. No one seemed to recognize that she wasn't that kid anymore. She'd actually made something of herself in the city. She no longer had time for volunteer work and sports…but it was because she was accomplishing great things. It was hard to feel proud of her success in the city when her family and friends in Brookhollow only seemed interested in her adolescent ventures. Collecting the plates from her mother, she pushed through the swinging kitchen door with her hip. She set the plates on the counter near the sink and leaned against it. Her cell phone vibrated in her pocket. *Oh, thank God. Her service must be back*. She reached for it. A new text from a Brookhollow area code.

Do you need help escaping through the kitchen window?

Tension seeped from her shoulders and a genuine smile formed on her lips for the first time that day. She glanced from the kitchen window to Luke.

Now do you understand why I stay away?

Luke smiled as he responded. You're even prettier than I remember.

She blushed, caught off guard by the compliment. Her thumbs flew over the keypad.

Nice try, but flattery won't work. Hitting Send she folded her arms across her chest. His smoldering, deep blue eyes were merely a speed bump on her way to another successful acquisition.

She fought to hide a smile as she read, Meaner, too.

Taking a sip of wine, he sat back in his chair.

Not mean, just determined to do my job.

Waiting for his reply, she turned and filled the sink with dirty dishes. Her parents still refused to install a dishwasher in the old home.

The phone vibrated on the counter and she reached for it.

No matter what it takes?

She hesitated. There wasn't much she wouldn't do for her career. After working from a junior associate to her current position, busting her butt with long hours, extended trips, living from a suitcase, never having time for anything else—including a real relationship—failing wasn't an option.

No matter what. Don't stand in my way, Luke.

She peered through the window watching as he read and replied.

Don't think I'll step aside quite so easily this time, Victoria.

Her heart pounded as she turned away. Were they still talking about the store?

Setting the phone aside, she scraped the dirty plates into the garbage can and stacked them in the sink. A moment later, out of the corner of her eye she noticed Luke pacing the back porch. He'd excused himself to take a call, and she tried to tamp down her curiosity.

Luke smiled, and she watched his moving lips, wishing she could read them.

Her mother hadn't mentioned otherwise, so she'd assumed he was single. But then again apparently her mother couldn't be trusted as a source of information about Luke anymore.

Of course he must have someone special in his life; he was gorgeous. She wondered who it could be. Every single woman in town would be vying for his attention. She bit her lip, watching as he picked up a shovel on the deck and, cradling his phone against his shoulder, cleared a path to the stairs leading to the yard. With his back to her, she took the opportunity to study him. In his faded jeans and leather jacket, he looked better than ever.

She'd always been attracted to him, but she hadn't remembered him looking quite so irresistible.

Luke set the shovel aside and turned toward the window. Seeing her watching him, he waved.

Victoria's cheeks flushed, and the wet dinner plate slipped out of her hands. She caught it before it hit the floor. Quickly, she turned her attention back to the sink.

A moment later, the back door opened and Luke appeared beside her. "Brrr. It's cold out there once the sun sets."

"Mmm-hmm." She nodded as she scrubbed the plate with a sponge.

Luke peered into the sink over her shoulder, his warm breath on the back of her neck. "I think those little pink flowers are supposed to stay on the plates." He picked up a dish towel.

"Oh, no, that's okay. I've got this." She laid the plate in the drying rack and motioned for him to give her the towel. "Go into the living room and relax with my parents." *Or leave. Either would work.* She just wanted him as far away from her as possible. Spending time with him was proving difficult. Beyond the physical improvements, he was even kinder, funnier and more familiar than she could have imagined.

"No way. It's the least I can do for supper." He moved the towel out of her reach and picked up a handful of forks from the drying rack.

His cell phone rang in his shirt pocket and he checked the caller ID. He slid the phone, unanswered, back as it continued to ring.

"If you have to get that, I can finish up here." She nodded toward his vibrating pocket. Her BlackBerry had once again lost signal and she was eager to return to the bed-and-breakfast to catch up on missed calls and emails.

"No, that one can wait," he said, placing the forks in the cutlery drawer and reaching for a plate. "My brother-in-law, Roy, is retiling their downstairs bathroom and he has a million questions." He laughed. "I offered to just do it myself—it would be faster and easier."

She hated that the sound of his laugh and the sight of his smile still had such a profound effect on her.

Luke sniffed the air. "Your mom is a fantastic cook." Opening the oven door, he looked inside at the pumpkin pie.

"You better close that before she comes in here and catches you," she warned, washing the last plate and setting it aside. She took the dish towel from Luke and dried her hands. "And I wouldn't let your mother hear you say that."

Luke closed the door and studied her intensely. "How about you? Have you acquired any new baking skills?"

"No." Victoria had never been the culinary wonder her mother was; she'd never had the desire to learn, despite years of working at Mrs. Norris's bakery in the summer. "I'm too busy to bake." She shrugged and removed the apron from around her neck, hanging it on the hook near the pantry.

Luke's gaze dropped to her waist. "Looks like you've been too busy to eat, too."

She tugged her shirt lower and cleared her throat. "So, I heard about your dad's heart attack last year. How is he?"

"Better," Luke said with a nod. "After his bypass surgery, he's feeling much better. It's one of the reasons I try to spend more time here in Brookhollow now, working on local construction projects…to help out. Dad won't admit he can't do certain things.… I was sorry to hear about your grandma. I would have attended the funeral, but it happened so suddenly, and I was away."

She dismissed that with a wave of her hand and said, "I barely made it myself. I flew in from an acquisitions trip to Minnesota, then took the red-eye back out." Her maternal grandmother, her last remaining grandparent, had died from a stroke several years before. As a child, Victoria had spent a lot of time with her, chattering away as her grandma planted flowers in her garden or sitting on the porch, holding her wool as she knitted hats for the maternity ward at the hospital. After she moved to New York the two had remained close, talking at least once a week. She missed those conversations.

Her grandmother had always encouraged her to do what made her happy, regardless of what others might think.

Wiping pie crumbs off the counter onto her hand, she said, "Dad told me you helped him with the deck last summer.… That was nice of you."

"Ah, your dad did most of the work. Even

retired, he's a fantastic contractor. Definitely knows his stuff," Luke said. "He told me about your promotion and that you bought an apartment a few months ago. Congratulations."

"Thank you." Victoria's gaze met his and she laughed.

"What's funny?" Luke asked. But he was grinning, too.

"Just that we haven't spoken in forever, yet we know enough about each other to write a book."

Luke laughed. "Small towns."

His cell phone rang again.

He took the phone out of his pocket, checked the call display and silenced the call.

"You're quite the busy guy. Your phone rings almost as often as mine…when I have service." She grabbed the oven mitts as the timer beeped on the stove. She took the pie out of the oven and set it to cool on the rack her mother had put out, as she made a fresh pot of coffee.

"Yeah, sorry…work." He shrugged. "This is a busy time of year."

"The store's closed," Victoria said with a frown.

"My other job." Luke didn't elaborate.

Victoria fought every last impulse to question him further. It was none of her business. The only thing she cared about was the store.

"Oh," she said simply, serving the first piece of pie and pushing the dish toward him. She plated the rest and carried them on a tray into the living room, where she served them to her parents and aunt and uncle.

Her mother raised her eyebrows. "You're not having any?"

"I'm stuffed from dinner." Victoria faked a yawn and glanced at her watch. It had been a long day and she had work to do. "Actually, Mom, I think I'm going to head back to the bed-and-breakfast."

Her mother glanced at the clock on the mantel above the fireplace. "I guess it is getting late. Oh, don't forget to take some stuff I thought you might like to have from your old room." She pointed to the box near the doorway.

Victoria cringed inwardly. Just recently, her parents had finally converted her old bedroom into a sewing room for her mother. The pink walls that used to hold posters of her favorite rock bands were now painted a light tan. Her cheerleading and soccer trophies that used to line the bookshelves were in the attic, replaced by her mother's collection of patterns. She suspected the pictures of herself and Luke and her friends had found their way into the overstuffed box near the door and she wished she could somehow escape without taking it. She'd purposely left all of this behind.

She bent and picked up the heavy box and turned with a forced smile. "Good night, Dad."

"Drive safe, honey. The roads are slippery," he cautioned. He reclined the leather recliner and rested his pie plate on his protruding belly.

"I will. Bye, Mom. Uncle Frank, Aunt Linda." She advanced toward the porch and gave a quick nod in Luke's direction. "I'll see you in the morning...at the store?"

His determined gaze met hers and he nodded. "You bet. You need help with that box?"

"Nope, I got it." She struggled to open the front door, balancing the box on one arm, then stopped. There was no escaping him. She closed her eyes and sighed. "Luke... you've got me blocked in the driveway."

He swallowed his mouthful of pie and set

the plate on the end table. "Sorry, I forgot." He grabbed his keys and met her at the door.

"Hey, look where you kids are standing." Her mother chuckled, pointing to the door frame above their heads.

Victoria looked up. Mistletoe hung about three inches above them. *Oh, you've got to be kidding me.* "Forget it, Mom," she said, shaking her head as she reached for the door handle. She doubted very much Luke wanted to kiss her, either. She took a step outside, but Luke's grip on her arm drew her back in.

He looked amused. "It's mistletoe, Victoria. It's tradition."

Her mouth gaped. He couldn't be serious.

He moved toward her, and she took a step back. His hand tightened on her shoulder, as he lowered his head.

He is serious. Her mouth went dry, and she licked her lips. "Luke…" Her protest was muffled as his lips landed on hers.

The kiss was quick and soft, but her knees weakened under its effect. Off balance, she reached out and grabbed his arm, starting to lose her hold of the box. Luke tightened his grip on her waist to steady her as he moved away and took the box from her.

Victoria's trembling hand flew to her lips where his had just been.

"That's the trouble with mistletoe," he said, his gaze piercing. "You can't always control who you find underneath it."

LUKE JUMPED INTO his truck and slammed the door. The heat of the simple kiss made him only distantly aware of the cold air inside the cab. He slid the key into the ignition. The memories of their past together had faded over time…and then she'd come back. That's all it had taken.

He'd had the urge to kiss her the moment he'd seen her shocked expression in the store earlier that day. But he hadn't expected his own reaction to the kiss, which had been meant to annoy her. The joke was on him.

The woman was here for one reason—to take his store away.

His cell buzzed on the passenger seat. "Hello?" he answered, cradling the phone against his shoulder as he turned on the headlights and backed out of the driveway.

"Hey, man, where are you?" His buddy Jim Bishop could barely be heard above the loud background of his surroundings.

"Just leaving the Masons' house." Luke shivered, finally registered just how cold it was. The heater in the old truck was cranked, but only chilled air came out of the vents. Ice crystals formed on the inside of the windshield and he rubbed it with the sleeve of his jacket, clearing a narrow chunk of window to see out.

"What were you doing over there?" Jim yelled into the phone.

Luke cringed and pulled the phone away from his ear. "Mrs. Mason invited me to dinner and you know how much good it does to argue with that woman."

Jim laughed. "I would love to be a fly on the wall when your mom finds out…and she will find out."

Jim was right. His mother would know soon enough and he dreaded the conversation that was bound to ensue. "Yeah, well, try to keep the news to yourself."

"You got it. Hey, if you're on your way home, why don't you stop by the pool hall? Bob's wife let him go out tonight and Darren's on his way."

Luke hesitated. "Who's on bar tonight?"

Jim laughed. "You know, if you didn't

break the hearts of all the waitstaff around here, you wouldn't have to ask that question."

"That's not what happens." Luke scoffed. "We date, we have fun, then we mutually agree to go our own ways…" Most of the time anyway. Of course there may have been women who'd been hoping for something more from him, but he'd learned his lesson about serious relationships the hard way a long time ago.

"Is that why you're still avoiding Hayley?"

"I'm not avoiding her… I just don't trust her to pour me a drink at the moment."

Jim's loud, hearty laugh came through the phone again. "Well, don't worry, you're safe. Melody's on bar tonight."

"Perfect." Luke pulled into a driveway and turned the truck around. A few games of eight ball were just the thing to clear his head. If he'd learned anything so far, it was that he would need his resolve when dealing with his ex-fiancée. "I'll be there in an hour. I have to stop by the house to let the dog out first."

"Great, bring your wallet."

"Sure. I have no problem taking your money."

CHAPTER THREE

VICTORIA SCANNED HER ROOM at the bed-and-breakfast, trying to figure where the noise was coming from. She glanced at her laptop screen. The annoying buzzing came from the cable Mrs. Harris had given her to connect to the internet. A timed-out error message appeared on the screen and the buzzing paused, then resumed. Her mouth fell open. *Seriously, dial up?* She rested her head in her hands as she waited. When Mrs. Harris had said the Brookhollow Inn had internet access, she'd assumed it was Wi-Fi.

The color-themed guest rooms, occupying the two upper floors of the four-level estate were still decorated in an intriguing mix of Victorian, French country and European Old World. Downstairs, the common areas consisted of a sitting room near the front of the house with a large stone fireplace, hand-crafted furniture and bookshelves lined with magazines and novels. These were the better-maintained areas of the house, and Victoria suspected it was because they saw the least amount of use.

The dining area with its six-round wicker table and chair sets extended onto a magnificent, large wraparound deck with a view of the big, fenced yard. She'd been disappointed to see that the large floor-to-ceiling, stained-glass windows were chipped, and the floral wallpaper was outdated and peeling in the corners. The weather-worn gazebo still stood in the center of the yard, near the rock waterfall overrun with weeds; it had been the location she'd selected for the wedding ceremony. In summer, the garden had been the perfect backdrop. Now, draped in mounds of snow and ice, the bare trees and neglected rock beds seemed just a sad shadow of a more elegant time.

The buzzing stopped and her home page opened at a snail's pace. She typed her remote access login and password and hit Enter. Nothing. The hourglass icon appeared on the screen. "Oh, come on." Her BlackBerry revealed thirty-two new messages, which the cell service here maddeningly prevented her from accessing. At this rate it would take her until midnight to read and respond to them all. Her voice mail could wait until morning; it was too late to return calls now anyway.

She stood and stretched at the bedroom window. The street below was dark and quiet—a typical Monday night in Brookhollow. In the city, the sound of traffic and the glow of lights were a constant reminder of life in continuous motion. She missed the noise and distraction. Here, the silence allowed her to hear her own thoughts.

Raising a hand to her lips, her cheeks heated. When she'd left home, she'd been certain the memory of Luke would plague her forever, but time and distance really did have a way of mending the heart and allowing you to forget. And then one simple kiss had shaken her.

A loud knock on the bedroom door made her jump and she released the thick curtain. Mrs. Harris? Her eyes widened as she opened the door. "What are you guys doing here?" Three of her best friends from high school stood in the hallway. She hadn't told anybody she was coming to town and guilt now washed over her. She was here for work and she hadn't wanted to mix business with pleasure. Rachel Harper was the only one she kept in touch with, and she'd been planning to stop in and surprise her at some point. Well, the surprise was on her.

"We went by your parents' place. I thought you'd be staying there." Rachel was struggling to catch her breath after the climb to the third floor. Her flushed cheeks held the glow of a woman eight months pregnant.

Victoria shook her head. "They finally transformed my old room."

"Anyway, we didn't want to wait any longer to see you," Rachel said, struggling to lean in to give her a hug, her belly making it difficult to get close.

"Hey, girl, long time," Lisa Cameron said as she hugged her next. "We haven't seen you since Rachel's wedding.... How long ago was that—three years?" Tall and thin, Lisa towered over the others, just as she always had. With her long, dark hair and slanted, hazel eyes, she could have signed a modeling contract anywhere in the world. It amazed Victoria that her beautiful friend had chosen Brookhollow and the domestic role of wife and mother instead.

"I know. I should visit more. I just travel so much for work, being at home in New York is a luxury." Besides, she didn't add, a vacation to Brookhollow couldn't be classified as a vacation. She'd be constantly checking around the corner for a member of the Dawson family. One in particular, the one she couldn't avoid this time.

Ava Miller took her hands. "Wow, you look even better in person than you do on Facebook," she said, laughing. "And those are the best pictures anyone has of themselves." She tossed her red hair over her shoulder.

Lisa nodded her agreement. "You're telling me. Kenny has his high school football picture posted. He refuses to believe he looks a day older, despite the receding hairline and beer belly, which gives Rachel's massive bulge a run for the money."

"Hey!" Rachel protested, swatting her friend's arm, as she joined them in laughter.

"It's true, Rachel, you are huge." Ava raised her eyebrows, staring at the protruding stomach fighting the constraints of the buttons on Rachel's coat. "Are you sure you're not having twins again? They say if you've had them once, the likelihood increases you'll have them again."

This would be Rachel's third pregnancy and fourth child and the Harper family didn't seem to be slowing.

"The doctor confirmed it—one baby." Rachel looked terrified as she patted her middle. "He better be right."

The playful interaction between her friends warmed Victoria. She hadn't realized how much she'd missed them. It shouldn't surprise her that they knew she was in town. She suspected by now everyone did.

"Um…did you guys want to come in?" She glanced at the stack of paperwork on the desk and struggled with a sense of obligation. She really had a lot of work to catch up on.

Rachel waved a hand. "No, your friend from New York…" She paused, thinking hard.

"Heather?" Victoria guessed.

"Yes, that's it. Sorry, I can't remember anything these days with this pregnancy. I swear it's like living in a fog for nine months. Anyhow, she messaged me on Facebook earlier today— I guess she found me among your thousands of friends." Rachel laughed.

Two hundred and sixty-four, and not real friends. Mostly business acquaintances. She actually knew only a handful of people on her friends list.

"Anyway, she confirmed the rumors that you were arriving today and agreed that we had to take you out for a night on the town." Rachel suppressed a yawn. She unbuttoned the top of her coat and fanned herself with her gloves.

Heather. She should have known. "You don't look like you're up for a night on the town." Victoria smiled sympathetically.

Rachel scoffed. "Nonsense. I'm the life of any party. Let's go."

"That's right, grab your coat," Lisa chimed in. "I got a babysitter for the first time in six years."

"Me, too." Ava high-fived Lisa.

The two looked giddy at the prospect of an evening out. Something she took for granted in New York. Other than her extensive travel schedule, she had no real responsibilities. She was lucky. She could come and go as she chose. Her friends' lives were foreign territory.

She didn't want to disappoint them, but the

messages in her in-box needed a response. She hesitated. "I wasn't planning on going anywhere. I have a lot of work I need to catch up on." A glance toward her laptop screen revealed the internet connection had timed out again. "Where would we go anyway?" she asked, eyeing them with suspicion. The choices in Brookhollow were slim. If they said the karaoke bar, she was locking herself in this bedroom.

"Just to the pool hall for a drink." Rachel rested her hands against the back of her hips and blew a lock of wavy brown hair off her forehead.

Victoria frowned as she studied her friend. "I thought you were supposed to be on bed rest?"

"No, I'm fine now. I'm past the thirty-six-week mark, so the doctor says I'm okay to deliver anytime now."

Victoria's eyes widened.

Rachel laughed again. "Don't worry, I won't. Believe me, this little one likes it tucked in under my rib cage. I'll be lucky to coax him or her out when it's time." She rubbed her side.

"I don't know…" Victoria hesitated. "You guys could just come in for a while."

Lisa glanced past her into the room and nodded toward the laptop. "They have free Wi-Fi at the pool hall."

"I'll grab my stuff." Victoria dove for her coat.

As LUKE DROVE past the Brookhollow Inn on his way to the pool hall, he stepped on the gas, ignoring the temptation to go see her. Of all the ways he'd envisioned her coming back to Brookhollow, he never in a million years would have expected this.

Noticing his gas light illuminated on the dash, he turned the truck into the lot of the only station in town. He had no choice, but before stepping out of the truck, he glanced through the front window of the minimarket, toward the cashier, holding his breath. Thankfully, Mike Fisher was working the night shift and not Mike's sister, Cheryl. He was running out of excuses for why he hadn't called her for a second date and, while he felt bad about it, he didn't think it would be fair to lead her on when they clearly had nothing in common. Eight years his junior, he'd been hesitant to even go on the first date, but it turned out she was a little too mature for him. The ticking of her biological clock had been louder than the music playing inside the café. And while he could respect and admire her for knowing what she wanted out of a relationship, he also knew what he wanted. And he hadn't given any thought to getting married and having children in a long time, not since Victoria.

Maybe Jim was right, he thought, as he jumped down from the truck and jogged into the store, he had to stop dating local women.

He pushed through the glass door and waved in greeting. "Hey, Mike." He took his wallet out of his back pocket and pulled out his credit card.

"Hey, Luke. My sister was just saying how your truck must get amazing mileage. We haven't seen you in here for weeks. Forty in gas?" he asked, taking the card and sliding it through the register.

Luke blushed. "I'm not avoiding her... Of course not... I'm just..."

Mike grinned. "Avoiding her?"

"Yeah." Luke looked away, embarrassed, as he replaced his card and slid the wallet into his back pocket. "Sorry, man. Your sister's great.... I'm just not really looking for anything serious."

His sisters had a theory about why that was. One they had no problem reiterating at each and every family get-together. Family dinners at the Dawson home often turned into an intervention, as they insisted on discussing his apparent fear of commitment. Ultimately, the blame always returned to Victoria and her untimely departure from Brookhollow.

While he couldn't deny the theory held water, he knew his choice to remain single couldn't be completely blamed on his ex. He just couldn't seem to find anyone he wanted to spend an extended period of time with. No one he'd dated in recent years had challenged or intrigued him enough. He refused to believe he had unreal expectations.

"She told you about her one-year plan from date to altar, huh?" Mike said, handing Luke a pen to sign the credit card receipt.

"About five minutes in," he confirmed, scribbling his signature and handing Mike back the pen.

"Well, you don't have to drive the truck until you're running on fumes. She's going out with a guy on my hockey team. They've really hit it off, so you're off the hook."

Luke released a sigh of relief. "Thanks. I owe you one."

"So, I noticed a green Infiniti rental with a familiar blonde at the wheel drive by this afternoon." Mike leaned against the counter. "Anyone we know?"

"Yeah, the town troublemaker," Luke confirmed with a wry grin.

"Aka Victoria Mason?"

"The one and only."

"She's here to buy out Legend's Sporting Goods, right?" Mike asked as the phone behind him rang.

"If I let her, yes." Once again he prayed he was up to the challenge of going head to head with her. The girl he remembered was persuasive and determined. He suspected she'd stop at nothing to acquire the store. She'd said as much, and that worried him.

"So what you're saying is, the store is hers." Mike grinned and answered the phone.

RACHEL YAWNED AS she stirred the ice in her virgin cosmopolitan.

Victoria glanced up from her laptop. "Are

you sure you're okay?" So far she'd sorted out many of the issues in her in-box, and she pushed aside her guilt for only half listening to her friends reminisce about the old days.

"Yeah." Rachel nodded, despite her tell-tale droopy eyes. "I just haven't been up this late in a while," she said, struggling to hide another yawn behind her hand.

Victoria laughed, glancing at the time on her cell phone. A little past ten-thirty. In New York, she and Heather wouldn't even have hit the clubs yet. Not that she would ever call the pool hall a club. Six pool tables were sand-wiched in a dark corner near the bar and a tiny wooden dance floor, just big enough to hold a dozen people, provided the club por-tion of the hall. The bowling alley occupied the same building to the left and the movie theater was on the right. Not exactly a trendy hot spot. But somehow, it put her at ease, after the stress of the day.

"No… Kenny, listen to me… His rash cream is on the shelf next to the changing table." Plugging one ear with her finger, Lisa yelled into her cell phone above the Christ-mas music blaring from the speakers.

Victoria picked up her phone, wondering

how Lisa was getting cell service in here. Nothing. She shook the phone to no avail, and set it aside. Her provider was getting an earful when she could finally call them.

Lisa rolled her eyes. "Yes, that's right…just put a thick layer all over his butt… Yes, bye," she said shutting her old flip phone and shaking her head. "Seriously, that man wouldn't notice something unless it jumped off a shelf and strangled him."

"Jeremy has a diaper rash?" Ava asked, sipping her white wine. She tucked a loose strand of hair behind her ear.

"Yes. Last week he had a stomach flu and his poop was runny, you know…that yellow color—mustard consistency." She wrinkled her nose.

Ava nodded her understanding. "With that rancid smell… I know it well," she said with a shudder.

Victoria stared at the two. She pushed away her plate of chicken wings. It was too late to be eating fried food anyway.

"The poop I can handle. It's the vomit. That curdled-milk vomit," Lisa added, sitting back in her chair.

Ava waved a hand and said, "I told Darren, I'd change dirty diapers all day long, but vomit was his department."

Victoria stared at her laptop screen, trying to drown out the conversation around her. Poop and vomit. Were these the same girls who'd refused to pick up their own dogs' crap when the town implemented that law?

"Girls, I think we are grossing Victoria out," Rachel said with a laugh. "Sorry. That seems to be all us moms can talk about these days. We're dying for a night out, but then we all miss our kids."

"It's no problem, really. Sorry, I've been attached to this computer for the last hour." Victoria scanned the remaining unanswered emails. She sighed and closed the laptop. She deserved a break.

"So, how about you? Any plans for kids in your future?" Ava leaned forward and a lock of her red hair fell into her face. She pushed it back and secured it with a bobby pin.

Victoria gulped her drink and shook her head. At this stage of her life, children weren't even a consideration, and the prospect of having a family someday grew smaller with each passing year. Wiping the condensation from the glass with a finger, she said, "Um…no.

My position at Clarke and Johnson takes up so much of my time. I travel a lot and there's hours of overtime almost every day."

"But you have a boyfriend," Lisa said. "I saw pictures of you with a guy on Facebook."

Pictures of her with a guy? *Oh, Rob.* She shook her head. "He's just a coworker I dated for a while." She should update her Facebook profile more often and maybe remove some of her older photos, especially now that Rob was engaged to another colleague. "Nothing serious."

"So, there's no one special in your life?" Ava asked, toying with the stem of her wineglass.

"Um…" She debated telling them about Jordan—a guy she'd connected with through an online dating site in a moment of poor judgment, self-pity and too much wine, four months before. With her busy travel schedule and his long hours on Wall Street as a trader, so far they'd managed to make time for three quick lunch dates and countless late-night chat sessions over Skype whenever she was out of town.

She was disappointed that those calls wouldn't be possible on this trip, with the dial-up access at the Brookhollow Inn. She'd emailed him explaining the situation, attaching an invite to her company's Christmas party on December 20. It would be their first real date and a chance to introduce him to her friends and coworkers. She hesitated. Her Brookhollow friends wouldn't understand why she'd had to turn to online dating when she lived in a big city, full of interesting, single people. Nor would they understand that work took priority over relationships. "Not really," she said finally.

Ava and Lisa shared a look.

It took all of Victoria's strength not to question the exchange. So, she wasn't married yet. She didn't have a house full of kids. Did that mean she was a failure? Her mother certainly thought so, but she'd expected her friends to be more open-minded. She'd chosen a different path and there was nothing wrong with that. Was there? The awkward silence spoke volumes. She couldn't stand it. "I mean, there *is* one guy."

The girls looked hopeful.

"Go on," Lisa urged, moving her chair closer to the table.

"Tell us about him." Ava nodded.

"Well, right now we've just been texting and video calling a lot...a few lunch dates..." Victoria blushed, praying the confession didn't sound as lame as she thought it did.

Ava looked disappointed. "But you *are* going to go on a real date?"

That was the plan. She prayed he'd be available the night of her Christmas party. The thought of going alone again this year was too depressing to contemplate. "Yeah. We're just so busy with work."

"That's good." Rachel sat straighter, apparently forcing herself to look awake. "Whatever, don't pay any attention to those two. With or without a serious boyfriend, I bet your life in New York is so exciting. Like an episode of *Friends*."

Victoria smiled. "Sure, something like that."

"I knew it," Rachel said. "Ow..." She grimaced and gripped her side.

"Are you okay?" Victoria hoped her friend hadn't chosen this moment to go into labor.

"It's fine." Rachel struggled to catch her breath. "Just a kick."

Ava and Lisa exchanged knowing looks. "I miss that part," Lisa said, her eyes filled with tears, and she laughed. "Look at me," she said, wiping her eyes with a paper napkin.

"It really is the best feeling, having life growing inside you. Don't worry." Ava touched Victoria's hand. "I'm sure you'll experience it someday."

Victoria's cheeks flushed. "Um…excuse me for just a second." She pushed her drink away and grabbed her cell phone. Sliding from the barstool she made her way to the bathroom. Inside, her phone beeped. Amazingly strong cell reception in the bathroom at the pool hall, of all places. Finding an empty stall, she closed the toilet seat and sat, dialing Heather's cell number.

Her friend answered on the third ring. "Hello? Vic?"

"I'm going to kill you," she hissed into the receiver.

"What? Why?"

"For telling my former friends to take me out on the town!" This night was turning into an intervention. Somehow, Victoria suspected her mother had set the girls up to remind her of everything missing in her life. It was working.

The door to the washroom opened and she heard someone enter the stall next to her.

She lowered her voice. "Do you even know what a night on the town around here means?"

Heather laughed. "So, it's not New York, it's your hometown."

"To say it's not New York is the understatement of the year. I'm at the pool hall, which is also the bowling alley, *and* the movie theater. They have a disco-ball, dance floor and get this—*arcade games*. The place hasn't changed at all since we came here in high school." She closed her eyes and rested her head in her hand. The familiarity of the place and the memories here made her chest hurt.

Heather was still laughing on the other end, unable to speak.

"That's not even the worst of it. I'm here with a pregnant woman, about to fall asleep at the table or give birth any minute—I don't know—and two mommies who can't talk about anything other than poop and vomit. And I can't participate in the conversation because I don't know anything about poop and vomit."

"Vic…stop…" Heather said, struggling to catch her breath.

"I'm glad you find this amusing," Victoria ground out.

"It can't be that bad."

"Oh, really?" Victoria rubbed her eyes. She had to get out of here. "I hate you for setting this up." She stood and slumped against the bathroom wall. Her eyes fell to a set of initials inside a heart, drawn in black marker on the opposite wall: V.M. and L.D. Forever. She shrieked. *They haven't painted the walls in twelve years?*

"What?" Heather sobered instantly. "What's wrong?"

"The graffiti on the bathroom wall is taunting me," she barked into the phone. "I'm seriously going to have a panic attack. Where are you anyway?" Her friend had also been assigned an acquisitions trip that week.

"You don't want to know."

"Heather." Her tone was stern.

"San Diego. But it's really not that great."

"Liar. How do you always get the good trips?" In the past three months her friend had been to Miami and Phoenix. Victoria had been to Amarillo and Bridgeport.

"I'm dating the boss. It means I'll never get promoted, but I get the good trips."

Victoria shuddered. If that's what it took, she'd rather be sent to Alaska.

"Don't worry, I'm sure you'll start getting sent to better locations in the New Year."

"Yeah, maybe." She wasn't so sure. "Okay, I have to get back out there."

"I'm sorry, Vic. I thought it would be fun for you to catch up with your old friends." Heather sounded disappointed. "You always talk about them and the fun you had in high school. Kind of makes me jealous. I was always the outsider at my school."

"I realize you meant well, but I just don't know these women anymore. We certainly don't have anything in common. I feel like my life is meaningless to them. My accomplishments mean nothing because I haven't done them with a baby on my hip." She let out a deep sigh and rubbed her forehead. She had to call it a night. The free Wi-Fi just wasn't worth it.

"Don't let them get to you. We will celebrate our lack of knowledge of poop and vomit at the Richardson the night you get back. First round of drinks and the cab are on me."

She doubted that another girls' night out

would so easily put to rest the idea triggered by her old friends that life was passing her by, but she just said, "Okay. Talk to you soon." Disconnecting the call, Victoria freed herself from the bathroom stall. She readjusted her pink cashmere sweater, relieved she didn't know the other person at the sink. She washed her hands and smoothed her wavy, blond hair before walking out.

"I'm not sure she's having a good time." Lisa was saying as she approached the table. "I don't think she finds our domestic life very interesting."

"Well, I don't see anything spectacular about being attached to a laptop and Black-Berry, either," Ava said. "And she's never going to get married and have kids if she can't even find time to go on a date."

"Remember who you're talking about. Victoria's never wanted those things. It's not like she didn't have the opportunity—she chose something different, that's all," Rachel said.

"Well, I still think she's crazy for leaving Luke," Ava replied.

"Speak of the devil, look who just walked in… Now this should be interesting." Lisa blushed, noticing Victoria behind them.

She followed the other woman's gaze toward the pool hall entrance and her heart sank. Couldn't she get through one disaster today without him playing a role in it?

Luke stood in the entrance, scanning the almost-empty pool hall.

Lisa held up a hand in greeting.

Ava swatted her arm down, with a quick glance in Victoria's direction. "Stop that," she said in exasperation as Luke approached their table. "Great. He's on his way over. Sorry, Victoria."

"It's nothing I can't handle." Victoria took a sip of her drink and fought to keep her hand steady. After all this time, despite her success in New York, her friends still thought she'd made the wrong decision. Well, she didn't expect them to understand her motivations and ambitions. They never had. At least she could count on Rachel to defend her. *Just get through this evening.*

"Hey, ladies. Glad to see you three finally got an evening out. Ava, I see Darren over at the pool tables. Who's with the kids?" Luke asked.

"They're spending the night at Grandma

and Grandpa's." She pumped her fist in the air, which made them all laugh.

"Rachel," he said, "you look beautiful as usual. Quite the pregnancy glow you have working for you."

"Thanks, Luke." Rachel turned a deep shade of crimson, but it was obvious the compliment had made her evening.

Traitors. All of them. Victoria watched in amusement as the three women chatted up her ex-fiancé. Squinting in the dim lighting, she took in his strong jawline and blue eyes reflecting the glow of the Christmas lights hanging from the ceiling.

"Hey, Luke. Quit flirting and get over here." Jim Bishop waved from the pool table and held up a beer.

Luke nodded as he moved around the table. "Excuse me, ladies. I have some money to win." He paused by Victoria's chair and lowered his voice to say, "I thought you were tired. Does your mother know that you lie to her?"

Victoria stared at the glass in her hand. "I don't know, Luke. Does *your* mother know you had dinner at our house?"

Luke cleared his throat as he unzipped his

leather jacket. "Well, our mothers don't need to know everything, now, do they?"

"Enjoy your pool game," she said, dismissing him.

He glanced at her computer on the table in front of her. "You brought your laptop on a girls' night?" he asked. "Real party girl. Enjoy your evening, ladies." He raised a hand and sauntered off.

Victoria resisted the urge to turn and stick her tongue out to his back. "I think we need another round," she said, draining the contents of her glass. She stood and had to grip the edge of the tall bar table for support against a dizzy spell.

"Not me. I just texted Nathan to let him know I'm on my way. Sorry, Victoria, I'm beat." Rachel slipped into her coat.

"No problem. Get some rest." It was almost eleven. In New York, the night would just be getting started. In Brookhollow's local hot spot, only a few quiet tables remained other than the boys shooting pool. She should call it a night, as well. She had the perfect excuse now with Rachel leaving. Turning toward the pool tables, her eyes met Luke's. She'd stay for one more drink with the girls. She had been a little rude.

"Okay. Be sure to stop by this week and we'll catch up some more." Rachel got up from the table, adjusting her purse strap on her shoulder.

Ava stood. "I'll walk you to your car."

"Another glass of wine?" Victoria raised an eyebrow.

Lisa and Ava hesitated. No doubt the gap between their lifestyles was perfectly clear to each of them.

"I'd love to see pictures of your children if you have them." She really was interested in their lives; she just hated that it stirred an unprecedented yearning in her.

The other two agreed.

"Okay then, I'll be right back."

"I'll save our table." Lisa was already digging around in her purse for pictures.

"Sure," Victoria said. As if that would be necessary. The place was dead.

Approaching the bar, she ignored the cat calls from the pool tables. "Hi, Melody. Can we get another round?"

"Sure, Vic. How've you been?" The bartender, Melody Myers, was another old high school acquaintance. With a yawn, she poured vodka into a shot glass and dumped the contents into a short glass, before reaching for a can of energy drink.

She looked older than her thirty-two years. The lines around her eyes and forehead were deep and she appeared to have aged more than the rest. With her thinning face and even a few streaks of gray in her light brown hair, it was hard to believe they were the same age and from the same graduating class. Having lost her husband in a car accident the year before, she was raising her twin seven-year-olds on her own.

"I've been good. Busy…"

"Yeah, I noticed the laptop."

Victoria ignored the hint of judgment she thought she detected in the woman's voice. "How about you?" she asked gently.

"Taking it day by day," Melody answered honestly as she shook a shaker and poured Lisa's fruity cocktail, then grabbed the bottle of house white wine to pour a glass for Ava. She placed the drinks on the bar.

Victoria nodded as she reached into her wallet. Melody's incredible voice had once kept her very busy at weddings and funerals. Victoria had always assumed she'd take it further. It saddened her to think that Melody's life hadn't turned out exactly how she'd planned. She hesitated before asking, "Do you still sing?"

Melody wiped down the bar and deposited the cash in the register. She tossed the change into the tip jar after Victoria refused to take it. "Well, I'm still a star at the church and with my kids every night. That's enough for me." But there was a note of longing in her voice.

Victoria noticed the pictures of the young boys behind her on the bar mirror. Cute kids.

Melody caught her staring and smiled. The effect softened her hardened features. "David and Joshua—twins. Must be something in the water around here. Be careful," she warned, nodding toward Luke.

Victoria's cheeks heated. "Thanks for the warning—" she indicated her drink "—I'll be sure to stick to this." And as far away from Luke Dawson as possible, which would be a challenge given the reason for her visit.

LUKE LINED UP a shot for the eight ball. He lowered his gaze to sight down the pool stick. Beyond the green felt, he saw Victoria saunter back toward their table, drinks in hand. Dress pants and a formal sweater for the local watering hole. He suspected she hadn't packed a single set of casual clothes in her no-doubt designer suitcase. But no matter how much he wanted to, he couldn't fault her—she seemed to be living the life she'd always desired and he respected that. Drawing back, he let the pool cue slide between his fingers. The white ball spun toward its target, directing the other ball straight into the left-hand, corner pocket. "And that's how it's done." He stood and grinned, as the other men booed.

Jim counted out the twenties in his hand. "Who invited you here tonight anyway?" he mumbled and turned to the group. "Come on, guys. One of us has to be able to take him."

Darren shrugged. "He's on fire tonight," he said. "And I've already lost more to him than I'm going to tell my wife." He drained his beer and stood.

"I heard that. I *am* just sitting over here," Ava called from where she sat with Victoria and Lisa.

Darren grimaced. "Sorry, honey." Joining their table, he wrapped an arm around his wife. "How about we head home and I'll

make it up to you?" he said, p
on her cheek.

Ava shot him a look. "Seriously? Y
lost a lot of money and you've been dri
ing and you think you're going to be romantic tonight?" She placed a hand over his face
and pushed his puckered lips away, hiding
her smile.

Luke joined them at the table. "How about
it, Ava? Want to try winning back some of
this guy's money for him?"

Ava grunted. "Luke, do you remember the
last time I played pool?"

"I do," Melody called from the bar. "By the
way, it's going to cost three hundred dollars
to fix that hole in the wall from the cue ball."
She pointed a finger.

"Shh…" Darren held a finger to his lips. "I
can't believe you reminded her."

Ava glared at him.

"I hadn't forgotten." Melody shook her
head and resumed filling the dishwasher with
the dirty beer mugs and glasses. "And guys,
this is last call."

"At eleven-thirty?" Jim sat on the edge of
Lisa's stool. She shuffled over to make more
room for her cousin.

"You usually close at one," Darren said.

"Josh and David have a dentist appointment in the city first thing tomorrow morning, so I'm kicking you out early."

"Okay, Mel. No problem. I guess I'm the winner here tonight." Luke shrugged and folded the bills.

"Not so fast." Victoria stood. "How much you got there?"

Luke's face lit up with amusement. "You? You think you can tear yourself away from your laptop long enough?"

"I asked how much you've got there."

Luke flipped through the bills. "Two hundred and eighty," he said, studying her face as she bit a thumbnail.

She dropped her hand. "Double or nothing."

He smirked. "You're serious? You think you can beat me?"

"Without a doubt," Victoria said confidently, moving closer to stand just inches from him. Defiantly, she stared him down.

She was even feistier than he remembered. Well, he had no problem taking her money, too. "You're on." He picked up her glass and drained it, then began choking and sputtering.

"That's disgusting. What was that? Cough syrup and vodka?"

"Red Bull and vodka." Victoria grabbed the pool stick out of his hand and sauntered toward the table in the corner.

"You do know that stuff can kill you, right?" Luke said, taking the empty energy drink can from where Melody had left it on the bar and following her.

The others followed.

Jim grinned. "This is going to be good."

Darren nodded.

"It actually says right on the label—Do Not Mix with Alcohol." Luke held the can in front of Victoria and pointed to the fine-print metallic ink.

Victoria squinted. "It does not." She pushed the can aside.

Luke was relentless. "It does."

"Are we playing pool or not?"

Luke set the can down. Had she been fine-tuning her eight ball skills in New York all this time? Pulling the rack out from under the table, he flipped it and tossed it to her. "Rack 'em."

Victoria caught it with one hand and busied herself collecting the faded, chipped, stray balls from the pockets. She leaned forward and arranged them inside the triangle. Her wavy blond hair fell over her shoulder and glistened in the light of the pool table. His gaze fell to her lips.

When she moved back, a dangling object above her head caught his eye. "Hey, Vic, look up," he said. Mistletoe was quickly becoming his favorite Christmas tradition.

Victoria paused and glanced toward the pool table light overhead and the thin, very old and worn piece of mistletoe hanging from the edge of the lampshade. She reached up and yanked it free, crumbling the brittle leaves as Luke approached. "Oh, no. You're not getting me that way again." She straightened and pointed a finger at him as he moved closer.

He lowered his head, enjoying the panic in her green eyes. "Don't even think about it, Luke." The words were strained and he heard her breath catch deep in her chest.

Luke moved his lips to the side of her face, against her flushed cheeks. Placing a hand on her waist, he drew her closer. "Don't worry, I'm not going to kiss you," he whispered in her ear.

Her eyes widened. "You're not… I mean, good," she said, evidently flustered.

Flustered was good. Gaining confidence, he dared to pull her even closer until his lips brushed her ear. "No. The next time I kiss you, you won't be fighting it."

CHAPTER FOUR

LUKE SHIVERED AS he trudged through the deep snow toward the service entrance of Doug's Motors, the best car repair shop in New Jersey. The sun had just crested the horizon, barely cutting through the early morning fog and lightly falling snow. He yawned as he opened the door and entered. He hadn't gotten to bed until one and he rarely stayed up past midnight anymore. The loud metal music playing inside the shop didn't help his throbbing head. Man, he was getting old.

"Hello?" he called above the music, scanning the shop. He noticed a pair of grease-stained coveralls and steel-toe boots sticking out from beneath a Dodge Charger toward the back of the bay. He kicked at one of the boots.

Bailey Sheppard sailed out, wrench in hand. "Luke!" she said, sitting up as she wiped her grease-stained cheeks with a dirty rag. It didn't help, only smeared the line of oil

across her nose. "Didn't hear you come in."
She stood and killed the loud music.

"How could you over that racket?" He
shook his head. "It's not even seven-thirty
in the morning."

"For you that's early, for me it's late. I
worked through the night," she said, suppressing a yawn as she poured a cup of tarlike coffee from the almost-empty pot.

He thought he recognized his cousin's vehicle up on blocks. "Isn't that Bryce's car?"

"Yeah, he has a court case in the city this
morning. He's picking it up at eight."

"Let me guess, he dropped it off late last
night." His cousin left everything until the
last minute, never concerning himself about
who he might be inconveniencing—in this
case the best mechanic in town. Also the prettiest.

"He caught me on the way out." Bailey
took a sip of coffee. "So what's up?"

"The truck heater is giving me trouble
again."

Bailey set the cup aside. "Bring her in. I'll
take a quick look."

"I'd appreciate that, thanks." Luke jogged
outside and drove the truck into the empty

work bay at the end. He popped the hood and jumped out, as Bailey approached with a tool kit and a new heater blower motor. "You figure it's the blower motor?"

"Nine times out of ten." She nodded, setting the tool kit aside and looking under the hood. "Luke, how are you still driving this old thing?"

Luke ran a hand along the roof and laughed. "You take good care of her, she's still running great."

"Not for long by the look of this engine," Bailey warned, wiping her hands on her coveralls. "Anyway, the heater will take a couple of hours to fix, so I'll just drop it off at Legend's on my way home around nine-thirty?"

"You're an angel, thank you. I'm meeting Victoria at the store, so I'll be there."

"That's right, I'd heard something about her coming to town. Actually, Darren texted me last night to say she'd almost kicked your butt in a pool game."

"*Almost* is the key word." Luke shook a finger at her. "You are still the only pool shark in town able to beat me. And by the way, I'm still waiting for my rematch to prove it was just a fluke."

Bailey laughed. "Not on your life," she said, cranking the music and sliding back under Bryce's Charger.

Leaving the shop, Luke almost collided with his cousin. "Hey. In a rush?"

Frazzled, Bryce ran a hand through his wet, wavy hair. Tiny pieces of tissue paper stuck to his chin and a blob of shaving cream slid down his neck. "Yeah, I got the time of my court case messed up. I need to be in New York by nine-thirty."

Luke often wondered how his cousin had ever gotten his law degree. He'd always been an absentminded professor—not exactly top of the list of qualities in a successful lawyer. Yet his law firm did well.

It helped that it was the only one in town.

"Don't sweat it, Bailey's been working on your car all night. I think it's just about done."

Bryce's shoulders relaxed. "Great."

"Hey, while I have you. I may have some documents for you to look at later in the week."

"About the sale of the store?"

"Not that I'm selling, but yeah—if you have time."

"No problem, I'll make sure you get a good price."

Was Bryce listening? "I don't plan on accepting the offer. I just may need a second set of eyes, that's all."

"Listen, Luke, I get that the store means a lot to you, but you really should at least consider selling. You must have a lot of your own cash flow tied up in the renovations." Bryce straightened his tie and tucked the edges of his shirt into his pants, fastening the belt.

Luke didn't expect Bryce to understand. Suffering from asthma from a young age, he'd never participated in sports and as far as Luke knew, his cousin had never even stepped inside Legend's. Others were sure to share his attachment though—anyone who'd played sports in school; anyone with kids. "Either way, I'll call Brenda if I need your help."

"Sure, I'll let her know to leave some time open in my schedule this week," Bryce said, plugging one ear against the blare of the music as he hauled the door open to step inside. "Maybe you should let Victoria have what she came for, so she can get out of here before you get attached to something else equally draining."

Head down against the blowing snow, Luke headed in the direction of the sporting goods store. Cut his ties with both Victoria and the store before either one or both ended up costing him more than he could afford? The memory of the night before, watching her laugh as she gave him a run for his money, and sensing she too was experiencing conflicting emotions gave him hope.

Of course, she'd loved him when they were engaged and about to be married.... Love hadn't been enough to keep her then so why would it make any difference now?

SUN SHINING THROUGH the blinds woke Victoria the next morning. She had trouble opening her eyelids. *Darn it.* Her contact lenses were stuck to her tired eyes. She must have forgotten to remove them when she arrived back at the bed-and-breakfast long after midnight.

She threw back the bed sheets and swung her legs over the side of the bed. At the bathroom mirror, she peeled the dry lenses from her irritated eyes.

Luke had been the ultimate charmer at dinner. No doubt show for her mother. He'd insisted they put business aside for the evening and try to forget the reason for her visit. Her mother had beamed. Talk about misplaced loyalty. She knew her mother still wished she and Luke had gotten married. Sheila Mason made no secret of the fact that she longed for grandchildren and was losing hope of ever having any. Victoria also suspected her mother missed the close friendship she once had with Luke's mother and hoped a reunion between their two children could mean re-uniting the families. She hated to disappoint her mother.

She felt as if she'd made a habit of disap-pointing her over the years.

After rinsing the lenses with saline solu-tion, she grimaced as she put them back in. Her tired reflection stared back in the mir-ror. Her shoulder-length blond hair lay limp around her face and her eyes were puffy and bloodshot. She'd been in Brookhollow less than twenty-four hours and the stress was al-ready showing. Splashing cold water on her face, she reached for her toothbrush. If last night had taught her anything, it was that she'd been right to keep her visits to a mini-mum.

The room phone rang.

Anyone from her office would call her cell phone. Not that they'd have much luck getting through. If the only place she could get consistent cell reception was in the pool hall washroom, she'd be spending a lot of time there.

She ignored the phone—likely her mother—instead smearing toothpaste onto her toothbrush. It was too early to discuss how fantastic dinner had been or how great Luke looked or the reasons she'd left him years ago.

Luke had made a choice, as well. He could have moved to New York. The full-time job offer from Clarke and Johnson Acquisitions after her internship had been what she'd been waiting for, working toward.

The phone rang again.

"Jeez, Mom!" She tossed her toothbrush on the counter, spit the toothpaste into the sink and dashed across the room. Answering on the fourth ring, she said, "Yes, Mom, dinner was fun, Luke looked fantastic and I'm an idiot for leaving Brookhollow. Did I forget anything?" She sighed. What would it take to convince people how fantastic her life was now?

A deep voice answered, "Well, I can't take

the credit for dinner, but thank you for the compliment, and it's about time you admitted moving to the city was a dumb idea."

She opened her mouth to speak, but Luke didn't pause to let her.

"I'm downstairs. Hurry up."

"What do you mean, hurry up? I'll meet you at the store in an hour."

She checked the clock on the bedside table. *Ten o'clock.* She hadn't meant to sleep so late. By ten any other day, she'd have put in a few hours' work already.

"I've been at the store waiting for you since eight o'clock. Does your company know you sleep in on the job?"

"Why didn't you call sooner?"

"I wasn't aware you relied on me to be your alarm clock. Had I known—" Luke lowered his husky voice "—I would have found a more enjoyable way to wake you."

"Luke!"

"I *did* call your cell twice. It went straight to voice mail, which by the way is full."

She groaned. She'd expected as much. "My service here is inconsistent," she said.

"Whatever. I'm here now. Get your butt downstairs in five minutes."

Dial tone.

Victoria stood staring at the receiver. She walked to the window. His truck was parked on the street in front of the inn, and unexpectedly, she smiled. She couldn't believe he still drove that beat-up thing. The truck had been old when he'd bought it secondhand from his cousin more than a decade ago, the same day he got his license. There had been many kisses in the cab of that clunker.

Luke got out to fix a wiper blade. Wearing faded jeans, a cable-knit sweater and a baseball hat, he looked like the boy she'd left a lifetime ago. But he wasn't that boy anymore. He was the owner of the store she was here to buy.

She pulled a pair of navy dress pants out of the closet and dug around in her suitcase to find her dark brown cashmere sweater. After tugging it over her head, she ran a brush through her thick hair. She applied her lipstick and mascara and checked her reflection in the mirror. Not bad for someone who'd encountered the ghost of Christmas Past the night before. She grabbed her coat from the chair next to the bed and glanced at the clock.

Four minutes. That stopped her. She sat in the plush velvet armchair.

She'd let him wait. Well, wait some more. Let him realize he couldn't boss her around. She would make this deal on her terms.

The ticking of the clock on the wall seemed louder with each passing second. She stood and paced in front of the window, checking her BlackBerry. Still no service. Her boss was probably wondering what was going on. She checked the clock again. Six minutes. *Long enough.*

Creeping down the main staircase, she avoided the creaky stair at the bottom. Mrs. Harris clanged pans in the kitchen and at the smell of raspberry muffins, her stomach growled. As soon as they hit Main Street, she needed food. She opened the side guest entrance door and the cold wind took her breath away as she stepped outside. Keeping her head down, she made her way to the truck. The door handle of the passenger side jammed.

Luke leaned over and opened the door from the inside. "Sorry, that one sticks sometimes."

"I remember," Victoria said as she climbed in. Light brown dog hair covered the seat and she cringed inwardly at the thought of the damage to her nice pants.

Luke handed her a cup from the Coffee Hut on the corner.

The strong smell of vanilla and cinnamon reached her nose. Her coffee tastes hadn't changed since she was a teenager, and apparently he remembered perfectly. "I wasn't sleeping. I was…working," she argued taking a sip of the hot coffee. *Mmm*… Much better than her usual, skinny, no-foam latte. More calories, as well. She put the cup in the holder.

"You still have pillow lines on your cheek."

She quickly glanced in the side mirror.

Luke turned off the side street onto the main road, heading away from the town center and the sporting goods store.

"Where are we going?" she asked as he pulled out into the traffic.

"It's a surprise." He didn't take his eyes off the road.

"Luke, I'm not much into surprises." She felt moisture bead on her palms. The only place she wanted to go was the store. She was desperate to start this process. There was so much to cover and more than a few details that needed sorting before she could get a sale offer. The thought of wasting any more time was torturous.

"Fine. It's not a surprise. I'm just not telling you."

"Why not?"

"Because I want you to ask me eight hundred times along the way." He studied her. "Look, it's only a few more blocks, okay? Just sit back and relax. Enjoy your latte."

"Fine." She was too tired to argue.

"So, where did you learn to play pool like that?" Luke asked after a moment.

"I lost, remember?" She wondered how long she could put off paying the utility bill that month, as the loss had created a gap in her monthly budget. It had been so close. She blamed the alcohol for the loss.

"Yeah, but you had me nervous there for a while. It was like watching myself play." He checked over his shoulder and changed lanes.

"That's because you taught me." Typical guy—he didn't even remember their first date. Guess it wasn't that memorable…to him. She, on the other hand, could recall every last detail, from him picking her up in this same truck to the first kiss they'd shared outside the pool hall. It had been Christmas then, too, during their sophomore year. The night of the first snowfall. The kiss had been nothing short of magical, with the big, soft snowflakes falling around them, feeling warm and protected in each other's arms.

Luke laughed.

"What's so funny?"

"The look on your face. Of course, I remember. I just wanted to see if you did." He winked.

Victoria cleared her throat. "Vaguely," she said, studying their surroundings to avoid his gaze. The junior high and high schools, across the street from each other, looked the same. The police station and fire department still shared the big old building on the corner of Oak and Pine Street. Even the shopping mall still boasted the same stores...Reitman's, Moore's... Time seemed to have stood still in Brookhollow. She longed for the faces of strangers, and neighborhoods she didn't know, to help her distance her emotions from the job she was determined to do.

"Do you drive at all in New York?" Luke leaned forward to turn the heat on maximum.

She was grateful for the blast of heat at her feet. "Thanks." She shook her head. "No, not often. It's faster to take the subway around the city."

"That explains that parallel-parking job yesterday."

She narrowed her eyes. "You're still on that? It wasn't that bad." So, she couldn't parallel park? Really, who could?

"If you say so. Do you live right in the heart of the city?" he asked, pulling the truck onto a side street.

The neighborhood was familiar.

"About three blocks east of Central Park on Lexington Avenue." Beautiful, big, century-old homes lined both sides of this street. A group of young boys played street hockey in the road and moved aside to let the truck pass.

Luke waved to the boys and turned the truck onto a cul-de-sac.

"Hey, isn't this the old Kingston property?" she asked.

Luke pulled into a long driveway she'd been down many times before. The Kingston family home had stood unchanged since the late 1800s on acres of land, extending to a riverbank at the far end of the property. As kids they'd fished the river in the summer months and skated it in winter. She'd always loved the home's splendor and history.

She was a fast-paced, career-minded, executive apartment-style woman, but this house brought out a different side of her. A more domestic side she chose not to entertain often. The view of the stone mansion, with its twin, arching peaks and wraparound deck off the master suite, all draped in a thin veil of snow and ice, was breathtaking.

Luke, who used to have a passion for history and architectural design, had said that if the Kingstons ever sold the home, he would buy it. It had been a dream of theirs years before.

"What are we doing here?" she asked coldly. This was the last place she wanted to visit.

He stopped the truck in the driveway and shut off the ignition. "I live here." He opened the truck door and jumped down.

Her mouth gaped. He lived here? He owned the Kingston property? When? Why? How? And why hadn't her mother told her? Why hadn't her friends told her? She couldn't depend on anyone for gossip anymore. Her head swam with questions as she watched him come around to her side of the truck.

He gestured for her to get out.

She opened the passenger door and hopped down. "Since when?" she asked in disbelief, following him up the walkway to the front porch.

"Last year," he said, opening the front door and ushering her inside. A big tan Samoyed greeted them with slobbering kisses.

Victoria cowered behind Luke at the sheer size of the animal. That wasn't a dog; it looked more like a bear.

On Luke's command, the dog sat. "Madi's harmless." He bent to pat her and pulled a treat out of his pocket. The dog lay on the floor and crunched her biscuit, ignoring the new visitor.

"I didn't even know the house was for sale," she said. Not that she would have been able to afford to buy it. Besides, the house was in Brookhollow and she'd never entertained the thought of returning. Not even in retirement.

"How would you have known?" Luke asked, leading her into the kitchen and turning on the coffeemaker.

Glancing around the room, Victoria took

in the original hardwood floor, the antique white cabinets and the old, mahogany furniture. "Mom usually mentions things like that." Her mother was certainly choosing her gossip carefully these days. "But I thought you were away last year?" She'd learned that much from her brief weekly conversations with her mother.

"I was." He leaned against the kitchen counter and motioned for her to sit. "I moved to Boston to finish my master's in architecture and in my last month at BU, I got a call from one of the architectural firms here offering me a contract job fixing up this place so it could be sold. Mrs. Kingston and her kids decided the expense of keeping up the house wasn't worth it when the kids all lived out of town, with no intent of returning. I didn't want anyone to destroy the integrity of the original house, so I jumped at it." He poured them coffee and joined her at the table.

"Thanks. Continue," she said. He still hadn't explained how he now owned the house of her dreams.

"When I met the family who intended to purchase the place, they had different ideas for their new home. They practically wanted to rebuild the entire house," he said.

"What? Were they out of their minds? You can't just destroy the history of this place!" She blushed at the passion she'd shown and, avoiding Luke's eyes, she picked up her cup and brought it to her lips. "Sorry, go on."

Luke cocked his head to the side. "It would be nice if you had that same opinion about the sporting goods store."

Victoria shook her head. "The store is different. Get back to the story."

Luke continued. "Well, I put in my own counter offer on the place and, knowing how much I loved the house, Mrs. Kingston accepted it. She was relieved her family home wouldn't be torn down—or modified beyond recognition." He sat back in his chair and crossed one leg over the other.

"But, how could you…um…" She hesitated. There was no polite way of asking where the funds had come from. "This house is on nine acres of land, how did you…"

"Afford it?" Luke shrugged. "I'd been working for the five years between my degree and master's program and I put almost every cent away. I'd been planning to move to New York myself…"

Her stomach lurched.

"…but then this happened…and then the store…" His voice trailed off as he studied her.

He'd been planning to move to New York? He hated big cities. Would he have looked her up if he had? Would she have cared? Too many unanswered questions ran through her mind. None of that mattered now. He hadn't moved to New York. He'd bought a house in Brookhollow.

Putting the cup down, she stood and checked her watch. It was almost eleven. "Well, congratulations, Luke. It's a beautiful home, but why exactly are we here?"

He picked up their empty mugs and placed them in the sink. "Right, business, of course. Follow me." He led her down the hallway and up the spiral staircase to the landing at the top. The house was breathtaking. Every room was more beautiful than the previous one, and as she stood at the top of the staircase, overlooking the main living area with its original stonework fireplace and double French doors dividing the space, it was hard to ignore what she was feeling. It was just a house. So what if Luke was realizing a dream they'd once shared?

"Watch yourself," he cautioned, reaching to pull a small cord hanging from a door on the ceiling. It opened outward, and a small ladder sailed out. "That wasn't much fun the first time." He headed up the ladder.

"Where are you going?" Victoria peered up into the darkness of the attic. A cold draft reached her, and she rubbed her arms.

Luke flicked a switch, and the attic illuminated with a dull yellow glow. "We need to find the paperwork for the store. Get up here," he said as he disappeared from view.

Victoria glanced at her new dress pants and sweater. She hesitated. Sorting through boxes in an old attic was not in her job description. Neither was spending time alone with her former fiancé in a house they'd once dreamed of as they planned a future together. *Why couldn't this acquisition have been easy, like the others?* A simple exercise in paperwork, not a treacherous trip down memory lane.

"Come on. You're wasting time. Don't you

want to get this over with so you can get back to New York?"

He had a point, but there could be spiders up there. Big ones. She placed her hands on her hips. "Why do I need to come up? Can't you find them yourself?"

"If your company wants to buy the store, you're going to need the original paperwork and blueprints. I stored them in a box up here. It will be much faster if we both look and you certainly seem in a hurry to get this done," he called down to her.

He was right. She was in a hurry and the more time she spent with Luke, the more urgency she felt. The pants were already covered in dog hair. How much worse would a little dust be? She held the wall as she climbed the old wooden ladder. The rungs twisted and creaked beneath her feet. "Are you sure this ladder is safe?" Gingerly, she crept her way to the top.

"Nope, but it's the only way up here."

"When did you accumulate so much stuff?" Victoria gasped. The attic was full of boxes and she squinted to read the labels. "Christmas decorations, family photos… What is all of this?" Swiping at a spiderweb, she hoped the occupant was long gone.

Luke shrugged. "Most of these boxes belong to the Kingstons. I said she could store them here as long as she needed. Her children weren't interested in keeping the bigger items, but they will be coming to get the photos and boxes of memories at some point. Who knows, I may even break out those Christmas decorations next week." He opened a box in the corner, looked inside, then closed it back up.

Victoria's heart sank at the mention of the Christmas decorations. The Kingstons' home was even more beautiful at Christmas, with white lights strung everywhere and the big evergreen tree in the yard decorated with hundreds of baubles and bows. The family used to host a decorating party each year and invite the neighborhood kids to help them. It was a tradition she missed this time of year when she allowed herself to remember. Usually each year she'd make a point of getting to Rockefeller Center and spend a few stolen, dreamy minutes watching the ice skaters in the sunken rink there. The enormous Christmas tree always made her think of the

Kingstons'. Grand in its own setting, theirs would look quite modest next to the massive New York City version.

"Maybe I'll even let you help decorate." Luke stopped opening boxes and searched her face.

Victoria cleared her throat and looked away. "I'll be gone by next week." She hoped. Christmas in Brookhollow would be too much. She had to be back in New York by then. The magic of the city would help her shake this feeling of nostalgia. The memory of the decorated Kingston tree would be overpowered by the magnificent display in Rockefeller Center, and the shopping therapy before her ski trip would erase any lingering sentiments she may have for her hometown and ex-fiancé.

"Well, you're here now. Start looking through those boxes on your right." He pointed to a stack on the shelf along the wall. They were unlabeled and the cardboard looked newer than the rest.

"What exactly am I looking for?" She opened a box and coughed, waving away a cloud of thick dust. Maybe they weren't so new.

"A big brown envelope with the name of the store on the front." Luke opened a small window and tied back the stained, lace curtain. "Let me know if you get cold. I just think we should air out some of this old dust we're stirring up."

The fresh, cool air made it easier to breathe in the confined space. "I'm fine." She sifted through three boxes of clothes and one of old encyclopedias. No envelope. Moving the boxes aside, she opened two more. Just old winter clothing and blankets.

"Hey, check this out." Luke held a photo album open in her direction. "It looks like their wedding photos."

Victoria made her way to the other side of the attic and took the heavy leather-bound book from him. Pictures of Mr. and Mrs. Kingston in front of the Catholic church on Maple Street. She touched a black-and-white photo. "Wow, she looked beautiful." The old-fashioned, lace dress she wore was simple and elegant. Classic Mrs. Kingston. With her hair tied simply at the base of her neck, she looked radiant. Her husband stood next to her, young, handsome and in love as he stared at his new bride.

Luke looked over her shoulder as she flipped the pages. His breath on the back of her neck made her shiver and she moved farther away before closing the book. She handed it back to him.

"Most people are happy on their wedding day. The unique thing about the Kingstons, was they were happy every day together." After fifty-eight years of marriage, they had remained in love until the day Mr. Kingston had lost his battle with cancer. A year ago. Victoria had been on an acquisitions trip in Arizona at the time and hadn't made it to the funeral. She struggled with the sudden guilt she felt and headed back to her stack of boxes. Fifty-eight years.

"You know, I think you and I could have made it that long together."

Victoria stared at the box in front of her. "No way. We fight too much." She opened the next box.

"So did the Kingstons. Don't you remember the stories Mrs. Kingston used to tell about their first years of marriage?"

Victoria shook her head. She didn't.

"Like how their eldest daughter got her name."

"Liz?" Victoria pulled out a box, wiped the dust away and sat.

Luke continued to dig through the boxes. "Mr. Kingston wanted to name her Ann, after his grandmother, but Mrs. Kingston wanted Liz…Elizabeth. They argued right up until the day of the christening, when Mr. Kingston finally said, 'I'm the man, I make the decisions.'"

She rolled her eyes. "That would never work these days."

"Funny, it didn't work then, either. Mrs. Kingston didn't argue. She waited until the priest asked for the baby's name and without pausing she said 'Elizabeth Ann Kingston.'"

Good for you, Mrs. Kingston.

"And in front of the priest and all of the friends and family, how could Mr. Kingston fight her?" Luke shook his head.

"So that's why he always called her Ann," Victoria said with a smile.

Luke nodded. "Drove her nuts…but she still loved him."

"Yeah, well, Mr. Kingston was better looking than you." The joke was meant to ease the tension between them, but it hadn't worked.

"Maybe." He nodded. "But I think we fight

because we're passionate about what we want, just as they were."

"Right." She couldn't disagree. It had always been the way between them. "But in our case, we want very different things."

Luke placed a hand under her chin and tilted her face toward his. "I think we wanted the same thing, we just had different ideas on how to get it."

Victoria's cheeks flushed. Removing his hand from her face, she stood, backing away from him. "Well, right now what we both want are those store papers and we won't find them this way." She pointed to the other side of the attic. "You go back over there."

She turned and tore into a box. She needed those papers and soon. Luke Dawson had always held her heart tight in his grasp and despite time and distance, that hadn't changed. Coming home hadn't been a good idea. *Jeez, now even I'm calling it home.* She had to get out of Brookhollow as soon as possible.

Four hours and countless boxes later, Victoria yawned as she stood to stretch.

"Do you want me to get more coffee?" Luke asked, glancing up from the box he was rummaging through.

"You went last time. It's my turn." She climbed backward down the ladder and made her way to the kitchen, pausing to look into the various rooms along the way. Alone, she took time to marvel at the home's beauty. Most of the rooms were still empty, as the house was far too big for one person. Many evenings they'd fantasized about filling those rooms with the sound of children and family. In truth, the idea had terrified her.

She ran a hand along the papered wall as she studied the old black-and-white family photos still hanging there. Luke hadn't taken them down.

Opening the door to the study, she took in the extensive floor-to-ceiling library on one wall, the antique writing desk in the center of the room and a small rose-colored, wood-rimmed satin couch in front of the large window, overlooking the garden. The old fireplace in the corner hadn't worked in years, but it was so cozy, regardless.

She closed the study door and continued past the spiral staircase to the kitchen. She set the coffeepot to brew and rinsed their mugs. She opened several drawers, looking for a dish towel to dry the mugs. One contained a stack of unopened mail addressed to the Kingstons. And sitting on top was the elusive paperwork. Legend's Sporting Goods was written in black marker across the manila envelope.

"You've got to be kidding me," she said, pulling the envelope out and slamming the drawer.

"What's that?"

Victoria jumped at Luke's unexpected appearance in the kitchen. "The papers we've been searching for all day." She slapped them against the palm of her hand, eyeing him suspiciously.

"That's great." His smile faded at her expression. "What?"

"You honestly expect me to believe you didn't know it was in here?" She threw the envelope on the table. What had he been hoping to achieve with their wild-goose chase through the attic? The pictures of the Kingstons, all the talk about the Christmas decorating... What had been the point?

"I had no idea. I could have sworn I put it in one of those boxes." He picked up the envelope and peered inside. "Looks like everything we need. What were you doing snooping around in my drawers anyway?" he asked.

"I wasn't snooping. I was looking for a towel."

Luke opened the only drawer she hadn't tried and removed a dish towel.

She scowled. Four hours in a dusty attic with him for nothing. Almost two days of this trip wasted so far. She shook her head. No more distractions. She had a job to do.

Luke poured a cup of coffee and handed it to her.

"Actually, no coffee for me. I need to get back to the inn. I'll just go through my documents with you so you can review them, and then I should have an offer tomorrow." She ignored the outstretched cup.

"An offer I *won't* be accepting." His voice was firm, as he set the cup down and leaned against the kitchen counter.

"We'll see." She opened her bag and took out the documents. Spreading the paperwork across the table, she highlighted the more important areas for Luke to review. She drew a big *X* next to the signature line. By week's end, his name would be scribbled across it, and she'd be back in New York. She cleared her throat and forced herself to think of him as just another business owner she intended to win over. "Okay, so here's the information about Play Hard Sports and the contributions they plan to make to the community… and this is my company's information and a sample contract…"

The Samoyed sauntered in and let out a deep bark.

Victoria moved to the other side of the kitchen, away from the animal.

"What's wrong, Madi?" Luke asked, ruffling the dog's ears. "Do you have to go outside?"

The dog yelped in response and danced from one paw to the other.

Luke opened the kitchen door and a cold blast of air swept through, scattering the papers to the floor. Victoria retrieved them as Luke coaxed the dog outside.

The big ball of fur whined in protest.

She couldn't blame the dog for changing her mind. Fat, wet snowflakes fell on the wooden porch, and the wind blew snow across the door frame.

"I hate to break it to you, Victoria, but I don't think you'll be going anywhere, not anytime soon." Luke closed the door after the dog and then reopened it a few seconds later to let her back in.

The dog shook the snow from her thick fur coat as she walked past.

"It looks awful out there." Her stomach clenched. She couldn't be stranded here with him. "How long do you think the storm will last?"

"I'm sure the wind will die down soon." Luke's tone was reassuring, but the look in his eyes suggested he suspected otherwise.

She picked up the steaming coffee cup and carried it to the table. "Well, I guess we could at least go over these papers now. No sense in wasting any more time." With any luck, by the time they finished going through the terms and conditions of the sale, the storm would have passed.

Luke took the proposal from her. "I have a better idea. Since we're both dirty anyway and it's a perfect pre-Christmas snow day, why don't you help me decorate this place? That way you'll at least get to see it before you disappear back to the city," he said. "I'll even make dinner."

"You? Cook?" Victoria's mouth dropped in

disbelief. The Luke she remembered couldn't even boil water.

"Yes, as a matter of fact." His smile reached his eyes.

Her knees weakened, and she sat at the table. "Fine. But tomorrow when I have the offer, we have to focus on business and business only."

What on earth was she doing? Dinner alone with her ex-fiancé, in this house, so full of memories, with a snowstorm raging outside? She stared out the kitchen window as the snow blanketed the yard. The trees were hardly visible, and the truck in the driveway was buried. The blowing snow would make travel dangerous. There was no escape. She was stuck there as long as the storm continued.

"Deal," Luke agreed, extending a hand.

She stared at it for a moment, then extended her own.

His rough grip tightened and made her hand seem so small. She'd made a lot of deals with a handshake in her career so far, but none felt as binding as this one.

CHAPTER FIVE

"How is it?" Luke asked a few hours after the snow had buried the truck, pouring red wine into two glasses and setting one down in front of Victoria. He laughed and wiped a glitter speck off her cheek. "From the Christmas decorations."

"Oh." She touched her face.

While Victoria had put up the Kingstons' old Christmas decorations, he'd delivered on his promise to cook dinner. Neither had broached the subject of the storm or the potential sleepover doomed to take place as the wind and snow raged on. The radio reported near-record accumulation and predicted the blizzard would continue through the night. As much as he sensed her apprehension, he was grateful for Mother Nature's untimely storm. Bringing her to his home, the Kingstons' home, the one they had always admired together had had the desired effect of reminding her of the past, but the storm helped to prevent her from escaping the nostalgia.

"The food tastes wonderful," Victoria said honestly, taking another bite of the pork roast he'd prepared in his slow cooker with vegetables and gravy.

"I'm glad you're enjoying it." He sat down and looked at her over the Christmas centerpiece of cinnamon-scented candles and boughs of holly. Keeping his eyes off her had been a challenge all afternoon. Either Christmas spirit or the magic of this old house had visibly relaxed her. He'd even caught her humming along to the Christmas music. The sight of her decorating the home had warmed his heart in a way he'd never expected.

Victoria shifted in her seat, dropping her gaze to the plate of food. "You're staring at me again."

Luke laughed softly. "Sorry, I'll try to stop doing that," he said though he knew it would be impossible. "So, I take it you don't cook much in the city."

"Why would you assume that?"

"Because when I asked you to hand me the gravy strainer, you gave me the pasta strainer instead," he said.

"You caught me," she admitted, raising her hands in defeat. "I'm a terrible cook. Most of my meals are either from a salad bar, a restaurant or takeout," she said. "I'm too busy, and besides, in the city, you can order anything you want and they'll deliver it right to your door."

"You work long hours?" Luke sat back in his chair, wineglass in hand, studying her. He wondered if she really enjoyed her life in the city and if she ever regretted calling off their wedding.

"Around the clock," she said. "But I don't mind, I love my job and that's what it takes to get ahead." She pushed a piece of pork around her plate.

"Is that what this trip is about?" Luke leaned forward and reached for the Snowman pepper shaker. "Getting ahead?"

She hesitated. "It's about doing my job," she said finally with a shrug, then quickly changed the subject. "I still can't believe you bought this house." She glanced around the dining room, still filled with the Kingstons' antique furniture. "And all these beautiful furnishings…" Her hand trailed along the fine mahogany wood of the table.

"I told you, it was a rescue mission. I really had no choice," Luke said. He stood and carried their empty plates to the sink.

"It's so peaceful out here." She leaned into the high back of her chair and rested her head against the cushion. "So different from the city, where traffic and sirens are the background soundtrack to life. I'd forgotten how quiet things were in Brookhollow." The only illumination came from the scattered streetlights and the glow from the neighboring houses. "I bet on a clear night here, the moon and stars look incredible from the front porch."

"But you love the city, don't you?"

"Yes, I do."

"Is that why you hardly ever come to town? Just can't tear yourself away from everything New York has to offer?" Luke filled the sink with water. An uninstalled dishwasher still sat in the packaging in the corner of the kitchen.

Victoria remained silent for a long time.

Luke shut off the water and waited. They had all night. Except that wasn't nearly enough time to convince her that Brookhollow was home. His heart ached, but he decided to take advantage of whatever time fate allotted them.

Finally, she cleared her throat and said, "When I left here, I was determined to become a new person, the person I always felt I was on the inside…but who I could never become."

"Living here."

She nodded.

"With me." His voice was low and filled with raw emotion. "I understand. I always did. Believe it or not, I always understood you and I knew you'd have resented me if I'd convinced you to stay." He firmly believed that and it was his only source of comfort when he wondered about his own decision to just watch her leave.

Their eyes met and he didn't look away for a long moment. A silent battle raged in him. He wanted to reach for her, wrap his arms around her, and erase the years in between. Nothing mattered at that moment except for the unspoken words held back in fear.

Her cell phone beeped with a new text message on the chair next to her. She jumped at the sound and reluctantly tore her gaze away. A small smile crossed her face as she read.

"Boyfriend?" Luke asked fighting to keep the jealousy he felt out of his voice.

"Just a friend," she said with a shrug.

"I don't smile like that when I get a text message from a friend. Do you have a picture on there?" Luke nodded toward the phone.

"Of who?" she stalled.

"Your *friend*." Luke came closer.

Clutching the phone to her chest, she shook her head.

"Sure you do. Come on, let's see," he urged, forcing her arm away from her body.

"Why do you want to see him?" She struggled under his strength as he pried the phone out of her fingers.

"Just to see what I'm up against," Luke explained, hitting the recall button on the phone. Jordan's message came to life, under the profile picture of him she'd stolen from the online dating site. His heart sank. The guy had success written all over him.

"You're not even in the running." Victoria choked out, reaching for the phone.

Luke moved it farther away. "Maybe not yet," he said as he studied the photo. Sure this guy may be good-looking and successful, but he had something no one else did—her past, her memories, her triumphs and failures. He'd been the one holding her hand at her grandfather's funeral and the one holding her hair back when she had food poisoning on grad night. He knew her, what made her laugh… old seventies sitcoms…and what made her cry…sappy commercials at Christmas. Their history had to count for something. "Really? This guy?" He handed her back the phone.

Victoria studied the picture. "What's wrong with him?"

He shrugged. "Nothing. He just looks a little boring, safe. You could do better. I happen to know someone…"

Victoria shot him a look and put the phone in her coat pocket, text message unanswered.

Luke laughed. "How about some music?" he asked.

"Sure. I'll start the dishes." Victoria stood and rolled the sleeves of her sweater. "It's the least I can do in exchange for the dinner."

Luke went into the living room and scanned the CDs along the shelf near the window. Finding the one he was looking for, he removed it from the case and slid it into the player. Seconds later, the sound of Bob Marley's "Stir It Up" followed him into the kitchen. Grabbing a dish towel from the counter, he dried a plate.

"I can't believe you still listen to Bob Marley."

"Bob Marley never goes out of style." Luke put the plate in the cupboard and dropped the dish towel onto the counter. Taking her wet hands from the sink, he spun her around the kitchen.

She stumbled and Luke pulled her into the heat of his solid chest to steady her. "You okay?"

Her arms went around his neck and her body pressed against his. "Yes," she whispered.

Luke's head rested on top of hers and his lips brushed against her hair. Competing emotions fogged his thoughts. In his attempt to make *her* remember, he was remembering—all of it. "Victoria, I've…"

The music stopped and suddenly they were in the dark.

"What happened?" Victoria pushed against his chest and out of his arms, feeling for the counter behind her.

Luke shut his eyes in the dark as he took a step back. "A power outage. The storm must have taken out a transformer," he said as he steadied her against the counter. "Just stay here. I'll get a flashlight." He felt his way into the living room and winced as his knee cracked against something solid.

"Ow... Victoria did you move furniture in here?" He limped, feeling his way carefully to the desk.

"Sorry, I had to move some things around to fit the four-foot nutcracker statue into the corner near the window," she called.

Retrieving the flashlights, Luke returned following two bright beams of light and handed one to Victoria. In the dim illumination, he searched her eyes for any trace of the moment they'd just shared.

Victoria refused to meet his gaze.

The moment had passed.

Luke cleared his throat. "Well, I guess you're stranded here tonight."

"I guess so," she said, avoiding his eyes. "We should probably call it a night."

"Come with me and I'll show you where you can sleep." Luke led her out of the kitchen and up the staircase. The only room properly furnished was the master suite. He paused outside the door and turned.

Victoria hesitated in the hallway. "Oh, I can't…"

"None of the other rooms are furnished yet. Mrs. Kingston sold a lot in an estate sale while the house was for sale. I insist." He turned the door handle and pushed the door open for her, then stepped back. "I'll sleep downstairs…on the couch." He shifted his weight from one foot to the other and shoved his hands deep into his pockets. The couch was as far away from her as possible.

"Okay…thank you," she said, stepping into the room. She turned and offered him a weak smile. "Good night, Luke."

His shoulders sagged as he moved away from the doorway. "Good night. The second drawer in the tall dresser has my T-shirts in it. Feel free to use one," he called over his shoulder.

He suspected that by morning all the progress he'd made in opening her heart to him… to Brookhollow…wouldn't matter.

CHAPTER SIX

VICTORIA TIPTOED DOWN the creaking staircase on the way to the kitchen. She needed coffee…and lots of it. The time on the coffeemaker blinked 2:56. That couldn't be right. She reached into her purse on the table and pulled out her cell phone. 11:02. *Crap.* Moving around the kitchen, she waved it in the air until she found a signal near the kitchen door. Three missed calls. All from her boss. She rubbed her forehead and paced. Erik would be expecting a status report, and she had nothing.

She peeked into the living room. Luke still slept soundly on the tiny couch, his legs draped over the side. She forced her gaze from his exposed muscular chest and stomach as she dialed the number to the New York office.

"Clarke and Johnson Acquisitions," the cheery receptionist said.

"Kim, it's Victoria. Is Erik available?" Victoria whispered.

"Victoria? Why are you whispering?" The receptionist's own voice lowered to a conspiratorial level.

Because the enemy is asleep in the next room. "Bad cell reception out here." She moved farther away from the living room and raised her voice just a little.

"Okay. Actually, Erik just left for lunch. Would you like his voice mail?"

"No, that's okay. Please just let him know I called and things are going on schedule." *Two lies in less than a minute. A personal record.*

"Great, I'll let him know." The other woman paused. "Are you okay? You don't sound like yourself."

She forced herself to sound more upbeat. "Yes—I'm great.... Not a thing wrong—I'll talk to you soon." She disconnected the call and tossed her phone back into the purse.

Madi joined her in the kitchen and went straight to the door. The dog looked up at her, dancing from one paw to the other. Victoria braced herself for a cold gust of wind as she let her out. But to her surprise, the sun was bright on the snow-covered yard and a cool yet mild breeze blew against her bare feet.

The dog looked at her as though she somehow had something to do with the sudden climate change. She bounded down the few steps leading to the snowy yard and found a favorite tree.

Victoria stood in the doorway admiring the beauty. Even covered with four feet of snow, it looked magnificent and inviting. Large oak trees lined the fence and a tire swing still hung from one of the thick branches. Luke had always said the yard would be wonderful for children. He had talked about building a tree house and putting up a jungle gym. The idea of a family and the domestic life he painted had meant sacrificing everything she'd wanted for herself.

Watching the kids in the yard next door building a snow fort, Victoria fought an unexpected feeling of emptiness. Her life was everything she'd hoped it would be in the city. The confusion she was experiencing was unsettling.

The sound of the back door of the neighbor's house opening startled her. A young woman stepped out onto the deck and glanced over.

Oh, no. Turning away, Victoria ushered the dog back inside. "Come on, Madi," she cajoled.

The dog licked an icicle hanging from the deck.

"Madi, let's go," she begged to no avail.

"Victoria? Victoria Mason? Is that you?"

Too late. Victoria ran a hand through her disheveled hair and forced a smile as she waved at Lindsay Harper, Rachel's sister-in-law. Another woman in town who could be counted on to know everything about everyone, and would share her knowledge without hesitation. As a nurse at the understaffed medical clinic, Lindsay worked hard, but she also played hard and her reputation for being a party girl in her off hours hadn't changed since their high school days.

"What are you doing at Luke Dawson's house?" A mischievous smile crept across the woman's face. "I get it. Relighting an old flame?" she asked. Her blond hair was piled high in a loose bun on top of her head and last night's dark mascara outlined her eyes, bleeding onto her cheekbones. She tossed an empty wine bottle on top of an overflowing recycle bin on the deck.

Victoria struggled to stay calm. In less than two hours, everyone in Brookhollow—including their mothers—would know she'd spent the night at Luke's house. "Um, no... Luke and I were just discussing business yesterday when the storm hit and I was forced to stay here." She hoped the truth sounded more convincing to Lindsay than it did to her own ears. Everyone knew the history between her and Luke, and now here she was standing on his back porch, wearing his T-shirt and pajama pants. Things couldn't get much worse.

"Oh, right. Of course, honey...business." Lindsay laughed. "Have a nice trip home. Make sure to stop in before you leave," she said as she turned to face a robed man in winter boots joining her on the snowy deck with two steaming mugs.

Victoria opened her mouth, then closed it. She dashed inside and closed the door. What a mess she'd created.

"Who were you talking to?" Luke, wearing only his jeans, said as he walked into the kitchen.

"Your neighbor, Lindsay Harper, who just saw me in your clothes and who has the biggest mouth in town and more friends than

Oprah. Within hours everyone in Brookhollow will know I spent the night here," Victoria said, pacing the kitchen linoleum.

"Don't worry about it." He cornered her and wrapped one arm around her shoulder.

She tensed at his touch and forced herself not to look at his toned chest and arms. *Where was his shirt anyway?* "Why not?" Maybe she was wrong about Lindsay Harper. Maybe she had changed since high school. Maybe she'd matured.

Luke shrugged. "It doesn't matter what people think."

"Maybe not to you, but our mothers are going to be furious and my boss would lose his mind…"

"Victoria, nothing happened and it's really not a big deal." Luke said, brushing a stray lock of hair off her face and placing a hand on her hip, as he drew her closer.

She batted his hand away and backed up until she hit the door frame. "I have to go. I must have been crazy to stay here last night." She stumbled past him, but he grabbed her arm to stop her.

His eyes blazed. "Fine, you're right. Maybe it wasn't a smart idea to start getting to know each other over again. I know *I* had been doing just fine, not knowing exactly what I was missing all this time. But it turns out my memory of you doesn't even come close to how wonderful you really are." He paused. "Look, all I know is having you in this house with me, the way we always talked about, was amazing and you can't tell me you don't feel anything when I do this." He pulled her into him and claimed her lips with his own.

Victoria struggled in his grasp, fighting to maintain control of her emotions. Her career was what mattered. Nothing else. Not Luke, not Brookhollow, not this house.

His tongue traced a trail along her lips and her knees buckled beneath her. He tightened his grip on her waist, and her body betrayed her as it curved into his.

She wouldn't allow this to happen. She pushed against his chest.

Luke pulled his head back, but kept hold of her.

Lifting her chin, Victoria stared into the eyes of the only man she'd ever loved. "Nothing." She shook her head. "Last night was amazing but it wasn't real. I have a life in

New York, Luke, and I feel nothing for you. Not anymore." *Last lie of the day.*

"SO YOU'VE REVIEWED the documents?" Victoria cradled her cell phone against her shoulder as she glanced at the town map on the passenger seat next to her. She'd have to figure out the GPS function on the BlackBerry when she got home. Scanning the folded sheet, she looked for the tiny sporting arena landmark. The arena was on the outskirts of town and she couldn't remember the correct turnoff. She checked the street signs. She was about two blocks away.

She'd just faxed her boss a copy of the floor plans and documents she'd gathered from Luke an hour earlier. Receiving a call from Erik so soon wasn't a good sign. From what she could tell from the documents, the buyout wouldn't be as simple as extending an offer and relying on some gentle persuasion to close the deal, even if the store owner wasn't her ex-fiancé. Her boss's tone suggested he too had underestimated the difficulty of this one.

"Yes. The original owners were very smart in their negotiations with the city when they purchased the building. They were protecting themselves from a situation exactly like this." Erik clearly wasn't thrilled, but he didn't sound discouraged, either. "It just means we have to work smarter, that's all."

Victoria recognized Erik's go-get-'em tone that she hated. He used it when he was expecting a lot from his employees.

"But we should still be able to get an offer soon…right?" She fought to disguise the anguish she felt. She could handle this acquisition. But staying positive was proving to be tough.

"Soon enough." Erik sounded noncommittal.

Her shoulders slumped as she pulled onto the arena parking lot, avoiding the potholes in the gravel. So much for being back in New York by the end of the week. The longer she stayed in Brookhollow, the harder this acquisition became and the more her personal life spiraled out of control.

"The problem is we don't have a legal leg to stand on in the original contract, which states that a competing chain store cannot occupy any space within fifty miles of Legend's Sporting Goods. While we're not technically opening a competing store next to them, we are trying to buy them out. The lines are blurry, but the bottom line is if they refuse to sell, there's not a whole lot we can do."

Fantastic.

"Do you think we should send in another rep...to assist you?" Erik paused. "Perhaps you're experiencing competing emotions on this one?"

You have no idea. She hesitated. Maybe another rep should take this one. Then she sat straighter in the driver's seat. *No.* The last thing she needed was for Erik to lose confidence in her abilities. She needed to close this deal and reaffirm her own belief in her abilities. She wouldn't let Luke Dawson and her guilt over the town's attachment to the store make her doubt her own choices. "Don't worry, Erik, I've got this. Just send the offer as soon as you can."

"There's the confidence I love. We'll talk soon," Erik said with a laugh. "And Victoria?"

"Yes?"

"Try to have a bit of fun while you're there. It is your hometown, isn't it?"

Fun? If he knew how much fun and how

little work she'd done so far, she'd be looking for a new job. "Sure thing, boss." She hung up and rested her forehead against the steering wheel. "Arrrgh!" *How is this happening?* This acquisition should have been a simple deal to close. Mr. Jameson had been long past retirement age. Play Hard Sports was offering Brookhollow a bigger, better sporting goods store just a short drive outside town. The store wouldn't even interfere with the quaint, picturesque community. And the employment opportunities it would provide... Could she convince the residents of that? Could she convince Luke?

She pounded her head against the cold plastic. Going head to head with him was going to be a battle, especially after the night before. *How could I have been that stupid and careless?*

The boys' bantam hockey team—the Brookhollow Blades—practice game would be over in twenty minutes. In San Diego, Heather should be up by now. She dialed her friend's cell phone.

Heather answered on the third ring. "Hello," she said through a yawn.

"Sorry, did I wake you?" Victoria bit her

lower lip as she stared through the windshield and watched as several families entered the arena. According to the schedule on their website, public skating was next, from one until three.

"Yeah, but I should be awake anyway. How are you?"

"In trouble."

"Okay, I'm awake." Heather sounded more alert. "What's happening?"

"This is an acquisitions nightmare." Victoria turned the rearview mirror and studied her reflection. Dark circles had formed under her eyes.

"Not as smooth as you'd hoped?"

"Have you forgotten that *Luke* owns the sporting goods store I'm here to buy?" She paused, waiting for her friend's reaction.

"Luke?" Her friend sounded confused.

Victoria tapped her fingers against the steering wheel and waited for the name to trigger recognition.

Heather gasped.

There it was.

"No way! Your ex-fiancé Luke?"

"Yes."

"You mean, the guy you talk about whenever you drink?"

Victoria frowned. Okay, maybe once or twice she'd told her friend about Luke, but it was only natural to share things about your past with a close friend. Luke had been a big part of her past, that's all.

"Fine. I may bring him up from time to time." Heather was missing the point. "Anyway, Erik says the paperwork stipulates that if he doesn't want to sell the store, he doesn't have to. What am I going to do?"

"Well, I know what you're *not* going to do, and that's let your feelings for him get in the way."

"I think they may already have."

"Victoria! I can't believe you." Heather sounded shocked. "You've been there two days... What are you thinking? You need to get it together."

"I know, I know." She readjusted the mirror. She couldn't even look at herself.

"Well, do you at least think it will work? If you fall back into his arms, will he sign the sale papers?"

"Heather! I'm not feeling this way on purpose in the hopes of convincing him to sell the store." She rested her head against the seat and shut her eyes.

"Then what's going on with you?"

"I don't know," Victoria groaned. "And it gets worse…"

"I don't see how it could."

"I spent the night at his house."

"You what?" Heather shrieked.

"There was a snowstorm…I was stuck."

"Victoria…what were you thinking?"

"I wasn't, okay… It's this place… I knew coming here was a mistake. I should never have accepted this acquisition."

"I don't think accepting the assignment was the mistake…"

Victoria's phone beeped with a call waiting. She glanced at the display. Her mother. "Listen, Heather, I have another call coming in. I'll have to call you back."

"But I'm not finished yelling at you yet."

"It's my mom. Trust me, she'll yell at me enough for both of you."

"Fair enough. Call me later."

Victoria hit the call waiting button. "Hi, Mom."

"Victoria Suzanne Mason, tell me it isn't true."

She glanced at the time. 12:43 p.m. *Not bad*. It had taken only two hours for her mother to find out about her spending the night with Luke. She hesitated, preparing for her mother's lecture. "You told me never to lie to you," she responded. "Where are you anyway?" Loud traffic noises in the background made it hard to hear.

"Walking to my car," her mother snapped. "I just left the fabric store, where I had the most unpleasant run in with Darlene Dawson. Maria told both of us. She heard it from Louise Parsons, who said her daughter Emily heard it from…"

"Spare me the gossip chain, Mom. I stayed at Luke's because of the weather. There was nothing I could do." She rubbed her forehead.

"But Maria said Emily said that Lindsay Harper saw candles in Luke's house last night."

"Yes, the electricity went out."

She'd have thought her mother would be jumping for joy at the prospect of the two reuniting. Not that that was what was happening.

"Nothing happened," Victoria reassured her. She rummaged in her purse for a lip gloss at the memory of Luke's kiss. "Besides, why are you upset? I'd have thought you would have started the wedding preparations by now," she mumbled.

"I already went through those preparations once before…in vain. But the reason I'm upset is because I know you, Victoria, and you are going to break that man's heart again and I'll never hear the end of it from Darlene. If I thought she was bad to deal with before… Your father and I may have to leave town."

"Oh, please. Quit being so dramatic. You and Dad won't have to leave town. Luke is a big boy—he can deal with his mother. Nothing happened between us and no one is breaking any hearts. Try not to worry, Mom. I'll call you later."

Victoria ended the call and dug in her purse for an aspirin. Her head ached. Luke, her boss, Heather and now her mother. Something had to give. She had to convince Luke to sell the store and fast, before she went crazy.

LUKE'S CELL PHONE vibrated in his jacket pocket. He cut the power on the chain saw and set it on the ground at the base of the tree. Retrieving his cell phone, he groaned. *His mother.* He contemplated not answering, wondering how long he could avoid her. With all the various Christmas gatherings around town, probably not long.

"Are you going to answer that?" Jim asked, setting his own chain saw aside.

"It's my mom," Luke said, tossing the phone back and forth in his gloved hands. If he didn't answer it, his sisters were sure to start calling next and they'd be worse.

Jim laughed heartily, his heavyset shoulders shaking.

"What's so funny?"

"You're thirty-four years old and still afraid of your mom." Jim took a soda out of the cooler and popped the lid. He sat on the plastic box and rested his arms on his knees.

The phone continued to ring.

"I'm not afraid...." Luke kicked a pile of dirty snow toward his friend. "Just give me a sec." He moved a little way down the path and hit the receive button on the call. Maybe she'd just heard about dinner at the Masons. Yeah, right. "Hey, Mom."

"Care to tell me what's going on with you and Victoria Mason?"

Luke cringed. He was a grown man, yet the sound of his mother's disappointment still struck a nerve. *Get a grip. You're capable of making your own decisions.* He closed his eyes. Who was he kidding? No, he couldn't. He was an idiot. In one day, he'd opened himself up to the heartache and disappointment sure to follow an encounter with Victoria.

"Well?" His mother's volume increased.

"I don't know what to say, Mom. Yes, she spent the night at my place, but it doesn't mean anything." The words were tough to say. He wasn't sure what he'd been hoping for or expecting from Victoria, but her hasty departure that morning had been a blow to his ego.

"How can it not mean anything?"

"She's just here to do a job. We were looking for the store papers when the storm hit." He kicked snow from the bottom of his steel-toe work boots.

Oh, man. He refused to talk about this with his mother. "Look, Mom, I gotta go. Jim's going to cut his leg off with the chain saw. I'll call you later, okay?" he said, clenching his leather work gloves.

"Just promise me one thing."

"What?"

"Please don't allow yourself to get hurt by that girl again. Watching you get over her the first time was hard enough. And dealing with her mother…" She sounded sad.

"I won't get hurt, Mom. And you and Mrs. Mason have to get over this stupid fight. It has nothing to do with you two."

"It's a family thing, Luke. You and Victoria are our children. Your happiness means everything to us, therefore your choices affect us, too."

"Mom, I'm a big boy. I was just a kid back then." He rested against a tree.

"You may be older now, but believe me, matters of the heart make no distinction between a lovesick schoolboy and a grown man who should know better. The heart wants what it wants."

"Well, I guess I'm in trouble then, because the only one mine's ever wanted is Victoria's," Luke admitted with a sad smile. It was true, despite the relationships he'd had over the years, the only real connection he'd ever felt was to Victoria. His youngest sister, Kayla, the romantic among the Dawsons, claimed it was because the two had shared a crib at naptimes when they were babies.

Darlene sounded defeated as she said, "I was afraid you'd say that. In that case, just try to make sure the store is the only thing she leaves with this time."

CHAPTER SEVEN

VICTORIA TUGGED OPEN the big, heavy metal
door to the arena. The air inside was just a
fraction warmer than the cold outdoors and
she rubbed her hands together for heat. She
wished she hadn't left her gloves in the car.
Division win banners hung from the ceiling
above the ice where the bantam hockey team
played. The scoreboard displayed the results
of the practice game so far with only fifteen
minutes to go. The away team led, 3–2.

The heels of her pointy-toed leather boots
clicked against the concrete floor as she approached the man behind the plexiglass window of the ticket counter. He looked up from
his newspaper and a smile spread across his
face. Standing, he opened the window. "Hi,
Victoria."

He looked only vaguely familiar. She
searched her memory for his name. He must
be in his early thirties, which would have put

them in high school together. Was it James? No, Jason? She forced the pretense of recognition, searching his shirt for a name tag. "Hi…"

"Jonathan…Turner," he said.

Her mouth dropped. *Jonathan Turner?* There was no way this glasses-free, acne-free, hundred-pound-lighter man was Jonathan Turner, her tenth-grade, science fair partner and one of the nicest guys in their high school. She couldn't find her voice. The transformation was incredible. This stocky, muscular man with a square jaw and hazel eyes flecked with gold had an air of confidence, quite unlike the shy boy she remembered.

"I know I've changed quite a bit. I don't blame you for not recognizing me," he said with a grin, displaying a beautiful row of straight, white teeth.

Braces-free, too. Victoria smiled and tucked a stray lock behind her ear. "I'd say." She nodded. "Wow." She couldn't believe her eyes.

Jonathan cleared his throat.

She was staring. "Sorry."

"What brings you by? The game is almost over," he said.

"I know. I actually just stopped by to talk to the team and coach…" She hesitated. "Is it still Ethan Bishop?" A lot had remained the same in Brookhollow over the years, but she couldn't assume everything had.

Jonathan nodded. He glanced toward the bag she carried. A sleeve of the new Play Hard Sports uniform stuck from the top. "You planning to show the boys those uniforms?" he asked with a frown.

Victoria hesitated. She hated this approach, but she had to try, especially if she wasn't making headway with Luke. Besides, the new uniform samples she'd brought along were gorgeous, bright red and gold—the team colors with embroidered lettering, not the stick-on type that peeled in the wash. "Only if Ethan says it's okay." She forced her voice to sound confident. "I have to try." Dealing with the store owners was challenging enough. Going around them to solicit community pressure to aid in the acquisition was nerve-racking.

"You're sure you want to go in there?" Jonathan looked concerned.

Victoria laughed and said, "Yes, I'm sure

it won't be that bad." Opening her wallet, she took out several bills.

He shook his head and opened the gate to let her in. "No way. Put your money away. The game's almost over and if you decide to stay for the family skate after, it's on me."

"Thank you." She waved as she made her way to the last set of wooden bleachers near the home team's box. Tucking the jersey deeply into the bag, she zipped her coat higher and found a seat on the cold, paint-peeling bench. She scanned the arena. Panels of plexiglass along the ice were held together with duct tape, preventing the pieces from shattering further. The team's crest in the center of the ice was faded to a light red and yellow and the scoreboard was barely lit, so many of the bulbs were burned out. She suspected at his age, Mr. Jameson wouldn't have even known that the arena was in such a bad state. He surely would have donated money to help fix it up if he had. She wondered if Play Hard Sports would also provide funding for upgrades and repairs to the arena. She made a mental note to ask.

Ethan turned behind the coach's bench. He

waved and nodded in greeting, but his eyes held a note of wariness.

She stood, straightened her coat and approached the bench as the horn blasted, signaling the end of the game. "Hi, Ethan," she said with what she hoped was a warm smile. "Nice to see you again."

He smiled as he stood to open the wooden door, welcoming the young players back to the bench. "Great job, guys." He patted each of their helmets as they passed through on the way to their locker room. When the last boy was gone, he turned his attention to Victoria and grinned. "I figured you'd stop by at some point." He collected the towels and water bottles from the bench and tossed them into a large equipment bag.

"Yeah, I was hoping to talk to you and the boys."

Ethan zipped the bag and tossed it over his shoulder. "About the big-chain sporting store?" he asked as he tugged a wool hat over his short dark hair and grabbed his gloves from the bench, heading toward the locker room.

Victoria followed. "Yes. More specifically

about what the store is offering in support for the local teams."

He frowned. "Legend's has always sponsored the teams." He stopped and shook his head. "I'm not sure you're talking to the right guy, Victoria. I mean, Mr. Jameson was a local hero. No one wants to see the store shut down." He resumed his pace.

In her heels, she struggled to keep up with his quick strides. She hopped over a huge crack on the concrete. "Yes, and I know that support was appreciated by the community. I even benefited from it myself at one time." She stopped and touched his arm.

Ethan sighed as he turned to look at her.

"But you can't argue the point that the uniforms are old and this stadium could use some improvements," she said gently.

Ethan's shoulders slumped as he scanned their surroundings.

She pulled the jersey from the bag. "Look at this stitching. It won't peel in the wash and each boy and girl will get two, one in the home color and one for away games." She held it toward him to inspect.

He stared at the uniform, but made no move to touch it.

"Plus, Play Hard Sports is partnered with some impressive talent scouts. The kids would get the opportunity to showcase their skills. I mean, there's got to be a few guys on the team who you think can make it to the Junior A leagues…or further." She held her breath.

Ethan's face lit up. "Young Cole Richards is a star. I've never seen a kid skate so fast… But, I don't know about this. The boys are happy with what they have."

"All I'm asking for is a chance to talk to them, show them the new uniforms, find out what they think. They deserve the best." She paused and waited.

"Okay…fine." Ethan nodded. "But Luke's not going to be happy about this," he warned her.

She waved away his concern, despite her pounding heart. "Luke's not happy with me anyway."

"Wait here. I'll go talk to the boys." Ethan pushed the locker room door open and loud voices and laughter floated into the hallway.

Victoria set the bag on the floor and pulled out the second jersey, straightening the fabric.

"What are you doing here?"

The deep voice inches from her ear made her jump. She turned and her hand flew to her chest.

Luke, smelling of pine and the outdoors, towered over her, scowling. He was wearing a thick, plaid jacket and his work boots, and Victoria could guess where he'd been that morning. It was tradition with her family, too, to have a real tree for Christmas.

"I came to talk to Ethan and the boys." She raised her chin, forcing any trace of nervousness from her voice. "What are *you* doing here?"

"I offered to pick up my nephew, Steve, from practice today."

Of course. Of all days.

Ethan poked his head through the door. "They say it's okay for you to come in." He saw Luke and winced. "Hey, Luke."

"Hey, yourself. What's going on?"

"We were just going to hear what she has to say, that's all." Ethan looked sheepish.

"As they should." Victoria shot Luke a look and grabbed her bag. She strode through the locker room door and forced a brave smile as twelve young boys stared back at her. "Hi, guys."

Luke followed her in and stood in the back of the room, his expression intense, his eyes never leaving her face. Quite the contrast from the adoring gaze hours before.

She swallowed a lump in her throat and passed the jerseys to the boys on either end of the bench. "Please pass these along. These are the new uniforms that Play Hard Sports is offering to donate to your team. And not just for hockey…for soccer and football, too."

The boys' faces lit up as they passed around the jerseys, whispering among themselves.

Victoria grabbed a stack of brochures from the bag and handed one to each of the boys. "This is their supply brochure. The new store will offer big discounts on hockey sticks and pads—"

"Legend's donates them for free." Luke folded his arms across his chest.

Victoria frowned as she stepped forward and picked up a goalie pad lying in the middle of the floor. The plastic was worn and the colors faded, the padded inside was thin from wear. "Yes, but they're mostly used equipment donated by kids who've outgrown them, and therefore dangerous. Someone could get hurt."

"No one has yet," Luke argued.

"That's not entirely accurate." Ethan scuffed his boots against the concrete floor. "Jeremy's knees are pretty bruised up." He shot an apologetic look at the young goalie.

Luke ruffled the boy's hair. "Ah, he's tough. Right, Jeremy?"

The boy nodded and grinned. "That's right."

Luke slapped the boy gently in the back of the head. Then he knelt in front of him and said, "Jeremy, I'm kidding. You should have told me you needed more equipment. I'll get you anything you need from the stock at the store." He stood and extended his arms. "That goes for all of you."

The young captain of the hockey team stood, too. "Um, can we have a few minutes? We'd like to discuss the new uniforms in private, if that's okay."

Gathering the jerseys and the extra brochures, Victoria nodded. "Of course. Take the time you need. Bring the brochures to your parents. There's no rush. Thanks for listening, guys," she said and left the locker room.

Luke was close on her heels. "I can't believe you. Trying to persuade children?"

"And what exactly were *you* doing? I'm just giving them a choice. You can't force people to do what you want. Maybe not everyone cherishes that old store or this small town the way you do, Luke." She pointed a finger at his chest.

His face fell and she immediately wished she could pull the harsh words back. They weren't true. Everyone in Brookhollow, herself included, appreciated the history of the store.

Luke's expression hardened. "You know, I'm starting to realize that." Turning, he walked away.

VICTORIA CHECKED THE address Rachel had given her and pulled into the driveway of the two-story bungalow at the end of the Cedar Creek Drive cul-de-sac. After the rough start to the day, she wanted to see a friendly face. Rachel could always be counted on to raise her spirits.

A moment later she knocked on the door and waited.

"Victoria, hi!" Rachel said, opening the door and ushering her inside.

"I hope I'm not intruding. I would have

called first but my phone is still giving me problems and without access to my contact list, I'm lost."

"No worries. Come on in." Rachel closed the door before hugging her tight. "I still can't believe you're here." She ran a hand through her disheveled, dark hair.

"Me, neither."

"Rough day?" Rachel asked, leading the way to the kitchen.

She hesitated. Her friend would have heard about her and Luke by now. Everyone else had, but she appreciated her reserve in not asking about it. "This town is just so small, you can't do anything without people finding out."

"Keeping a low profile was never your strong suit," Rachel said, offering a sympathetic grin. "Want to talk about it?"

"No." That's not why she was here, and Rachel was right. She should be used to being the topic of conversation around here. Besides, she wanted to catch up, not burden her friend with her issues.

"Would you like some tea…coffee…?" Rachel poured water into the kettle and set it on the stove.

Removing her coat, Victoria draped it over a kitchen chair. "Coffee would be great if it's not too much trouble."

"Not at all." Rachel hit the button on the coffeemaker.

The smell of spices as something baked in the oven made Victoria's stomach growl. "Whatever you're cooking smells delicious."

Rachel gestured toward her messy kitchen. Mixing bowls and pans littered the counters. "Sorry, if I'd known you were coming, I would have tidied up." She sighed. "I've been baking all day. The kids have a gingerbread house decorating contest at school tomorrow and in a moment of complete insanity at the PTA meeting last night, I offered to bake all of the house parts," she said, laughing as she shook her head.

"Well, if it tastes as good as it smells, I'm sure the kids will appreciate the effort. Can I help you?" Not that she knew anything about baking, but she could wash dishes or something.

"No way, have a seat. With three kids, I'm used to my house being a mess." Rachel took two mugs from the cupboard, poured Victoria's coffee and carried the cup to the table. "Cream or sugar?"

"No, thank you. Black is fine."

The kettle whistled and Rachel made herself a cup of tea. "Must be how you stay so skinny." She heaped two spoonfuls of sugar and replaced the lid on the sugar bowl.

Victoria smiled as she took a sip of the strong liquid and glanced around the kitchen. The house was small, decorated with antique furniture she recognized from Rachel's grandmother's house. "Your home is beautiful." She didn't need a tour to see the main living area, as the open-concept dining and living room were across from the kitchen, past the entryway.

"Thank you. I love it here, but we're outgrowing it," she said, patting her stomach under her apron.

Four children would definitely fill the space. *Four children.* She couldn't even begin to imagine how hectic and challenging the house could be and here Rachel was, baking. The woman was amazing.

"Nathan is thrilled. He always wanted a big family," Rachel said. "Of course, it's been a while since we've had a baby in the house.

Melissa just turned five in November and the twins are four."

"Wow, I can't believe how long it's been." The children were just babies the last time she'd been in Brookhollow for her friend's wedding.

"I know. I've missed you." Rachel reached forward and squeezed Victoria's hand. Tears sprang to her eyes and she wiped them away. "Look at me, pregnancy hormones." She shook her head. "Hey, guess what I found." She stood and struggled to reach above the fridge. "Our high school yearbook." She moved her chair closer to Victoria's at the table.

"How embarrassing," Victoria groaned. Her copy had remained buried somewhere at her parents' house. Though, she was willing to bet it had somehow made its way into the box of her old belongings. Opening the book, she scanned the pages of the teachers' photos. Outdated hairstyles and big dark-rimmed glasses. She touched the picture of the creative writing teacher who'd been at the school for thirty years. "Mrs. Kingston...Luke and I were talking about her yesterday when we were looking for the store paperwork in the attic of that old house." She paused and shot an annoyed look at her friend. "Which—you should have told me—he now *owns*."

Rachel looked sheepish. "Sorry. I thought it might upset you and I didn't think he'd end up taking you *there*."

"Yeah, it certainly wasn't how I'd pictured being in that house with him," Victoria said with a sigh. "Anyway, she was an amazing woman." She pointed to the picture.

"She's living in the seniors' complex on Maple Avenue. You should visit if you have time. The kids and I stop by every Sunday." Rachel added more water to her cup.

"Yeah…maybe." Victoria continued to flip through the pages.

"Wait, stop." Rachel held out a hand and pointed to their cheerleading squad. "Look how skinny we were. Well, you still are," Rachel said as she opened a cookie tin on the table and pushed it toward Victoria. "Here, let's fix that."

She took one. "Thanks," she said, studying the old pictures of herself smiling as she ate. *When was the last time she'd been that sincerely happy?*

Rachel flipped forward a few pages to their

graduation photos and covered her eyes with her hand. "Just look at my hair."

Her friend's hair stood about four inches from her tiny face in a frizzy, unruly mess. "Crimping was in style back then." She laughed, covering her cookie-filled mouth.

"That wasn't crimped—it always had that stupid kink in it. I straighten it now. Thank God for modern technology," she said, smoothing her short, straight dark hair. Then she pulled a Cheerio out of it and shook her head. "Though, I don't know why I bother."

"Hey, read your caption."

Rachel's eyes skimmed the blurb. "Yeah, how life can take a different turn, huh?"

"Says here you wanted to open a bed-and-breakfast." Victoria studied her.

"Don't you remember how every time we passed by Mrs. Harris's inn, I always talked about owning it. How I'd fix it up and all the stars would flock to Brookhollow."

"Why didn't you do something like that?" Taking a sip of her coffee, Victoria helped herself to another cookie. Was it her imagination or did food actually taste better in Brookhollow?

Rachel gestured around them. "Life had

other plans." She smiled, touching the bump under her shirt. "And I wouldn't change a thing. Maybe someday… How about you? Are you happy with where your life has led you?"

"Most days. This business trip is proving more challenging than most." Victoria hoped her friend didn't share Luke's opinion about her reason for her visit.

"Personally, I think the new sporting goods store will be great." Rachel gave a reassuring nod.

"Hopefully more people feel that way." She hated the idea of upsetting the people here.

"I think most do," Rachel said. "Maybe not everyone, though."

"The owner of the store isn't very impressed with me right now." Victoria smiled. For more reasons than one. She tried to forget the image of his angry scowl. "Luke's refusing to sell."

"And since when has he ever been successful in saying no to you? If you really want that store, all you have to do is ask. Last night might have been a good time."

Victoria gave her friend a dirty look. "Couldn't resist saying something, huh?"

Rachel held up her hands. "I'm just stating a fact as a nonjudgmental bystander."

Victoria stared at the picture of her and Luke at her graduation. So happy, so in love, so oblivious. "I don't think I still have that power over him."

"So, I HEAR VICTORIA'S back in town." John Bentley shined his monogramed bowling balls and set them in the holder. He took off his company jacket and draped it over the back of a chair. The Bentley's Electric logo was peeling off the back.

"Yes, she is," Luke said simply as he bent to tie his bowling shoes.

Another guy from the bowling league team, Ralph Miller, chimed in. "My sister said she saw her at the post office this afternoon using the fax. She said Victoria is looking really good." He ran a hand over his balding head and hiked his faded jeans higher on his thin waist.

"I hadn't noticed." Luke pulled on his bowling glove and scowled at his teammates. Admitting his feelings about Victoria to his mother was one thing, but he wouldn't give his friends that kind of ammunition. "Can we bowl now?"

For the next two hours he just wanted to forget about Victoria. All he wanted was to destroy some pins, blow off some steam and force thoughts of her from his mind.

The men exchanged knowing looks.

The waitress brought their beers and set them down on the round table behind them. "Lindsay Harper said Victoria spent the night at your place." She waited.

All eyes were on Luke.

He sighed. "Look, we were looking for the paperwork for the sale of the store, the storm hit, she was stranded, end of story." Small towns and their gossip. He picked up his beer and took a swig.

"Is she still strongheaded as a mule?" asked Russ Corbett, a middle-aged man and captain of their Wednesday-night bowling league. He picked up a ball and wiped it with his rag.

Luke groaned before finally saying, "I guess so." He'd never thought of Victoria's strength of character as a bad thing. He'd always respected and admired her no-nonsense attitude and willingness to get her hands dirty for a cause she believed in. This time though, he was the one blocking her path to get what she wanted. Sitting, he programmed their names into the electronic bowling system. The setup was new and the older men refused to learn how to use it.

"How long will she be in town?" Derek Hughes asked. "Is she staying for the holidays at least?"

Why did they assume he knew anything about her plans? Why did they care? The only thing he knew for sure was that seeing her and being with her again had opened an old wound and he wasn't sure what to do about it.

He looked around at the expectant faces. "Guys, I don't know what to say. She's here to buy out the store. She didn't come back here for me, or to stay. As soon as she realizes I'm not selling, she's on the road back to New York." His tone was nonchalant, but the thought hurt. A lot.

The men exchanged silent looks.

"What?" Luke asked.

"Nothing," Derek said.

"Those looks meant something." Luke looked from one man to the next. "Come on."

Silence.

Melody answered from behind the bar. "They want you to sell the store."

Shocked, Luke studied his bowling buddies. They avoided his eyes. It was true then. "Is that how you all feel?" His gaze fell on Steve and his father, Roy, who'd just arrived.

"What did I do?" Steve asked.

"Turns out, the boys here want me to sell the store. Do you feel that way, too?" He couldn't believe this. "Did those fancy new uniforms get to the team?"

Steve stared at the bowling shoes in his hand and shook his head. He toyed with the lace. "No. We agreed we'd rather have our old uniforms and keep the store open instead of wearing those awesome new ones."

Sighing, Luke glanced at his brother-in-law.

Roy shrugged. "At least the kids are loyal." He handed Steve several bills and said, "Go get yourself a soda, buddy."

Steve dashed off.

Roy lowered his voice. "Or at least, they *want* to be," he said, reaching into his pocket and producing a Play Hard Sports brochure. He handed the crinkled paper to Luke.

"What's this?" Luke frowned.

"His Christmas wish list."

Circled in black ink were a new pair of high-performance skates and a red helmet with flames decorating the side.

Luke stood and handed the brochure back to Roy. "You feel the same as these guys… as the kids?" He valued his brother-in-law's opinion.

Roy looked sheepish. "I know I told you it was a good investment to fix it up, but I think I was wrong. Have you seen the flyers for Play Hard Sports?" He shrugged. "Having the big store would save us a trip to the city for fishing gear in the spring."

The older men nodded their agreement.

Luke held his hands up. He couldn't continue to fight for something only he wanted. He refused to be the guy Victoria had accused him of being. If he was honest with himself, selling the store would be a huge relief financially. He'd have the funds available to take on some of the riskier projects his firm had bid on that year. "Okay, you guys win. I guess I should have asked your opinions, instead of just assuming everybody shared mine." Everyone seemed to think they'd be better off with the chain store. He disagreed, but either way, he wouldn't stand in the way of what his friends wanted. Mr. Jameson had always done what was best for the community. So would he. "I'll think about selling the store."

That didn't mean he was going to let Victoria win without the appearance of a fight though. She could deny her feelings as much as she wanted, but there was no denying how she'd looked at him the night before. He just had to remind her again. Remind her how great they were together. How great life could be in Brookhollow.

Lucky for him, he knew Victoria. The more he fought her, the harder she'd fight back. He smiled, a new plan forming in his mind. He'd wait and let her come to him. She'd have to, if she wanted the store. He would allow her to think she held all the cards, and before long he'd have his opportunity to show her she belonged here with him. If she wanted the store, she could have it, but not before she realized she also wanted him. He smiled for the first time all day.

"Luke!" Russ punched his shoulder.

"Ow." Luke rubbed the spot where he'd been hit. "What was that for?"

"You're up," the old man said with a grin.

CHAPTER EIGHT

"Is it your personal mission to make sure everyone on this street has their Christmas lights up this year?" Victoria asked Luke early the next morning. At Legend's, Steve had negotiated a hefty price for information on Luke's whereabouts. The kid drove a tough bargain. Twenty dollars for information she could have gained just by looking down the street.

"Yes, and I'm on a deadline. The downtown Christmas parade is next Saturday and the street looks better once the lights are up." From his perch on the ladder, Luke stapled a string of multicolored lights to the roof of his family's pharmacy. He didn't stop or turn to look at her.

"Why don't you take a break for a minute? I brought cinnamon-eggnog lattes," she tempted him, squinting in the early morning sun reflecting off the roof and extending a cup to him. She knew the combined scent of cinnamon and coffee escaping from the cups was enticing. She took a sip of her own.

"Actually, Vic, I need to get this done. I have contractors coming to the store in an hour," he said, positioning another set of lights along the roof.

He was still mad from the day before. Understandably so, but she refused to be discouraged. "Okay, well, let me help you then," she offered, placing the lattes on the sidewalk close to the building and picking up a set of tangled lights.

"I haven't checked that set yet." Luke gestured for her to drop them.

"I can check them." She looked around the side of the pharmacy for the outdoor outlet.

"Victoria, I don't need your help. If you have papers for me to look at, just leave them at the store."

"Okay." She bit back an argument and set the lights back in the cardboard box before picking up the lattes.

Luke grunted and went back to the lights.

Steve joined them on the sidewalk, nail gun in hand. "You found him all right then?" he asked Victoria.

She rolled her eyes.

"I'm here to help, Uncle Luke. Sorry I took so long." He picked up the same set of lights Victoria had just dropped.

"He said he doesn't need any help," Victoria informed the kid. "Cinnamon-eggnog latte?" She held out a cup.

The boy wrinkled his nose at the smell and shook his head.

"I said I don't need *your* help," Luke said as he descended the ladder and grabbed the latte. "I thought this was mine." He took a big gulp and then turned to Steve. "Can you check that set before we start on the other window?"

"Sure, Uncle Luke." Steve disappeared inside the pharmacy, trailing the string of lights behind him as Luke reloaded his staple gun and headed back up the ladder.

Victoria shuffled her feet on the slushy sidewalk. "I wanted to apologize about yesterday." The words came out in a rush through clenched teeth. Apologies were not something she enjoyed or did often. But she felt this one was warranted. She made a mistake, letting things get out of hand, but they needed to move on. They had a business matter that still needed resolving.

"Forget about it." Luke waved dismissively.

Through the pharmacy window, she could see Alisha Dawson standing behind the counter, watching them, a phone cradled against her shoulder. From the guarded look on her face, Victoria could guess what was being said. The Dawson family had never fully gotten over the fact that she'd canceled the wedding and now they probably saw her being in Brookhollow as yet another opportunity to hurt Luke. She doubted they would believe that this had nothing to do with him. She was just here to do a job. "Could you please stop for one minute and let me say something? Then I'll go and leave you to your work." She called up to him.

Luke descended the ladder. "What?" He stopped in front of her, rubbing his bare hands together for heat.

Now that she had his attention, she wasn't sure what to say. The intimidating stare from inside the pharmacy had her tongue-tied.

Luke glanced at his watch and placed his hands on his hips above his tool belt. "Victoria, I don't have all day. Do you have something to say or don't you?"

"I just wanted to take you out for dinner tonight…a business dinner. You know…to talk." She studied the ground.

"About what exactly?" Luke advanced toward her. "The stuck-up, better-than-everyone attitude you strolled into town with? Or trying to recruit young kids to do your job for you?" His face was inches from hers as he towered over her. His breath warmed her cheek.

Victoria looked around them, hoping his sister couldn't hear. "Talking to the team was part of my job." She refused to apologize for that. She truly believed that despite the history and nostalgia around the store, the kids would benefit more from having the support of the big chain store.

Luke stared at her then moved away. He stood looking up at the Christmas lights for a long, excruciating moment as she shivered on the slushy sidewalk.

"Luke?"

"I'll pick you up at the bed-and-breakfast at eight o'clock." Without so much as a glance in her direction, he climbed back up the ladder.

"But I wanted to take *you* out…" Victoria

didn't want to leave the planning of their evening in his hands. There were a few places in Brookhollow she'd rather not eat—like his uncle Joey's diner or the Fireside Grill, the only steakhouse in Brookhollow and the place he'd proposed years before.

"Do you want to make it up to me or not?" His eyes flared with anger, daring her to argue.

"Yes." She nodded.

"We do it my way or not at all."

"But—"

"I won't take you to Fireside Grill if that's what you're worried about."

"Okay, then." Her relief mixed with an unexpected sense of disappointment.

"Now, I'm busy. Go away," he said abruptly, as he tossed his empty cup past her into the trash can on the sidewalk.

"Okay, see you tonight." She made her way back to her vehicle, aware of his eyes following her.

THAT EVENING, Victoria paced the lobby of the inn. She pulled back the heavy, living room drapes. No Luke. The neighborhood boys were playing hockey a block away, but other than the sounds of their laughter, the street was silent. A typical Thursday night in Brookhollow. *Thursday.* She almost groaned. She'd been here four days already and hadn't accomplished anything.

Not true. She'd fallen back into the arms of her ex-fiancé and her heart was overflowing with emotions she hadn't experienced since… well…since she loved Luke. *Where was he? Had he changed his mind?* The idea that he'd stand her up had occurred to her. He'd been really angry earlier that day.

Headlights lit the street in front of the bed-and-breakfast. The old truck came into view and Luke pulled into the guest parking lot. Letting the drapes fall back into place, she bolted toward the door.

"Have a nice evening, dear," Mrs. Harris called from the hallway as she opened the door.

Victoria paused. "It's just a business meeting…dinner…thing." She shrugged, trying to act nonchalant. She hated that she felt the need to explain everything to everyone. The whole town was like extended family. A nosy family.

"Whatever you say, dear," Mrs. Harris said,

sitting back down in the wing-backed arm-chair near the fireplace and picking up her knitting needles. She propped her feet up on her footstool.

Victoria opened the front door. "Okay, see you. I shouldn't be late." Was she really promising her landlady an early night? This was a bed-and-breakfast, she reminded herself. She had a key to the guest entrance. She could come and go as she pleased.

"Just a second, Victoria." The woman struggled to get up from the chair and then disappeared into the kitchen.

"Mrs. Harris, I have to go," Victoria called, as Luke honked the horn.

The woman returned. "Could you give these to Luke? He helped me with the Christmas lights on the house last week," she said, handing Victoria a tin. The smell of chocolate and wafers escaped through the closed lid.

Mrs. Harris's cookies rivaled the best bakeries in New York. "Sure." She took the tin and headed outside.

"Luke is such a nice boy." The woman gave her a pointed look and the silent warning rang loud and clear. No one wanted to see the sweet boy-turned-handsome-Christmas-light-hanger-extraordinaire hurt again.

Victoria just nodded as she closed the front door behind her.

Luke waited by the open passenger door.

"Here," Victoria said as she handed him the cookies and ignored his outstretched hand to climb into the truck on her own. The dog fur had been wiped from the seat and the interior of the cab was spotless. He'd gone to some trouble.

"What is this?" Luke asked, opening the lid. "Cookies?" His eyebrows shot up. "Did you bake these?" His surprise melted any tension in the air between them.

Victoria laughed. "Of course not. They're a thank-you from Mrs. Harris for hanging her lights. Seriously, you could sell the store and start your own business hanging Christmas decorations."

Luke bit into a cookie. He closed his eyes. "Mmm."

Victoria reached toward the tin. She'd resume her diet once she got back to New York.

He pulled the tin out of reach and snapped the lid back into place. "Uh-uh, they're mine. Besides, I'm still mad at you," Luke said, shutting the passenger door and disappearing behind the truck. He opened the door behind the driver's seat and slid the tin under the backseat, well out of Victoria's reach.

She shot him a look, as he climbed in behind the wheel. "Quit being a child, and give me a cookie."

"No." He shoved one end of the cookie into his mouth as he put the truck in Reverse.

Victoria reached across and pulled it out of his mouth, then popped the whole thing into her own.

"I can't believe you just did that." Luke's stunned expression made her laugh.

"You wouldn't share," she said, struggling to talk with her mouth full of chocolate and wafers.

"Well, enjoy it." Luke pointed a finger at her. "It's the only one you're getting."

"We'll see." Victoria swallowed the mouthful and her stomach growled.

"Hungry?" Luke asked, pulling the truck onto the street.

"Starving." She'd been busy going over the acquisition paperwork all day at the inn and she'd skipped lunch. She'd also emailed her client contact at Play Hard Sports regarding possible funding for a new arena. The VP, Greg Harrison, was a generous man and within hours, he'd approved the request. She was eager to tell Luke about it, hoping it might sway his decision a little.

"It's going to be a bit before we eat."

"Why?" Everything in Brookhollow was within five minutes. "Where are we going?"

"You'll see," Luke said as he turned the truck onto the freeway, heading out of town.

"Luke…" *Where was he taking her?*

"Victoria, don't start this again. You were the one who wanted to make it up to me, remember?"

She wanted to argue that dinner and a road trip were two different things. She'd only agreed to dinner. Besides, she was really hungry. She bit her lip and nodded. "Okay," she agreed reluctantly, glancing toward the tin of cookies. "Can we at least have another one?" She thought she'd pass out from hunger otherwise.

"Fine," he grudgingly agreed. "But just one. Mrs. Harris doesn't bake often anymore."

Victoria unbuckled her seat belt and leaned over the backseat, stretching as far as she could until her fingers touched the edge of the metal tin. The truck swerved, sending her toppling over the seat. She glared at Luke. "What was that?" She looked through the windshield. There were no other cars on the street.

"Sorry." Luke's eyes were glued to the road ahead.

"Was there an animal on the road?" Victoria asked, straightening her twisted coat as she peered out the back window. She didn't see anything.

"No, it was your incredible body inches from my face that distracted me." Luke flicked on the windshield wipers as light snow covered the glass.

She punched his shoulder. "Okay, I'm going back there again. Do you think you can keep your eyes on the road this time?"

"Doubt it."

Leaning as far as she could, Victoria reached the tin and took out two cookies. She replaced the lid and slid the tin back under the seat. Handing a cookie to Luke, she put her seat belt back on.

He ate it as he took an exit off of the highway.

The sign read Riverside Drive—16 Miles

East. He was taking her to Riverside Drive? She'd heard the only restaurant on the river had closed the year before. Maybe it had re-opened? New owners? Her mother hadn't mentioned it. Wherever he was taking her, there'd better be food.

Victoria cleared her throat and said, "So, I contacted Greg Harrison today, the VP of Play Hard Sports."

Luke's jaw hardened.

"He's approved funding for new arena up-grades."

Luke swallowed his cookie and nodded. "I won't argue that the place could use some work," he said simply.

Finally they agreed on something. She'd let it go at that for now, taking her small vic-tories when she could, storing them as am-munition for later.

"Has your mom mentioned that she signed you up for the gift-wrapping station at the Christmas craft fair on Sunday?" Luke asked, clearly changing the subject.

"You're kidding right?"

Luke laughed. "I didn't think so."

The last thing she wanted to do was re-claim her old post at the gift-wrapping table.

Brookhollow did Christmas in a big way and the craft fair was one of the major highlights of the season. Luke's mother ran the event every year.

"Nope. She handed the volunteer form to my mother two weeks ago when she knew you were coming to town. Actually she handed it to Louise Parsons to hand to my mom." With a glance in the rearview mirror, he switched lanes, turning the truck onto the river road.

The old sugar-mill-style restaurant must be open. It was the only thing on this road, except for a few lookout points where they'd used to…

"Luke, where exactly are you taking me?" she glanced at her high-heeled, suede boots. She'd walk back to town if she had to.

Luke laughed at her terrified expression. "Not where you're thinking."

She blushed. Her cell phone rang in her purse and she dove for it. *The office.* This time of night, it must be important. *An offer?* Her stomach sank a little at the thought. *Don't be ridiculous—the faster you can get an offer, the faster you can get out of the craft fair.* "Victoria Mason," she said into the phone.

Static filled the line.

"Hello?" She had to change cell phone providers. "Hello…Kim?"

"Vic…I can barely hear…"

The crackling static turned to a high-pitched squeal. Victoria pulled the phone away from her ear. Frustrated, she disconnected the call and redialed the office number. If the receptionist was still at the office, Erik must still be there, too. *Please, let them have good news.*

Come on, pick up. The line rang until finally disconnecting without completing the call. Victoria sighed and shook the phone.

Laughing, Luke took the device out of her hand.

"What? You think you can fix it?" Victoria asked. Men. Always thinking they could fix everything. Though, if he could, that would be great. Her other clients would be having mild anxiety attacks by now with the lack of contact with her.

"Nope." Luke rolled down the window and casually tossed the phone out, where it landed in the bed of the truck.

"Are you crazy? It's going to get wet out there and not work at all." Her phone was her lifeline, her connection to the office, her email… Even sporadic service was better than no phone at all.

"Relax," he said, opening the glove compartment at her knees and taking out a shiny-new iPhone. "Here."

"What's this?" Victoria took the white phone she'd been eyeing in stores for months and turned it over in her hands.

"Your new phone…with a service provider we all use here." Luke turned the wipers on high and switched lanes again, taking an exit off the highway.

"You bought me a new phone?"

"Yes."

"Why?"

"Because you were driving me crazy shaking and waving that other piece of crap around."

"Oh."

"It's programmed with your number already, so you just have to cancel your current provider's service when you get back to New York." He hit the button on the phone. "I took the liberty of programing my number in there for you and I thought you'd like this wallpaper."

A picture of him appeared on the screen, a goofy grin on his face.

Victoria laughed until her sides hurt. "Thank you," she said.

"Don't thank me. I bought it with the money I stole from you playing pool."

Victoria shook her head and said, "Jerk— you can't let it drop, can you?" She looked at the guy staring back at her from the phone. He'd bought her a phone, with a service provider that worked. Her heart stopped. "Um, Luke?"

"Yeah?"

"What about my contact list? Did that transfer to this phone, as well?" She didn't think that was possible without manually inputting all of the information.

Luke turned a shade paler. "Um…no. Sorry." His gaze landed on the old phone in the rearview mirror. "Oops."

Victoria turned in the seat. Her cell phone lay in a puddle of melting snow. "Luke," she said through a groan. "I don't know anyone's number." She rubbed her forehead. It would take hours to look up her contacts and add them in.

"Maybe the other phone still works." He looked sheepish.

"I can't believe you," Victoria said, tossing the phone into her purse. How was she going to reach anyone now? All she could do was wait until they called or texted her.

"Sorry, princess. I was just trying to help."

"Well, don't." Victoria tossed her blond hair over one shoulder. She glanced at Luke's set jaw and softened. It *had* been a nice gesture. Really nice. "I'm sorry. Thank you for the phone," she said, touching his arm.

His eyes met hers. "You're welcome," he said, before pulling the truck into the Riverside Restaurant parking lot. The sign out front was off and the place was dark and deserted.

How had Luke not known? Even she had known the restaurant had closed for business months ago.

Luke undid his seat belt and cut the engine of the truck. Tugging on his gloves, he zipped his jacket higher. "Come on."

"Come on *where?* Luke, the place is clearly closed." She looked through the windshield. A no-trespassing sign was nailed to the fence. The last thing she needed was to get arrested on this trip.

He opened the door and jumped down. "Get out."

And she was getting sick of his bossy rudeness. "Quit telling me what to do," she said, shivering from the cold air blowing through the truck.

"I thought you were hungry."

"I am." He should know how cranky she got when she was hungry.

"Well, just trust me and get out of the truck." His expression was pure annoyance.

"Fine," she said through clenched teeth as she unbuckled her seat belt and took his hand, allowing him to help her down.

He kept it tucked into his as he closed the door and led her up the path to the restaurant. At the door, he reached into his pocket and pulled out a key.

"You have a key?"

"Yes." He didn't offer any more information as he opened the door and ushered her inside. "Wait here."

Victoria raised a brow.

"Please."

She sighed. "Where are you going?" She didn't like the idea of being left alone in the dark restaurant in the middle of nowhere. A shiver ran through her as she moved to stand close to the wall, keeping an eye on the door.

"Just give me a second." He disappeared inside and a moment later the room in front of her was illuminated with a thousand white Christmas lights.

A gasp escaped her lips as the stone fireplace came to life, radiating instant heat. The place was empty except for a thick red-and-white-checkered blanket spread out in the center of the floor. A picnic basket and bottle of wine lay in the center. "What is this?"

"Dinner." Luke unwrapped the cashmere scarf around her neck.

"Luke, it's beautiful, but I don't think it's a good idea…" *Definitely not a good idea.*

"What's the worst that can happen?" he whispered in her ear as he took her coat from her shoulders.

Goose bumps covered her skin under her thin, black, V-neck sweater. "So, how do you have a key to this place anyway?" Victoria turned, putting distance between them. She traced a finger along an old mahogany beam in the entranceway. The restaurant was designed to look like it was carved from the remnants of a seventeenth-century sugar mill. Large crystal chandeliers hung from the peaked, exposed beamed ceiling. The candlelight glowed against the stone walls in the dining room, and, best of all, the floor-to-ceiling glass walls on one side provided a scenic view of the river's edge. "Don't tell me you bought this place, too?" Nothing would surprise her anymore.

"My company is handling the remodeling for the new owners. A young couple from Boston is moving here to start a family next month." Taking her hand, he led the way into the main dining area of the restaurant. He motioned for her to sit, then lit a vanilla-scented candle on the fireplace and joined her on the blanket.

Her eyes widened. "Dawson Architecture?" She'd seen his company's name on several new restaurants being designed in the city, but she hadn't made the connection. His company must be doing well. She was impressed.

"Yeah—my office is above the sporting goods store." He opened the picnic basket and took out a roasted chicken and several containers with mixed vegetables and potatoes. He opened the wine and handed it to her along with two plastic wine goblets. "Sorry, I know it's not Fifth Avenue dining."

No, it's better, Victoria thought as she poured the wine. "You've been keeping yourself busy," she said before taking a bite of potato. First the roast, now this.

"Work has been the major focus of my life for quite a while." He nodded, cutting into his chicken. "How's the food?" He paused, holding his fork in midair.

"Delicious," she said, putting her fork down and taking a sip of the wine. "Business must be slow in Brookhollow, though." Maybe that was why he needed the store, but somehow she didn't think so. Luke had a master's degree in architecture—he could easily find a job.

"My company has projects in New Jersey, Boston and New York. Mostly new-home designs and renovations. We've started taking on several restaurant remodels, as well. I stay busy." He shrugged, taking a bite of his chicken. "Mmm, this is good."

"And you still have time to own a store, learn to cook and somehow live in Brookhollow?"

Luke laughed. "It's not as hard as it seems,

really. And I'm actually on vacation right now, until after Christmas. I usually spend more time working on job sites, but things have slowed a little in the past month. I'll get busier again in January. I won't have as much time to cook…in case you were planning to visit for a home-cooked meal sometime."

Victoria smiled but remained silent. She'd assumed Luke hadn't even been aware of life outside Brookhollow. But apparently, he was. He used the big cities to his advantage without having to live in one. The house… the store…he could easily afford whatever he wanted. She glanced outside. And yet, he still drove that old beat-up truck, parked out front now, collecting snow. She laughed.

"What's so funny?" Luke asked, leaning back to study her.

"Nothing."

"No, really what?"

"I just can't believe you own a successful business, and you still have that old truck." Victoria set down her fork and wiped her mouth with her napkin.

"What can I say?" Luke glanced toward the truck with a smile. "I'm attached to the old beast. Some great memories were made in that truck."

Victoria's eyes met his.

His eyes remained locked with hers as he moved the plates aside and crawled toward her on the blanket. Taking each of her hands, he brought them to his lips and kissed each palm.

She closed her eyes. This wasn't supposed to be happening, yet her palms tingled from his simple touch.

His fingers left a soft trail of goose bumps up her arms.

"Please don't," she pleaded, moving away from him.

"I love you," he whispered, wrapping his arms around her waist, pulling her closer. "I always have."

What he said didn't surprise her, but hearing it saddened her. What they'd had was long over. Twelve years was a long time. She lived in the city. He lived in Brookhollow. They didn't know each other anymore. They couldn't be around each other without arguing. All of this shouldn't matter if she loved him, but it did.

"Luke, I…"

"Shh." Placing his finger to her lips, he said, "Don't say anything. You don't need to."

He brushed her hair away from her face and rained kisses on her forehead, her nose, her eyes.

"Luke, I can't move back to Brookhollow…"

"I'm not asking you to," he said.

Not yet. But he would. And when he did, her answer would be no. She couldn't, wouldn't, give up everything in New York. She'd worked too hard to prove to herself that she could handle city life and, more than that, she thrived there. Luke's feelings for her were undeniable. She was sure of it, of him. She just couldn't trust her own emotions.

She loved him, there was no doubt, but was love enough? It hadn't been before. She wrapped her arms tight around him, not wanting to let go.

"I can't stay, Luke."

CHAPTER NINE

VICTORIA HUMMED "Frosty the Snowman" as she lathered her hair in the shower the next morning. Their dinner date the night before had been nothing short of incredible, and while she fought the urge to read too much into the rekindled spark between them, her mind reeled. Luke traveled to the city for work. Maybe they could keep some sort of relationship going when she returned to New York? She could visit Brookhollow more often… Meet him halfway, when she wasn't traveling.

Applying her lavender-scented shave gel to her legs, she ran her razor along her skin. A long-distance relationship wasn't ideal, but certainly anything was better than not being together. And over time they could figure things out…. She hoped he shared her opinion.

Her iPhone rang in the next room. With

her new, consistent service, that thing hadn't stopped ringing. Luke had turned it off during their restaurant picnic. The night before they hadn't discussed the store or the battle of wills they found themselves in. She still needed this acquisition. She wondered if this turn of events would make Luke more willing to sell. She could explain that once this deal was done, they could move forward with… whatever this was. But the bottom line remained the same—he needed to sign the sale papers for the store.

Victoria turned off the water and drew back the shower curtain. Reaching for her towel, she wrapped it around her body and grabbed a second towel to dry her hair.

Then the room phone rang. Her mother? Her brain was frantic as she tried to remember if she'd done anything incriminating in the last twenty-four hours? Nope.

"Hello," she answered, cradling the phone against her shoulder as she dressed.

"Good morning, pretty lady." Luke's husky tone suggested he'd just woken up.

"Good morning to you." Victoria glanced at the clock. It was after nine. "Sleeping in this morning are we?" she asked with a laugh.

"I was having a fantastic dream and didn't want to wake up. You were in it."

Time to change the subject. "So, any more Christmas lights need hanging today?"

"Nope, today I need your help with something."

"My help? With what?" She sat on the edge of the bed and slid her legs into the only pair of jeans she'd packed.

"Well, until your company has an offer for me to refuse, I still need to go ahead with my store renovations and I could use a woman's opinion on paint colors."

"Luke, you can't be serious. That would be a huge conflict of interest," she said. Wet hair fell against her shoulders. Obviously their dinner hadn't put a dent in his resolve not to sell the store. She picked up her cell phone from the bedside table. One new voice mail and Erik's cell number appeared on the screen. "Besides, my boss left me a message this morning. I'm willing to bet it was an offer." She hoped it was true. Once they could put this acquisition behind them, they could entertain the idea of a relationship, not before.

Luke chuckled. "Okay. How about this—if it *is* an offer, I meet you at Loni's Coffee Hut in an hour to discuss it, otherwise you come help me with paint colors," he bargained.

Victory hesitated. The idea of spending the day with him was tempting. Too tempting. She pulled the curtain back from the window. It was a sunny, crisp day. More snow had fallen the night before and covered the town like an image on a Christmas card. She'd never been sentimental about Christmas, but the scene outside her window that morning was breathtaking.

"I'm telling you, it *is* an offer," Victoria insisted, though her resistance and confidence were fading.

"If you're so confident about that, it should be easy for you to take this bet."

Envisioning his smile on the other end, she caved. "Fine. I'll call you back in five minutes." She hung up the room phone and picked up her cell phone to dial her voice mail.

The message from her boss was less than promising. The legal department had looked over the documents she'd faxed in, and they didn't see a way around the original agreement.

To acquire the store, Luke had to agree to sell and he could drive the price as high as he wanted. They weren't as confident about this acquisition as they had been about the others. Her boss's advice was to hang in there for another few days until they could reach a more reasonable number, and to stay close to Luke. He suggested she try to find out how much he'd be willing to sell the store for.

She deleted the message. Her boss was asking her to get personal information from Luke, and she didn't know how she felt about deceiving him. Besides, she doubted Luke's financial state would help their deal. Her ex-fiancé owned a successful company. His reasons for keeping the store had nothing to do with finances, but trying to explain that to her boss would be futile. Erik was not the type of man who would understand the community's desire to keep one of their own. To Brookhollow, the store was a landmark, a part of their history. In a way, it was all that remained of Mr. Jameson.

There wasn't much she could do about the acquisition at this point. Pulling her tank top over her head, she slid her white-lace blouse over top. She picked up her cell phone and dialed Luke's number.

"What time should I pick you up?" he

asked after the first ring. The confidence in his voice suggested he knew they were heading to the paint store.

"Give me twenty minutes and bring coffee."

THE LOCAL HARDWARE store was one of the biggest retail hubs in the community and a popular shopping place for the local residents. Selling everything from paint and tools to housewares and home decor, Fix-It Hardware had a reputation as a one-stop shop. As she opened the truck door and jumped down, Victoria hesitated. The possibility of running into many familiar, curious faces was high.

Luke reached for her hand and she tugged it away. "Don't. It's bad enough that I'm even here with you." How had he convinced her to do this? Was the time they'd been spending together making her soft?

He laughed and held his hands up. "Okay," he said, moving closer as they walked through the revolving door. "But don't think it's going to be easy for me to keep my hands off of you."

"Try," she said through clenched teeth as they passed Mrs. Grant and her oldest son, Mitch, leaving the store. The Grants owned the hardware store and it had been passed from one generation to the next for over sixty years. Mitch would take over the daily operations in a few years once his father, Craig, retired.

Their smiles didn't quite reach their eyes.

Can I really do this? She fought every urge to turn back to the truck and glared at Luke.

"What do you think they're thinking?" Luke asked, leading the way to the paint department.

"It's taking all my strength *not* to think about that." Victoria scanned the display of paint swatches eyeing the selection of red tones. *Hmm...maybe we should go with their high school colors.* She frowned. *He* should go with those colors...not *we*.

"Well, I'll be...Victoria Mason," a familiar voice said behind her.

Victoria turned. "Hello, George." Her smile was genuine. George Baker had worked behind the paint counter of the hardware store for over twenty years. He knew everyone in town *and* the color of their bedrooms. The best thing about George was he kept all that knowledge to himself. His wife, Lorette, was a legal assistant at the only small law firm in town owned by Luke's cousin, Bryce, and their son Lee worked at the medical clinic as a psychologist. The family was a gold-mine for gossip-worthy information, yet they were the only ones in town who never revealed the secrets they were privy to. Victoria wished more people around here were like the Bakers.

"I didn't know you were back," he said, wiping his hands on his paint-splattered apron.

Victoria suspected this was a white lie. Everyone knew she was back by now. "Got in Monday evening."

"How long are you staying?"

"I'm not sure yet. Only a few more days, though, at most." Victoria shot a glance in Luke's direction.

Luke studied the paint colors displayed on the wall. He reached for the same red palette she'd been considering.

"Well, it's sure great to see you." The old man smiled. "All the young folks are leaving this place. I often wonder why Luke here has stayed so long." George nodded in Luke's direction. "Can't be much work for an architect around these parts."

"But Luke is a store owner now." Victoria hoped she might get some information from the older man. Everyone in town seemed to know the motivation behind everything that happened in the community. George certainly knew a lot more than he repeated.

George frowned and said, "Not for…"

"Hey, George, what are the chances of getting some paint today?" Luke interrupted the old man.

Victoria gave him a curious look perturbed by his interjection. She was interested in hearing what George had been about to say.

George turned his attention to the paint samples Luke was holding out.

"I was thinking a dark red for the walls. What do you think of Crimson Lake, Victoria?" Luke asked, holding the swatches for her to see. He pointed to the darkest red on the palette of four different shades.

She gave him her honest opinion. "I think it might be a little dark for the small space." She studied the options on the various swatches Luke had displayed on the counter in front of them. "Um…how about Red Sky?" she suggested, pointing to a paler shade. "It's also a closer match to the local team colors."

"Perfect," Luke agreed, collecting the sample colors and setting them back on the display rack on the wall. "See, that's why you always bring a woman with you to do this kind of thing." He winked at George.

"Great. What else do you folks need? Primer? Paint rolls or brushes?" George asked, scribbling the name and number of their paint color selection on the order form.

Luke shook his head. "Nope, I have all of that already." He paused. "But actually, while I'm here..." Luke hesitated when he looked almost sheepishly at Victoria. "Well...I thought... See, I'm repainting most of the rooms in the house, as well...and I thought since I was here...maybe I could get that paint, as well. I'd love your opinion on color."

Victoria couldn't believe what he was asking. He couldn't possibly expect her to help him pick out paint for a bedroom he could very well end up sleeping in with another woman, in the house of her dreams no less. He was asking too much. She'd already broken too many of her own professional rules. She refused to break a personal one, as well.

"I don't remember that being a part of the deal." Victoria forced a tight smile for George's benefit.

"Just a second, George." Luke held up a finger and pulled Victoria into an aisle. He nodded to a couple passing by then turned back to her. "I know it's a lot to ask, but it doesn't have to be awkward. You would just be like a…consultant," he said, taking her hand in his.

"What did I say about touching me?"

He dropped her hand. "I'm absolutely no good with color, as we've just witnessed. I could really use your help." He put on a sad-puppy-dog face.

Why was she always torn between wanting to kiss him and slap him at the same time?

"Please," Luke begged, bending onto one knee, a mischievous smile playing on his full lips.

He knew he had her when she laughed. "Oh, all right. Get up." She pulled him to his feet.

"Thank you." He kissed her hand, holding it once more.

"Luke and Victoria! What a surprise."

Lindsay Harper strolled down the aisle toward them, a sly smile on her face.

Fantastic. How was this woman always around at the worst moments? She must have radar for gossip.

Victoria yanked her hand out of Luke's. "Hi, Lindsay."

"Wow, I must say you two have been joined at the hip lately," she said, eyeing Victoria with open curiosity and a hint of what appeared to be jealousy. "What brings you both to the paint section?"

Victoria shot Luke a pointed look. Anything he could possibly say as an explanation would be turned into tabloid fodder by his neighbor. She prayed he would come up with something fast.

"Um…" Luke began, obviously enjoying Victoria's discomfort.

"Hey, you two." George appeared behind them. "I'm going to help the Sanders for a moment, just holler when you've decided on a color for the bedroom," he said, disappearing around the corner.

She swung around to face Lindsay.

The woman wore a grin from ear to ear.

"YOU KNOW, YOU *COULD* turn this space into a museum." Victoria scanned the large collection of sports memorabilia as she stood in the sporting goods store in a pair of Luke's oversize coveralls, paintbrush in hand. Christmas music played from a small portable radio on the counter. Taking a sip of her peppermint mocha, she glanced around the store. The shelves had been pushed to the center of the room and draped in tarps, and green painter's tape covered the windows and moldings. If her boss could see her, poised and ready to help paint a store they were trying to buy, it would be definite grounds for immediate dismissal.

Luke opened the can of red paint and poured it into a clear, plastic tray. "You know, I think I'll keep it as a store." He stood and handed her the tray. "Here, you can start on the far wall."

Victoria set the tray aside and approached the shelves of valuable keepsakes. "Okay, but let's just say for argument's sake that you like the offer and decide to sell the business, the building is still yours and this place is the perfect size and location for a sports museum," she said as she picked up the football team's division win trophy from that season. "You could put the town's accomplishments on one side and use the other side for Mr. Jameson's extensive collection."

Luke placed his hands on his hips.

She picked up an autographed team photo from Mr. Jameson's time as a New York Giant. "I mean, look at all of this cool stuff. Rare baseball trading cards in mint condition, autographed photos…" She ran a finger along the shelf and raised an eyebrow. "When was the last time anyone saw any of this stuff, hidden away in the back of the store?"

Luke shrugged. "People know it's here," he insisted, dipping a paint roller into the tray. A frown furrowed his eyebrows as he pushed the roller back and forth.

Victoria pushed on, sensing she was getting somewhere. "Yeah, but you keep saying you want to keep this store for its history and what it means to the community…well… the value of this place is in these items," she pointed out, waving a hand toward the memorabilia. "They should be displayed properly Luke." She waited, holding her breath.

Luke hesitated, his gaze locked with hers. He opened his mouth to speak, then shook his head and cleared his throat. "Nothing's going to be displayed in time for the reopening if you don't get to work. Less talking, more painting." He nudged her toward her side of the store.

Victoria sighed. She'd keep working that angle. "How *did* you convince me to help you? I must be losing my mind."

"Hey, at least I didn't ask you to help me paint the house...yet," he said as he turned the Christmas music louder on the portable CD player they'd brought along for the job.

Lashing out with the paintbrush, Victoria slapped red paint on his coveralls. Luke retaliated by grabbing her and smearing a thin red line of paint across her forehead. She shrieked in response, struggling to break free.

He pinned her arms to her body to prevent further attack and trailed kisses along her neck.

Victoria wiggled to release herself from his firm hold as she giggled. "No fair—let go."

The bell chimed above the door and Luke turned them both around, not releasing her from his grasp. "Hi, Mom," he said.

Victoria gulped and her laughter ceased. *Crap.* This was not the way she'd been hoping to run into her ex's mother. In truth, she'd been hoping not to run into her at all. "Hi, Mrs. Dawson," she said as she freed herself.

"Hi, Victoria." The woman smiled politely. "Nice to see you again." The greeting was said between clenched teeth.

Yeah, right. "You, too."

"Your mother has volunteered you for your old wrapping station at the craft fair on Sunday. If you're still here then."

It looks that way. She forced a smile and nodded. "Yes, I will. I'm happy to help." She searched the store for an escape. Breathing became difficult with such awkward tension filling the tiny space. She had always felt on edge and nervous around Luke's mother, even when she and Luke were dating. Her expression of disappointment and caution was one Victoria had seen many times.

Luke grunted. "Yeah, right. Quit being so nice to my mom."

Victoria swatted him with the paintbrush. "Don't pay any attention to him, Mrs. Dawson." Didn't he feel intimidated that his mother had caught them fooling around? Now was not the time for his jokes.

"I never do, dear." Mrs. Dawson softened just a little.

At least they had that in common.

"So, what brings you by, Mom? Need a new football or hockey stick?" Luke laughed at his own joke.

Both women rolled their eyes.

"Quit being smart, Lucas."

Victoria hid a grin behind her hand. Lucas? Only his mother could get away with calling him that.

"I was just at Ginger's bakery and I thought I'd stop by to remind you about tonight. The men are asked to be at the recreation center by seven." She glanced at the paint in the tray. "That color looks too light." She shot a suspicious look at Victoria.

Victoria wished the floor would give way beneath her.

Turning, Luke rolled the paint along the wall. The vibrant red added instant life to the old place and the color was almost an exact match to the team colors.

His mother squinted. "Actually, it's quite nice once you see it up."

Victoria let out the breath she hadn't realized she was holding.

Luke shook his head. "Mom, I already told you I wasn't participating this year."

"But you do it every year. You're a top seller," Mrs. Dawson argued, setting her bags on the counter and readjusting her purse strap on her shoulder.

"I'm not doing it." Luke continued to paint.

Victoria looked back and forth between mother and son. "Not doing what? What's happening at the recreation center tonight?" Her curiosity was piqued. What was Luke determined to get out of doing?

"Tonight is the annual Christmas Charity Bachelor Auction," Mrs. Dawson said. "Last year Luke brought in over six hundred dollars for the medical clinic." The woman beamed with pride.

Victoria laughed. "Who paid that much for him?"

Luke dropped the roller and set up the ladder along the wall. "I'll have you know I'm in hot demand around here with the ladies."

His mother laughed. "Mrs. Harris bought him last year."

Victoria bent at the waist, laughing so hard tears streamed down her face. "Mrs. Harris?

Luke!" She fought to catch her breath. "How did that date go?"

"She had him fix shutters on the bed-and-breakfast and sent him home with a baked chicken," Mrs. Dawson explained, also holding her sides in fits of laughter.

"Laugh all you want," Luke said, pointing a paintbrush at Victoria, "but that was probably the best date I've had in…twelve years."

Victoria couldn't remember the last time she'd laughed so hard.

"Anyway, there's your father. I have to go set up at the center. Seven o'clock, Lucas. Don't be late." His mother picked up her shopping bag.

"Mom, I said no." Luke shot Victoria a look. "Can you help me here? Tell her we have plans."

"Apparently, we only have plans if I outbid Mrs. Harris, and I'm not sure you're worth six hundred dollars," Victoria said. "Don't worry, Mrs. Dawson, he'll be there on time."

"Wow, THERE ARE a lot of women out there." Victoria ducked her head through the curtain on the makeshift stage at the recreation center.

"Yeah, it's quite the highlight of the season around here." Luke wore a scowl. "I still can't believe you're making me do this." He grabbed her and pulled her into him.

The smell of his musky cologne filled her head. She snuggled into his chest. It felt so good to be in his arms. "You do it every year. Besides, I'm trying to get in your mom's good graces," she said with a shudder. "The tension in the store today was unnerving."

"I'm not worried about Mom. She'll come around. But I had been hoping to be doing something else tonight," he said as he brushed her hair aside.

Victoria pushed against his chest. "Well, I only have three hundred in cash on me, so I hope that no one goes above that," she said, reaching forward to unbutton the top few buttons of his blue-and-gray plaid shirt.

"You think this is funny, don't you?" Luke asked, tickling her.

"Yes." She wriggled away and looked around the curtain again. Out on the floor of the recreation center, the runway was covered in a red stretch of fabric with a string of white lights around the edge. Round tables with six chairs each were placed in front of the T-shape catwalk to allow ample viewing of the "product" on display. Strands of Christmas lights hung from the ceiling, providing the only illumination other than the spotlight at the end of the catwalk. The atmosphere in the room was electric as the women took their seats, chatting excitedly among themselves.

The front tables were already crowded with women. She noticed Rachel among them and waved.

"I saved you a seat," Rachel called out.

Victoria smiled and nodded. She held up a finger indicating she'd be only a minute. "I see some married women out there, too. Their husbands don't mind them buying a date for the evening?"

"Actually, some of their husbands are on display here tonight."

"How does that work? I thought this was a *bachelor* auction?" She frowned.

"Well, there are very few genuine bachelors around here, so the event committee will enlist the help of anyone they can force into this. Married men included. Their wives generally buy them back at a hefty price," he said, rolling his eyes. "This is ridiculous." He buttoned one of the lower buttons.

Victoria grabbed his hand to stop him. She ruffled his sandy-blond hair to mess it up. "This is fun." This *was* fun. In New York an event like this would be black-tie formal and the bachelors would be arrogant, rich men who'd be auctioned off for thousands of dollars to socialites. The press would then have a field day with the scandal stories the following morning. Not in Brookhollow.

She gave Luke a last once-over. A small streak of red paint remained over one eye. "Stand still," she insisted, licking her finger and scrubbing it away.

"I guess that's the closest thing I'm getting to a kiss?"

"Yup." She patted his butt. "Have fun." She blew him a kiss and disappeared behind the curtain.

"Bid on me," he called after her.

Victoria took her seat next to Rachel at the table on the left of the stage.

"Did you see the bachelor lineup?" Rachel asked, handing Victoria the homemade brochure containing the pictures and biographies of all twenty men up for auction that evening.

"No." Victoria's eyes lit up as she scanned the brochure.

Beer bellies, bald heads and mustaches filled the pages. Definitely not the New York, top-ten, eligible bachelor list.

Rachel pointed to the picture of her husband. "Poor guy's been stressing over this for weeks. Even dusted off the old treadmill in the basement," she said, laughing until tears formed in her eyes. Shaking her head, she added, "Then he tells me to clean out our bank account if I have to, to save him from anyone else." She took a sip of her soda.

"Which number is he?" Victoria scanned the line up. Nathan was fourth. Luke, of course was last.

"So, are you betting on Luke?" Rachel gave her a sly smile.

"He says I am."

"You may have a fight on your hands," Rachel warned, nodding to the group of twenty-something girls at the table nearest the stage, pointing to the pictures of the bachelors. "Pretty sure they're not here for Nathan."

Victoria felt a small surge of jealousy as she studied the young, carefree girls. The last time she'd been here, Rachel and she had been like them. "Well, if they want him, they can have him." *As long as they have an un-*

limited cash flow, she thought, mentally reviewing the remaining balance on her credit card. She sat back in her chair as the lights dimmed.

Mrs. Dawson, host of the event appeared from behind the curtain. Dressed in a long, dark green sequined gown, her light blond hair piled high in loose curls on her head, she looked beautiful. It was hard to believe Luke's mother was in her sixties. "Welcome to our fifteenth annual Christmas Charity Bachelor Auction," she said, waving and smiling at the attendees.

The crowd—women of all ages—cheered.

"If you've had time to glance through tonight's brochure, I'm sure you've noticed we have a terrific lineup of men braving the catwalk in support of new equipment for our medical clinic." She held up the brochure.

"Bring out Luke!" someone yelled from the back of the room.

Rachel shot Victoria a look.

Victoria scoffed.

Shading her eyes from the bright spotlight on the stage, Mrs. Dawson peered toward the back of the room. "Someone's excited to get started. I like your enthusiasm." She smiled. "Yes, once again my son Luke is up for grabs, so you better have brought your checkbooks."

All eyes turned to their table. She covered her face with a brochure.

"First," Mrs. Dawson continued, "we have a local hero. You all may know him as Fireman Jim. Please give a big welcome to our first brave bachelor—Jim Bishop." She waved a hand as the curtains opened, then moved away to the side of the stage where she picked up her gavel.

Jim, dressed in his firefighter gear, squirmed and fanned himself as he approached the front of the stage. Squinting in the bright lights, he wiped a bead of sweat from his forehead.

"Let's start the bidding at ten dollars."

Victoria covered a giggle as Jim's hat fell off, and he bent to pick it up.

Jim's girlfriend, Jill, raised her auction wand. "Ten dollars."

He gave her a grateful look and pleaded with his eyes for the crowd to let her have him for ten dollars.

Mrs. Dawson wouldn't allow it. "We have

ten dollars… Let's see twenty. Come on, ladies, Jim saves lives for a living."

The crowd cheered and Jim turned a deep shade of crimson.

"When was there ever a fire in Brookhollow?" Victoria whispered to Rachel. She suspected Jim played a lot of poker.

"The school alarm goes off once a month, but it's only a drill for the children," Rachel said, rubbing her belly.

"You okay?" Victoria looked concerned.

"Yeah. Just a kick. This little one is going to be a soccer player. He—or she—is much more active than the other babies were."

Victoria watched her friend's stomach ripple as the baby moved. *Fascinating.* A dull longing in her awakened, and she touched her own flat abdomen.

"Want to feel?" Rachel asked, reaching for Victoria's hand and placing it on her belly.

A second later a little foot-shaped bulge kicked Victoria's hand.

"Oh, my God! That is hard. Does it hurt?" She looked at her friend in awe. She'd gone through this twice before? And with *twins.* She admired Rachel's strength.

Rachel shook her head. "Not really."

"Going once…going twice… Sold to Jill Vanderwolf for forty dollars," Mrs. Dawson was saying on stage.

The next few men following Jim looked just as awkward and uncomfortable and relieved once their catwalk stint was over.

"These guys are really great for doing this," Victoria said, taking a sip of her wine as she crossed one leg over the other under the table.

"They really are. You couldn't pay me enough to auction myself off—charity or not." Rachel shifted in her seat. "Nathan's next." She pointed to the stage as the spotlight lit and Nathan appeared.

In a suit and tie, he hardly looked like the same ball-cap-wearing guy she'd gone to high school with. His dark hair was gelled and pushed back off of his forehead. "Wow, he looks great."

He waved in their direction as he approached the front of the stage.

"That's the only suit he owns. It's the one he wore to our wedding." Rachel laughed as she reached for the paddle.

"Let's start the bidding at twenty dollars," Mrs. Dawson said.

"What happened to starting at ten?" Rachel muttered, holding up her paddle.

"Great. Twenty dollars to his wife." Mrs. Dawson laughed. "Most women are trying to sell their husbands...must be newlyweds still. Do I hear thirty?"

Someone in the group of giggling girls raised a paddle.

"Seriously?" Rachel looked puzzled.

"Maybe the treadmill worked."

Nathan's expression became cocky.

"Forty dollars." Rachel held up her paddle.

"Fifty." The giggling girls again.

Nathan approached the twentysomethings' table and removed his coat. Flinging it over his arm, he winked.

Rachel's mouth gaped. "Oh, no, he doesn't. Sixty dollars." She turned to Victoria. "If that jerk thinks he's hanging out with those girls tonight, he's sadly mistaken. He has a nursery to finish painting."

Victoria hid her amusement at her friend's jealousy. Twelve years together and the couple still had enough passion to be jealous. It was endearing.

"Eighty dollars," the girls bid.

Rachel held up her hands. "This is ridiculous. I love him, but he's not worth that much." Rummaging in her purse, she held up a handful of bills. "Nope, charity or not, eighty is my limit." She dropped the paddle on the table as Mrs. Dawson started the final bidding.

Nathan glanced at them.

Rachel shrugged.

His face fell and panic crossed his features.

Oh, jeez. "Three hundred." Victoria raised her paddle.

Mrs. Dawson seemed surprised.

So did Nathan.

So did Rachel. "What are you doing?" she asked, tugging on Victoria's arm. "Save your money for Luke."

"The man has a nursery to paint." Victoria patted her friend's arm. "I'll just use my credit card for Luke."

Rachel smiled in gratitude. "Thanks." She yawned.

"No problem, now go collect your husband

and get home to sleep. You look exhausted."
Rachel's eyes had been barely open all evening.

"Yeah, good idea. I tell you, you don't
know what tired is until you're pregnant."

All of a sudden Victoria hoped she'd someday know the feeling. She nodded. "Good
night."

Nathan mouthed a thank-you as they left.

Victoria waved and sat back down.

The woman on her right leaned toward her.
"I just wanted to let you know they only take
cash here at the auction," she said apologetically. "They aren't set up for credit-card pay-
ments."

Victoria's eyes widened. *Oops. Sorry,
Luke.*

LUKE PACED BACK AND FORTH behind the curtain on the auction stage, readjusting the tool
belt his mother insisted he wear as a joke to
last year's event and then decided he should
keep the look. He couldn't wait to get this
over with and take Victoria back to his place.
He had a late dinner planned in front of the
Christmas tree and fireplace. He hoped the

more time she spent at the Kingston home with him, the faster she'd realize it was where she was meant to be.

He still couldn't believe how things were progressing between them. Every day her company didn't present an offer for the store was one more day he had to convince her that she belonged in Brookhollow, with him.

Regret washed over him. He knew keeping her here longer than necessary was wrong. No matter what the offer was, he was willing to sell the store, if it was what the town wanted. Her idea about turning the store into a museum was perfect, too. But all he could think about was how amazing it had felt to hold her in his arms the night before, as they'd stared out at the frozen river until close to midnight, neither of them broaching the subject of why she was there.

He pulled back the edge of the curtain and watched her laugh with the other women at the table. She was by far the most attractive woman he'd ever seen. He'd been a fool to let her go. What if she wanted to leave again after the papers were signed? Would he have the strength to let her walk out of his life knowing it was what she wanted? He shook his head. He couldn't even think about that now.

He heard his mother announce his name and the curtain disappeared. He plastered a fake, confident smile on his face as he made his way down the runway he'd built years before. Stopping at the end, he flexed his biceps.

The women cheered.

"Yes, that's right, ladies, he's not only devilishly handsome, but also handy." His mother winked at him.

He turned his back to the crowd and conveyed his exasperation to his mother.

"Let's start the bidding at one hundred," she said, ignoring him.

One hundred? He still couldn't believe women would pay actual money to date him. Women were crazy.

Paddles flew in the air.

"One hundred."

"One fifty."

"Two hundred."

"Three hundred."

Stunned—even though every year it was the same—Luke paused and looked among the paddles rising all over the recreation center. He glanced toward Victoria. She was scanning the crowd, as well, but her paddle remained on the table.

Why wasn't she bidding? Maybe she was waiting until the final bid. No sense entering the bidding war. He relaxed. That had to be it.

But when his gaze met hers, his confidence faded.

She mouthed something to him but he couldn't make out what she'd said.

Squinting in the bright lights, he shrugged to show he hadn't understood.

She shook her head as she continued to watch the war among the other women.

"Eight hundred."

"I have eight hundred from Lindsay Harper." His mother's voice was strained.

Lindsay Harper? Why did she want him?

Mrs. Dawson glanced toward Victoria, but Victoria still refused to engage in the bidding.

Paddles dropped all around them.

"Going once…" Mrs. Dawson announced, staring at Victoria. "Going twice…"

Lindsay smirked and winked at him.

Oh, no. He couldn't go to Lindsay. He

fought to disguise his panic. Even if nothing happened—and nothing would—the whole community would hear a different story the next morning. *Come on, Victoria.* He pleaded with his eyes.

She shrugged hopelessly.

"Going three times... Do I have eight-fifty? Anyone?" His mother stalled, scanning the crowd.

"Hey!" Lindsay interjected.

That's it, Mom. Get me out of this. Victoria sure isn't going to.

"One thousand" came a voice from the back of the room.

"Going once, going twice, gone to whoever that was." His mother beamed and rapped the wooden mallet against the podium.

Luke's shoulders relaxed. *Thank God.* Scanning the crowd for the bidder, he smiled when he saw Mrs. Harris approaching the stage. Good old Mrs. Harris.

She accepted his hand for help onto the platform and he wrapped her in a big hug.

"Now, don't go getting any ideas young man," she said, struggling to free herself.

The crowd roared with laughter.

"Thank you," he said, experiencing a flood of relief. Of course he would rather have been sold to Victoria, but given the choice between Mrs. Harris and Lindsay Harper, the older woman was definitely the safer bet.

"Well, I couldn't let you go to that girl could I? I would have thought Victoria would have rescued you. That's why I waited so long to bid." She looked confused.

"You and me both," Luke said, spotting Victoria making a hasty rush for the door. *Oh no, she doesn't.* He wasn't letting her off the hook. "Just give me a second and I'll be right with you."

"Take your time." Mrs. Harris pulled a sheet of paper out of her pocket. "I just thought of a few things to add to my to-do list."

Luke almost groaned. By the time he finished the chores on Mrs. Harris's list, it would be after midnight.

He caught Victoria's arm as she got her coat from the coat check. "Where do you think you're sneaking off to?"

"The bed-and-breakfast." Her tone was nonchalant. "You have a date, remember?"

"Yes, I know. But if I remember correctly,

I was supposed to have a date with *you*. Why didn't you bid? Did you see who I almost got sold to?" he asked, lowering his voice and helping her into her coat.

She collapsed against him in a fit of laughter.

"That wasn't funny. I was terrified. Last year she won Mike Fisher. After their date, she stalked him. I mean, he was close to getting a restraining order."

That made Victoria laugh so hard, she had to pant, trying to catch her breath. "She's not that bad."

"No, she's worse." Luke shuddered at the possibility of spending an evening with Lindsay. "Anyway, don't think I'm letting you off the hook. Why didn't you bid? I would have paid the final amount." He lowered his voice. "I wanted to spend the evening with you."

"Well, I'll be at the inn anyway. Once you're done with the list Mrs. Harris keeps adding to over there, come get me." She nodded in the direction of the stage where the older woman was scribbling furiously.

"I've seen the list, it could be pretty late before I'm done." He wasn't sure how many other opportunities he would have to spend time with her, to talk her into giving them another chance.

She stood on tiptoe and kissed his cheek. "It doesn't matter how late it is, I want to see you," she whispered in his ear.

Luke felt his insides turn to mush. Gripping her shoulders, he planted a firm kiss on her beautiful lips. "I'll be fast."

CHAPTER TEN

WHERE AM *I?* Luke squinted as he glanced around the room and touched the down-filled, flower-patterned duvet draped over him in the armchair. The Brookhollow Inn. Victoria still lay sleeping in the queen-size bed several feet away, her hair across her face. Luke smiled at the sight, as a ringing sound filled the room.

His cell phone. *Where is it?* Tossing the blanket aside, Luke slid his hand along the end table next to the chair. He reached the phone and silenced it, checking the call display. Darcy, his contractor on the New York restaurant project. He sent the call to voice mail. It had been well past midnight when he'd completed the long list of chores Mrs. Harris had planned for him. She definitely got her money's worth out of him. Victoria had been asleep when he'd let himself in and though she'd told him to wake her, he couldn't bring himself to do it. Instead, he'd settled into the armchair and sat awake listening to the sound of her breathing until he couldn't force his own eyes to remain open a moment longer.

She moaned in her sleep but didn't wake up.

Luke stood and traced a finger down her bare arm on the bed. His emotions swelled just looking at her. He loved her, always had. He placed a gentle kiss on her forehead and brushed her hair away from her flushed cheek.

I can't stay. Her words had torn a hole in him. He was desperate to convince her Brookhollow was home. A place where they could raise a family, start a life together—a real life. Not the crazy, busy, concrete jungle thing she had in New York. The task seemed impossible. She loved the city—the fine dining, Wall Street, designer-suit men, the magnificent skyline, the opportunity and excitement. She wouldn't give any of that up... not for Brookhollow, not for him.

His cell phone buzzed again.

Victoria stirred.

Not wanting to wake her, he tiptoed out of

the room, onto the heated balcony and closed the double French doors.

"Luke Dawson," he answered.

"Hey, Luke, it's Matt."

Another contractor on the restaurant renovation in New York. First Darcy, now Matt. They didn't bother him when he was on holidays unless there was a problem. "Matt, what's wrong?"

"The restaurant owner…"

"Mr. Luis…yeah?"

"He's complaining about a problem with the blueprints. We've explained the design layout to him but he's insisting on meeting with you…today."

Today? New York was a two-hour drive away. If he left by ten…eleven, twelve… "Tell him I'll meet him at twelve-thirty." He'd have to rush, but this was important. Mr. Luis owned a chain of restaurants in New York and Boston. It was the first remodel job he'd done for the man. If he made him happy, more work was guaranteed in the New Year. It was business he couldn't afford to lose.

"Sorry, man. I tried to tell him you're hours away, but he wants to clarify the issues before we go any further."

"You did the right thing by calling. I'll see you soon." Luke heard the double French doors open behind him. At least he wouldn't have to wake her. Disconnecting the call, he turned.

Victoria yawned. She had the comforter from the bed draped over her shoulders, but she still shivered in the cool air.

He crossed the balcony and wrapped his arms around her. He kissed the top of her head. "Good morning."

"Who were you talking to?" she asked, looking up, her arms around his waist.

"My contractor in New York. I have to drive in—there's a minor issue I need to deal with." He touched her cheek. "Sorry to rush off." He'd been hoping to spend the day with her. Take her to a few of their favorite places, help her get into the Christmas spirit. Remind her that Brookhollow was a great place to be.

"That's okay. In fact, I'm dying to get back to the city, even for just a few hours. Do you mind if I come with you?" she asked, blinking her sleepy green eyes.

She missed the city.

He hated the idea of taking her there. The

last thing he wanted was to remind her how fantastic New York was this time of year.

"Come on. A road trip will be fun," she coaxed, snuggling into his chest and sliding her hands under his shirt.

He got goose bumps under her touch and he hesitated. He *did* want to spend the day with her. Two hours to New York and back would give him plenty of time to find out where their relationship was heading. He needed to know where her head, and her heart, was. And he needed to tell her that he was willing to sell the store. She deserved to know that. Keeping her in Brookhollow under false pretences was wrong. He wanted her to stay because she loved him.

"Please, Luke. It will give me a chance to get appropriate clothing for the craft fair tomorrow," she said as she kissed his hands and waited.

"Fine, go get dressed. I just have a couple of calls to make." Reluctantly he broke away from her. At least she was still planning to help with the craft fair. Maybe when she was hit by Brookhollow Christmas spirit, she'd realize how great life could be here, too— though he suspected the possibility was slim.

She'd lit up like a Christmas tree at the prospect of going back to the city.

"Thanks." She dashed back into the bedroom and grabbed her clothes from a suitcase on the floor, then disappeared into the bathroom. "Luke?" She paused before closing the bathroom door.

"Yeah?"

"Do we have time for breakfast? I'm starving."

If he wanted to be in New York by twelve-thirty, he had to be on the highway soon. "No, but we can grab a coffee on the way and Mrs. Harris gave me another batch of her chocolate chip cookies."

She grinned. "Perfect."

"I'LL BE BACK here to pick you up in an hour," Luke said as he pulled his truck to the curb in front of her apartment building on Lexington Avenue two hours later.

"Great. That will give me time to shower and grab some more clothes, check my mailbox, that kind of thing. Thanks again for letting me tag along." She leaned toward him and planted a kiss on his cheek.

"You're welcome," he mumbled. "See you in an hour." He looked at her pointedly.

She laughed as she grabbed the box of mementos from the backseat of the truck. "Okay. Don't worry, I *have* to go back to Brookhollow." She suspected he'd been worried about bringing her to the city. All the way to New York, he'd talked about the craft fair, assigning her various tasks.

"You do?"

She experienced a twinge of guilt at his hopeful expression. "Yes, I left my rental car at the bed-and-breakfast. See you soon." She closed the door and raced up the steps to the building.

Inside her apartment, Victoria set the box onto the kitchen counter and sighed as she looked around the small space. She'd been so excited about finally owning her own place when she got it a year ago. The eight-hundred-square-foot, one-bedroom apartment had never seemed this...small...before.

Heading into her bedroom, she grabbed a suitcase and filled it with some casual clothes. She packed extra, just in case. If she couldn't get Luke to agree to an offer soon, she may be stuck in Brookhollow longer than she expected. The thought didn't bother her as much anymore. Humming a Christmas carol, she continued to fill the suitcase.

She grabbed her keys and took the stairs to the lobby.

The super, Ken, smiled when he looked up from a bill he was signing for a delivery guy. "Hey, you're back."

"Just for an hour. I'm heading out again this afternoon," she explained, opening her mailbox. Bills, Christmas cards and her latest issue of *Vogue* were crammed into the tiny space.

"That's right, your ski trip is this week, isn't it?" he said with a knowing nod.

Victoria's eyes widened. The ski trip. The vacation had slipped her mind. Most of her friends would be heading to the mountains that weekend. She'd planned to join them once this acquisition was wrapped up.

She bit her lip. Well, guess she wouldn't be going this year. Strangely, the realization didn't upset her. If this work trip kept her in Brookhollow over the holidays, it wouldn't be that bad. "No. I'm still working."

"Oh, that's a shame," Ken said. "You could use the break. You work too hard, you know."

He nodded to a couple entering the building. "I mean, since you moved in here, you've been away more than you've been home."

Ken was right. With sixteen acquisition trips and the yearly company retreat in Miami that year, she'd been away from her new home for a total of thirty-three weeks…and counting. "I'll try to take some time off after this," she vowed. "Happy Holidays, Ken." She bounded back up the stairs.

Inside again, she opened her Christmas cards and displayed them along the propane fireplace. She smiled at the one from Jordan, then a small pang of guilt struck her. She hadn't even replied to his text message from earlier in the week. They often went days without communicating and she suspected he was just as busy and probably hadn't read too much into her lack of contact, but she knew it was more than her work schedule or lack of cell service that had prevented her from responding.

She liked him, more than she'd liked anyone she'd dated in years. They had a connection, similar goals and ambitions. Both career-driven and successful, he understood her and she suspected a family life was the last thing on his priority list right now. And up until a week ago, that was perfect with her. She ran a finger along the gold-embossed lettering on the red, satiny card, marveling at how quickly what she longed for in life could change so dramatically.

Placing the card with the others, she struggled with her conflicting emotions. As much as she cared about Jordan, she knew only one man made her heart race. She debated calling him… What could she say? She'd fallen back in love with her high school sweetheart and now all she could think about was how they could be together. She bit her thumbnail.

She'd at least have to tell Jordan she wouldn't be attending the Christmas party if this acquisition dragged on much longer.

As she searched for her cell phone, rehearsing the best thing to say, she heard it ring. She dashed to answer it. *Her office. On a Saturday?* "Hello?"

"Hi, Victoria. It's Kim." The receptionist sounded tired.

The poor woman was as overworked as the rest of the staff. Maybe even more so. "Hey, Kim. Why are you working on a Saturday?"

"Erik asked me to call you with the good news."

Good news? The offer. Her stomach turned and she struggled with a competing sense of relief and disappointment. "We have an offer?"

"Yes. He said to tell you that while it's higher than the rate we paid for the others, not to worry about it. I sent the documents to the bed-and-breakfast by courier, this morning. Just have the owner sign them and get them back here."

"That's great. Thank you, Kim. See you soon," Victoria said, ending the call and sitting on the edge of her bed. They had the offer. Now all she had to do was get Luke to sign the sale papers. She could be back in New York and on her way to the mountains in a couple of days after the company Christmas party, if she wanted to...if she was successful with Luke.

She lay back and stared at her bedroom ceiling. Luke didn't need the store. He owned a profitable architecture firm and the town seemed less opposed to the big, chain store than she'd anticipated. Her guilt over the acquisition had subsided and she had an idea.

Maybe her mother knew more than she was letting on. After all she hadn't told her about Luke's company or about buying the Kingston house… She dialed her mother's cell.

"Hello?"

"Why didn't you tell me Luke owned his own architecture firm?"

"Hello to you, too, Victoria. Well, you always say you're not concerned with local news."

She could sense her mother's sly look even through the phone. "Mom." She was unimpressed.

"I didn't think you'd care…. Really, Victoria, why do you? Is Luke more appealing now that he's a millionaire?"

She rolled her eyes. Luke was far from a millionaire. Leave it to her mother to exaggerate his success. Dishes rattled in the background and she struggled to suppress her growing irritation. "Yes, except he isn't a millionaire, he's just successful and can you please leave the dishes alone?" Luke would be back to get her in fifteen minutes. Going through the apartment, she flicked off lights.

"When did money and status become so important to you? I remember my daughter telling me she would be happy with Luke, even if she had to live in a cardboard box."

"That was forever ago." Her days as a romantic were well behind her. "I was sixteen. What did I know?" Besides, it wasn't Luke's money that appealed to her now. It was the fact that his projects brought him to the city… Maybe he could reconsider his home base. There had to be more work available to him in New York than just about anywhere else. She grabbed a few sweaters from the suitcase and stuffed them back into the drawer. She wouldn't need the extra clothes she'd packed, if the offer was waiting for her back in Brookhollow.

"That sixteen-year-old knew what was important in life." Her mother sounded sad.

She was a success. Her career was under full sail. She loved her life. When and how had she become such a disappointment to her mother? Because she wanted more out of life than to marry Luke Dawson and live in Brookhollow, raising babies?

"What about Luke? You were with him again last night." It wasn't a question.

"Yes, I was and it's nothing, Mom. Just two old friends having…fun." For lack of a more appropriate description. Being with Luke had been fun, but it was more than that. Much more.

"Maybe for you, but I doubt Luke sees it that way." The clanging of dishes resumed.

"Luke can take care of himself, Mom. I think he's a lot stronger than you give him credit for." Victoria did a final check of the apartment to make sure things were unplugged. She planned to be back the following week—Christmas.

She hoped she wouldn't be returning alone. He was working on a project here in the city, maybe he could come stay with her…at least until her next acquisition trip.

"Okay, maybe Luke can handle this all over again, but what about us—your family? Me?"

"Mom, you knew I was only staying long enough to take care of the acquisition."

"So, you really won't consider staying. This 'having fun' with Luke was just a means to an end?"

Victoria hesitated before saying, "Yes, Mom. I'm coming back to New York. I'm not moving home."

The loud creak of the swinging kitchen

door drowned her mother's reply. Victoria turned.

Luke stood in the entryway. "I guess that answers my question, as well." His face fell as he left the kitchen, letting the swinging door close behind him.

"Who was that?" Her mother asked.

"Luke. I have to go, Mom. See you later." She disconnected the call and grabbed her purse and bag. The apartment door was still open and Luke was striding down the hall.

"Luke, wait," she called as she locked her apartment.

Men carrying a heavy couch grunted as she blocked their entranceway to the apartment down the hall.

"Sorry," she mumbled as she squeezed past them. The outside door of the apartment building was propped open with a brick. That's how Luke must have gotten into the secure building.

She was tempted to take the brick and toss it. Leaving the building open to strangers was dangerous. Someone could get hurt.

Someone *had* gotten hurt.

Out on the busy street, Luke climbed into the truck.

Victoria struggled with the passenger door. The handle didn't work. "Luke the door's stuck again," she called through the glass.

He rolled the window down a fraction. "No, it's not, the door's locked."

Locked? "Well, unlock it. Let me in. I didn't..."

"Didn't what? Mean what you said? Oh, I'm pretty sure you did," he said, staring through the front windshield as he started the truck.

"I did...but, well, I'd like to discuss alternatives...how we can..." Tears welled up in her eyes. How did she tell him how she felt? Her feelings were so confusing. She had no idea what she planned to do or what she expected from him. "Luke, open the door. We really do need to talk about what's happening between us."

He stared at her, expressionless. "Nothing's happening. Don't kid yourself, Victoria. You never considered a future with me."

Swallowing the lump in her throat, she straightened. "How am I supposed to get back to Brookhollow tonight?" Anger was the better of the two emotions she felt.

He stiffened and ran a hand through his

hair in frustration, "I'm sorry," he said as he rolled up the window and pulled the truck away from the curb.

He's actually leaving me here? Her eyes widened. She paced the sidewalk looking after the truck. Stopping, she picked up a lump of dirty, slushy snow and tossed it at the moving vehicle. It missed by a mile, but Luke stopped and got out.

He stopped in front of her and pulled out his wallet.

"What are you doing?" If he gave her money to get back to Brookhollow, she would lose her mind.

Instead, he handed her a wrinkled business card and refused to meet her eyes.

"What's this?" She read the card. Bob Smith. Who was Bob Smith?

"One of my contractors. He's from Brookhollow, and he's heading back tonight for the holidays. Call him. I'm sure he'll give you a ride," he said as he walked away, ignoring her openmouthed disbelief. He paused and turned back. "I can't spend two hours with you right now." He jammed his hands into his jean pockets as he trudged back to the truck.

"You expect me to ride with a stranger?" Bob Smith… She didn't recognize the name.

"He's one of my best friends. You'll be fine."

At that moment she wasn't sure she'd ever be fine again. "Luke!" She stomped her foot in a puddle of slush. Wetness seeped into the impractical leather boots.

Ignoring her, Luke disappeared down the busy street.

What was she going to do now? She hated the idea of a bus back to Brookhollow. She looked at the card. Driving with a stranger wasn't much better. She made her way back inside the apartment and slammed the door. She couldn't believe Luke had left her like that.

She sat at her computer. Maybe there would be a flight back to New Jersey that evening. Her father could pick her up from there. Crossing her fingers, she opened the flight website. The pricing this time of year would be ridiculous, especially last minute, and she wouldn't even be able to expense it to the company. It had been her choice to take this opportunity to come back to the city. She'd trusted Luke. She'd never thought in a million years he'd leave her in the city when he wanted her to stay in Brookhollow. She punched the required flight information into the keyboard.

Processing…

She scanned her apartment and shivered. The heat had been turned down and all the lights were off. It was dim and dreary inside her home. She wished she'd at least decorated for Christmas. Coming back to an empty, unfestive apartment next week would be disheartening. She pushed the thought away. She'd be too busy at work to notice…as usual.

She glanced back toward the screen.

Still processing…

"Come on." She bit her thumbnail as she waited.

The screen displayed the results.

Victoria scanned the flights to New Jersey.

Nothing. The first available flight was January 2.

Shutting down the screen, she rested her head on her arms. *What was she going to do?* She sighed and sat back in the chair.

Her cell phone vibrated in her purse. Luke? Had he come back for her? He'd better be bringing a good apology with him. She grabbed her phone, but didn't recognize the number. "Hello?"

"Victoria, this is Bob Smith."

Ah, the famed Bob Smith. His voice didn't ring any bells. "Hi."

"Luke called, said you might be looking for a ride to Brookhollow tonight." The hammering and yelling in the background made it difficult to hear him.

"Yes, but…well…"

"It would be my pleasure. The drive can be pretty boring alone. I'll pick you up somewhere at seven?"

"Seven?" she asked, glancing at her watch. That was almost four hours away. They wouldn't even get back to Brookhollow until after nine.

"Yeah, I have to finish up here first." He sounded apologetic.

She was the one needing the favor. Stranded people didn't have the luxury of being demanding. Forcing her tone to sound more pleasant, she said, "No problem. Seven is fine. How about I meet you at the Starbucks on the corner of Fifth Avenue?" Maybe she'd go shopping. Christmas was only a week away and she'd neglected her shopping, confident she'd be back in the city by now.

"Great, see you then. I drive a blue Jeep with a New Jersey Devils license plate."

"Thank you, Bob." Victoria still felt uneasy as she hung up the phone. She didn't even know this guy. But he was from Brookhollow...not that that meant anything anymore.

Needing some serious retail therapy, she grabbed her purse and left the apartment and, twenty minutes later, she got out of a cab on Fifth Avenue. The large store windows were lit up with colorful Christmas displays and white lights and big snowflake ornaments decorated the lamp poles lining the street. New York was nothing short of magical at this time of year. Groups of friends ducked into their favorite watering holes and Christmas shoppers whizzed past, struggling with too many bags. A couple walking hand in hand stopped in front of her at the cross light. The man turned and placed a kiss on the woman's cheek. The signal turned to *walk* and they strolled through the busy crossing.

Victoria let out a deep sigh. For the first time, she felt lonely here, even surrounded by so many people. As much as she loved living in New York, she loved Luke more. Always had. *Would he consider a long-distance relationship? Would* she *consider it?*

She needed to set things right with Luke. If he wanted her, she'd consider giving all this up for him. The city, her job, her new apartment, everything. What she wanted most, *needed* most, was to be with him. She was sure of it.

And if that meant moving back to Brookhollow, then the decision was made.

HITTING THE STEERING WHEEL, Luke flicked on the wipers in his truck. A light snow fell on the windshield. He resisted the temptation to turn the truck around. *She'd used him.* The thought made his blood pressure soar. He'd been so stupid. She wanted the store and he'd been standing in her way. He should have known she'd stop at nothing to get what she wanted. Even if it meant breaking his heart again. Deep down he'd known all along she'd never move back to Brookhollow, but he hadn't expected her to. If this last week had taught him anything, it was that he would do anything for Victoria Mason.

He'd let her go once, he wouldn't be that

fool again. Even if it meant leaving Brookhollow. He was in the city a lot anyway and his
job would be easier without the commute. He
could be more involved, more hands on. And
the city did have its own charm. If she asked,
he would follow her anywhere this time. He
frowned and shook his head. But she wouldn't
ask. He'd been just a means to an end. Nothing more.

"I REALLY APPRECIATE THIS," Victoria said as
she buckled her seat belt in Bob Smith's Jeep
Wrangler hours later. She glanced toward the
backseat where six large shopping bags full of
presents for her family and Rachel's children
were squeezed into the limited space next to
Bob's tool kit and lunch tin. "Sorry about
all the bags. I think I may have gotten carried away with the shopping." The sights and
sounds of the season had improved her mood.
With each couple or family she'd passed, her
decision to leave the city and start a life with
Luke in Brookhollow became easier. She
wanted that. Now, she had to convince him.

"No problem, really," the young man said,
turning the Jeep out into traffic.

Victoria took a sip of her coffee and settled back against the seat for the long drive.

"Are you cold?" Bob asked as he reached for the heater and glanced in her direction.

"No, I'm okay. Thanks." She set her coffee cup in the cup holder. "So, I feel bad asking this, but...should I know you?" She couldn't place him, but people could change a lot in twelve years.

Bob laughed. "No. My wife and I just moved to Brookhollow from Chicago last year."

"Oh." Victoria nodded, relieved. "Why?"

"Well, Luke invited us there for a weekend when we started working together and we thought it would be a great place to raise a family. My wife is three months pregnant," he said proudly. "So, believe me, I'm used to not being able to see out the back window through the shopping bags."

"Congratulations," Victoria said quietly, swallowing a lump in her throat. Everyone she knew had someone special in their life... children...a home... She hadn't realized how much she'd been missing out on. She'd fooled herself into believing the casual relationship she entertained with Jordan would be enough for now.

"Do you have kids?"

"No," she answered. She hadn't even had a serious relationship since Luke, nor had she even given the option much thought.

"I was surprised when Luke said you needed a ride back," Bob said, changing the subject.

Victoria was grateful. She was sure Bob wouldn't want to hear about the sudden ticking of her biological clock the entire way to Brookhollow. "Yeah, we just couldn't be in the same truck together tonight." Bob must have heard at least part of the story, so she didn't elaborate.

He nodded. "Yeah, I heard, but I meant I was surprised you were heading back at all. I mean, I thought your work would be done by now. You must be planning to spend the holidays with your family?"

"Unfortunately, no, I'm still working on the acquisition. It turns out that the original documents for the sale of the store protects it against an acquisition like this. So unless Luke willingly sells the store..." She shrugged.

At this point, it didn't even matter. Finishing the acquisition now wasn't important. Not if it meant hurting Luke. She bit her lip. Erik would just send someone else in to take over the project, but she couldn't worry about any of that now. The most important thing was getting to Brookhollow and telling Luke how she felt. The idea both excited and terrified her.

"But Luke *is* willing to sell the store," Bob said, confusion clouding his face as he turned the Jeep onto the highway.

"What?" She narrowed her eyes. "Did Luke tell you that?" she asked in disbelief.

Bob's expression changed. "Oh…I mean, I thought he was considering it…maybe," he stammered.

"Bob, are you telling me Luke wants tc sell the store?" Victoria demanded again, her anger rising. He'd been lying to her, keeping her in Brookhollow for no reason. All the trips down memory lane and the house… Her head hurt.

If he loved her enough to keep her in town in an attempt to make her fall in love with him again, he was going about it all wrong. What she needed was an honest confession of how he felt. To be sure in his love and that if she gave up the city for him, they'd be successful in making things work this time.

"I shouldn't have said anything. I really don't know for sure." He cringed.

Victoria relaxed her clenched fists. "I can't believe him."

"I'm sure he had his reasons for holding out." Bob smiled weakly. He reached forward and turned on the wipers as large wet snowflakes hit the windshield.

"I'm sure he did," Victoria mumbled, staring out the window.

Bob's cell phone rang. Picking it up from the charger, he glanced at the call display. "Speak of the devil. Hey, Luke," he said into the phone.

What was he calling for? To make sure she was getting back safely?

"Yeah, we're just leaving the city…"

Thanks to him, she was leaving four hours later than planned. She fought the urge to grab the phone from Bob and give Luke a piece of her mind.

"You're kidding," Bob said. "No, that's no problem… Where are you?"

Victoria's head spun in Bob's direction.

Bob looked at her apologetically. "Sure, we'll be there in a little over an hour," he said, ending the call and turning to Victoria. "The truck broke down."

LUKE LEANED AGAINST the truck, the hood open. Smoke billowed from the engine and the motor was hot. Wiping his grease-stained hands on his jeans, he grabbed another cookie from the tin. An hour outside Brookhollow, the truck had sputtered and died.

He didn't usually believe in karma, but who could argue that this was justice? He'd abandoned Victoria on the side of the road and here he was hours later—stranded. Although it could be argued that ultimately he'd saved her from being broken down on the side of the road with him, he knew she wouldn't see it that way. He was lucky his contractor was on the road. He could imagine the look on Victoria's face when Bob announced their next stop. She was probably still furious with him. But he was mad, too. He crunched the cold cookie and kicked the slush from his boot. Mad *and* hurt. Mostly hurt.

He'd had a change of heart and had spent the afternoon in the city, looking for her, as her cell phone continued to go straight to voice mail. The attempt was futile, but leaving without at least trying to find her felt wrong. He ran a hand through his snow-soaked hair. *Man, I've really made a mess of things.*

Bob's Jeep pulled up behind the truck and, seconds later, his eyes met Victoria's menacing glare. *Wow, she's really angry.* Maybe walking back to Brookhollow would be a better option.

"Hey, man, what happened?" Bob asked, jumping down from the Jeep.

Victoria stayed inside.

"The engine died about half a mile from here. I managed to push her out of the traffic, but she refuses to start." Luke shook his head and popped the rest of the cookie into his mouth. "Thanks for coming."

"Hey, no problem." Bob peered under the hood of the truck. He fiddled with the starter. "Yep, that engine's done. Looks like a boost would be futile. Better off just to call a tow truck." He wiped his hands on the back of his work coveralls. "How old is this truck anyway, Luke?"

"Old." Luke bit his lip, glancing in the direction of the Jeep. Victoria stared out the passenger side window. "She's angry, isn't she?"

Bob avoided his gaze. "You could say that." He shuffled his feet in the snow and shoved his hands into his pockets.

"I shouldn't have left her. She just makes me so crazy, you know?" Opening the back of the truck, he removed his toolbox and locked the door.

Bob slammed the hood of the truck and offered to take the toolbox.

"Thanks, I got it." Luke tucked the tin of cookies under his arm. Maybe he could give them to her as a peace offering. Though he suspected it would take more than cookies to make this right.

"Actually, Luke, I may have made things worse," Bob answered, placing a hand on Luke's arm as the two headed toward the Jeep.

Luke stopped. "I don't see how you could." Inside the truck, Victoria's head was down and she rummaged in her purse. He hoped she didn't have anything sharp in there.

"Well, I kind of told her you were planning to sell the store," Bob mumbled.

Luke's face fell. No wonder her face was a deep purple. Despite the cold, under his coat pools of sweat gathered on his back. She deserved an explanation, but the look on her face suggested she wasn't interested in hearing one.

"Sorry. It slipped," Bob said with a shrug.

"It's okay. I should have been honest with her."

"That doesn't always work. Trust me, you learn to be *creative* when you're married."

"Yeah, well, if you have any *creative* ideas on how to get out of this one, I'd love to hear them." Luke turned and waited for his friend. Any suggestion at this point would be appreciated.

Both men stared at the Jeep where Victoria had put her earphones on and rested her head back against the seat, eyes closed.

"Sorry, buddy, I think you're on your own." Bob slapped Luke on the back and jumped into the Jeep.

Luke opened the door behind the driver's seat and stared at the bags. Putting his tool kit on the floor behind Bob's seat, Luke pushed against them and climbed into the warmth of the truck.

Victoria didn't move.

"Bob, can you crank the heat? I'm freezing," Luke said, breathing warm air onto his cold, bare hands. His fingers were red and it hurt to bend them. His toes had gone numb inside his boots and his nose and eyes watered from the icy wind. He'd never get warm again.

"Sure." Bob adjusted the heat.

A blast of hot air seeped through the truck.

Victoria reached forward and turned it off, then huddled deep into her coat.

Bob shot Luke a look in the rearview mirror and shrugged. He mouthed the words *I'm sorry* and gestured toward Victoria.

Luke cleared his throat and leaned forward between the seats. "Victoria…" He tapped her shoulder when she didn't open her eyes.

She shimmied away in the seat, refusing to turn to face him.

Maybe now was not the time. Maybe it was best to just give her time to cool off a little. Judging by her actions, a year might be enough. He glanced at Bob.

Bob shrugged and motioned for him to try again.

Luke hesitated. Bob was a braver man than

he. "Victoria…" He reached for the earpiece and she caught his hand in midair, pulling the headphones off with her free hand. She tossed them into her open purse.

"*Don't* touch me and *don't* talk to me…unless you're ready to be honest."

Luke swallowed hard. His tongue seemed to swell in his mouth. "Look, I'm sorry I left you there…and for not telling you I was willing to sell the store."

Bob turned his attention to the wipers.

"I was just…hurt when I heard you on the phone." Luke lowered his voice. Talking about this in front of Bob wasn't ideal.

Victoria flung herself around in the seat. "So which is it? Are you sorry or were you justified?"

Luke gritted his teeth. She wasn't going to make this easy. What had he expected? An apology of her own? This was *Victoria* he was dealing with. It didn't matter that what he did was out of love; it had been the wrong way to approach things. "I'm sorry."

"Well, don't worry about it," she said with a wave of her hand. "While I was in New York, the office faxed the offer to the bed-and-breakfast. Tomorrow morning I'll drop the papers off at the store. Once you sign them, I'll be leaving Brookhollow."

Luke studied her stubborn, unyielding expression and his heart sank. It really was just about the acquisition for her. She was getting what she'd wanted and within a few days she'd be gone. *Grab her, tell her you love her. This could be your last chance.* He hesitated.

She turned to stare out the window.

Luke raised a hand to touch her arm, then dropped it. "Okay," he said, slumping back against the seat.

The fight in him died as he watched the snow fall outside. Maybe the old saying was right. Maybe sometimes love wasn't enough. Especially unrequited love.

CHAPTER ELEVEN

"HEY, HONEY. What brings you over?" Al Mason asked, opening the front door and enveloping his daughter in a hug.

"Mom asked me to stop by to help her decorate the tree this morning before the craft fair," she explained, scanning the living room. No tree in sight. Had her mother changed her mind? Or forgotten? Either would suit her fine. She was far from a tree decorating mood.

She rubbed her swollen red eyes and yawned. Sleep had eluded her the night before as she replayed the day's events in her mind. She'd tossed and turned, fighting competing emotions. She was furious with Luke for not being honest with her...for leaving her in New York...for not following her to New York years earlier. But overshadowing her anger was a dull sense of longing and hopelessness—he thought she'd used him. Staring at his goofy smiling face on her phone until long after midnight, she'd fought every impulse to call or text him.

Taking off her coat, she tossed it over the back of the rocking chair in the living room. "Where's Mom?"

The house was quiet. A sure sign Sheila Mason wasn't here.

"She's still picking out the tree. I'm on call to go collect it," Al said with a laugh, leading the way into the kitchen. "Tea, coffee?"

Victoria rubbed her aching forehead as she dug around in her purse to retrieve her bottle of painkillers. "Coffee would be great, Dad." She shook out a couple of pills and followed him into the kitchen. Tossing the pills into her mouth dry, she choked them down. "Here, I'll make it," she offered, taking the can of ground coffee from him.

"Thanks. Your mother always says I make it too weak."

It was one thing the two women had in common: they liked their coffee strong. She set the coffee to perk and joined her father in the living room.

Good Morning America was on the television. The background, behind the news anchors, of the snow falling on the busy street in Times Square made her heart ache. The day before, her choice to leave New York had been so clear, until they'd fought...once again. Their greatest success was in messing things up between them. Would they ever get it right? Were they meant to?

A phone rang in the den and Victoria glanced at her father. He made no motion to answer it.

"Dad, do you want me to get that?"

"No, no. That's your mother's work line. She gets angry if I answer it. I can never get the messages correct," he said with a laugh and shrugged. "I'm a retired contractor. I never claimed to be a good receptionist."

"Work line? What's that about?" Her mother was working again?

"Her sewing business." Her father gave her a surprised look. "She didn't tell you she started taking on business again?"

Victoria shook her head, as the coffee timer chimed. "Hold that thought." Dashing into the kitchen, she collected two snowman-shaped mugs from the cupboard. She poured their coffee and headed back into the living room. She set a mug down on the end table next to her father as she sat on the couch. "Okay, continue."

Al took a sip and grimaced. "Ack… You drink it like your mom." He set the cup down. "Maybe you should ask her. I'm sure she'd love to tell you about it."

Victoria wasn't so sure. Her mom had chosen to keep it quiet this long. "Why hasn't she told me about it already?" she asked, wrapping her hands around the mug and curling her legs under her on the couch.

"I would assume she just didn't want to bother you with it. You're always so busy with your work, your friends, that Jordan fellow," her father said as he flipped through the television stations.

"She still could have told me." She sat back in the chair. Her mother had real talent, and a creative eye for fashion. Victoria had always wondered why her mom hadn't gone further with her passion. Now, it seems she had.

The phone rang in the den again.

"Are you sure we shouldn't answer that?" She wouldn't want her mother to lose business.

Her father shook his head. "No, it rings all the time. It's best to let it go to voice mail."

He settled on an old black-and-white Western starring John Wayne.

"So, business must be going well then?" She couldn't let the subject drop. She was dying to know more.

"Yeah, well, it didn't take long for her old clients to hear she was back in business and start placing orders." He clamped his mouth shut.

"Old clients? You mean the people she used to make things for?" As a young child she remembered her mother making aprons and tablecloths to donate to the church craft fairs and she'd made a few prom dresses for some of the graduating girls in town.

"Okay. The truth is, before you were born, your mother ran a very lucrative sewing business. She even sold some of her designs to a clothing store in Newark."

"Mom?" Victoria's eyes widened and she pointed to her chest. "My mom?"

Her father nodded. "Yes. Your mother. You two are a lot more alike than you may realize."

"Wow." Victoria sat back in the chair. First Luke, now her mother. Running a successful business *was* possible living in Brookhollow. Could she, too, have had it all?

The house phone rang and her father answered it. "Hello? Okay. I'm on my way." He replaced the receiver and stood. "That was her. We'll be back in a few minutes," he said, opening the front closet and taking out his hat and scarf and coat. He grabbed a set of work gloves and some tie-downs for the tree. "Remember, not a word about her business." He slid into his coat and wrapped the scarf around his neck. Burying his balding head deep inside his hat, he added, "She's really proud of herself and she'll tell you about it when she's ready."

"RED RIBBON OR GREEN?" Victoria held the options in either hand and tapped her foot, waiting for the ten-year-old girl on the other side of the wrapping table to decide. It was only two o'clock and already she'd had enough of this. She wished for the millionth time she hadn't agreed to participate. Luke had the papers. All he had to do was sign on the bottom line and express post the forms back to New York. She should have been on her way back that morning. Yet, here she was, wrapping gifts.

Her mother had set up her craft table a few feet away. Despite spending time together as she helped decorate the tree, her mother had yet to address the topic of her new business.

"I'd like the red...no wait...green," the young girl said, pointing to the ribbon.

Victoria picked up the large gift-wrapped box.

"No, red." The little girl held out a hand to stop her from cutting the green ribbon. "Yes, definitely red."

"You're sure?" Victoria paused, scissors in midair. *Was I this annoying at ten? Probably.*

The cause of her anxiety stood about twelve feet away from her, manning the food concession stand. The *only* food concession stand. She craved a coffee, and the smell of cinnamon rolls reaching her nose was almost irresistible, but she refused to go to him. He'd barely given her a nod when their eyes met hours before. Now, he flirted with a short, bubbly brunette and Victoria fumed despite her best efforts. Two nights ago he'd confessed his love for *her*. Now look at him.

Laughing and joking with this woman she didn't recognize.

Cutting the ribbon, she wrapped it around the package. She tied the bow on top and handed the parcel to the little girl.

"Thanks." The young girl beamed at the present. "My mom's going to love it."

"I'm sure she will." Victoria didn't look at the girl, too distracted by the flirting across from her. The brunette touched Luke's arm and giggled at whatever he was saying. And giggled…and giggled. *Oh, come on, he isn't that funny.*

The little girl looked in the direction of the scene holding Victoria's attention. "Her laugh is annoying."

Victoria studied the child in surprise. She couldn't resist. "I agree. Who is she?"

"Megan Thompson. Her younger brother Michael is in my class at school. He is just as annoying. Last week he borrowed my…"

"Yeah, yeah, that's awful," Victoria interrupted. "How old is she?" She couldn't be more than twenty-two.

"Not sure. Michael says she's home from university for Christmas," the girl said with a shrug.

A university student? Really, Luke? Well, at least she wouldn't be in Brookhollow long. She didn't want to read too much into the relief she felt.

"Michael says they're getting married."

Victoria's head snapped around to look at the girl. "Who?"

"Luke and Megan." The little girl played with the roll of green ribbon. "Maybe green would have looked better," she said, studying her package.

Victoria snatched it away. "You got red. Why would he think that?"

"Who?"

"Her brother...Mitchell."

"She doesn't have a brother Mitchell... Do you mean Michael?"

"Yes, Michael, Mitchell, whatever... Why would he think that?"

"Think what?"

Victoria resisted the urge to strangle the child. "Why would he think Luke was getting married?"

"Oh, right... Because he says Megan loves Luke. They dated last summer I think." The girl tucked the present under her arm and moved away from the table.

"Hey, wait a sec…"

"There's my mom, gotta go!" The little girl waved as she dashed off to rejoin her family.

Great, badger a little girl for information about Luke's love life. That's mature. She brushed her hair away from her face and studied the young woman. She was cute. *He'd dated her?*

"How's it going over here?" A familiar voice startled her.

She jumped, placing a hand to her chest.

Mrs. Dawson grabbed Victoria's arm. "Sorry, dear. I didn't mean to startle you." She looked in the direction of Victoria's gaze. "Megan Thompson," she said with a frown. "That girl's nothing but trouble. I won't be sad to see her go back to university in the New Year."

"Really? Why's that?" The last thing she wanted to do was question Luke's mom for information about the two, but she was curious. Too curious for her own good. *Just wrap presents and mind your own business.*

"She's after his money." His mother picked up an empty ribbon roll. "She's just not good enough for my son." Darlene stopped. "Although, I seem to think that about everyone

Luke dates…even though sometimes I may be wrong."

Victoria felt tears threaten to brim over her eyelids and she cleared her throat. "She's pretty." Her eyes fell to the gift on the table in front of her as she reached for a roll of paper and scissors.

Mrs. Dawson wrapped an arm around Victoria's shoulders, surprising her. "Luke has loved you for a long time. Presented with the choice, he would always choose you…we all would." Victoria's chest tightened at the kind words. "The truth is, no one could light a fire under my son the way you could…and still can. I wanted to thank you for getting him to the charity auction the other night."

Victoria nodded, wiping a tear from the corner of her eye. "You're welcome. It really wasn't hard. Luke would do anything for the community."

"Yes, I know. Even sometimes when he's fighting for the wrong cause," she said. "We all think the big store and the support it can provide is a good thing. And remember what I said, my son's always been partial to blondes."

Victoria's smile was weak, but the words warmed her heart. Forgiveness came in different forms and she teared at the sincere gesture from Mrs. Dawson. But as much as she wanted to take comfort in her words, she doubted Luke was interested in *this* blonde anymore.

VICTORIA STOOD IN the back of the children's play area at the craft fair. Luke, dressed as Santa Claus, sat in a plush, red-velvet chair, handing out presents to the children. Squeals of delight echoed through the hall as they tore into the colorful wrapping.

Victoria felt a sense of longing that had become all too familiar in the past week. In the past, she hadn't realized how important family could be or how badly she wanted one of her own. Now she feared she might never have the things that she now knew mattered. Tears sprang to her eyes as she watched Luke with the children. He'd make a terrific father.

The anger she'd felt the day before had long ago dissolved. She understood why he'd lied to her. He loved her…or at least he had. She didn't dare hope that somehow they could work everything out. Life was complicated and love was messy. Sometimes the past should remain in the past.

Victoria wiped her cheeks and moved away from the doorway. The last thing she wanted was for anyone to see her cry. Checking her watch, she saw it was after six. Only a handful of families and workers remained. She made her way to the volunteer hut where she removed her coat from the hook on the wall. She tossed it over her arm and paused. Maybe she should stay until after Christmas. Her family would enjoy having her celebrate the holidays with them; she could visit Mrs. Kingston at the seniors' complex and spend more time with Rachel and the kids... She hesitated. No, she couldn't. The longer she stayed, the harder it would be to leave.

"Are you heading out now?" a deep, familiar voice said from behind her.

She bit her trembling lip and turned. "Yeah. Nice outfit," she said with a small smile, gesturing to the Santa suit.

Luke removed the hat and beard. "Thanks," he said, running a hand through his disheveled hair and toying with the fur on the rim of the hat. He hesitated, then reached into his Santa suit and pulled out an envelope. "Here."

"What's this?" she asked, taking it and opening it. She peered inside. The familiar

Clarke and Johnson letterhead peeked from the top page. Her stomach dropped.

"The signed store papers. That is what you wanted for Christmas, wasn't it?" His voice was low and void of emotion.

Their eyes met and Victoria didn't trust herself to speak. This was what she *had* wanted... She struggled with the lump in her throat.

Luke took a few steps toward her. "Isn't it?" His gaze pierced hers.

He was giving her what she wanted and letting her go again. She cleared her throat. "Um...yes, thank you." She held up the documents and forced a smile as she searched his face for any indication he wanted her to stay.

Luke's eyes revealed nothing. "Okay then. Bye, Victoria."

CHAPTER TWELVE

"So HE HANDS you the sale papers and you leave? Just like that?" Heather's dark brown eyes were wide and disbelieving as she stared at Victoria.

"Yes." Victoria threw her hands in the air. "What else was I supposed to do?" she asked, reaching into the open box of chocolates on her coffee table. Taking two, she popped them both into her mouth. "He was...*furious* with me." Chocolate dripped down her chin. She wiped it with her finger and licked it off.

"Yes," her friend said with a nod, "but he also told you he loved you and wanted you to stay in Brookhollow." She poured more wine into their glasses and put the lid back on the chocolate box.

"Hey!" Victoria reached for the box.

"You've had enough," Heather said, tucking the container beneath the cushion of the armchair she sat in. She took a sip of her wine and shook her head, studying Victoria.

"Whose side are you on anyway? He lied to me, remember, *and* left me stranded in New York." *Hadn't she been listening?*

"Yes, but his lie was to keep you in Brookhollow long enough to remind you that it's where you belong." Heather closed her mouth tight.

Victoria's eyes widened. "Well, it's great to hear that's how you really feel," she grumbled, folding an arm across her stomach. It ached from too much chocolate.

Her friend stood and joined her on the couch. "Look, Vic, I'm your best friend and I love you, so take what I'm about to say in the context that I only want you to be happy, okay?" Heather laid a hand on her shoulder.

She wasn't going to like this, but she was getting the speech anyway. "Fine," she mumbled.

"Your mother is right."

"What?" She'd expected a lecture, but that was worse. Friends really did know how to push your buttons.

"Let me finish." Heather slapped her gently on the back of her head.

Wine sloshed out of Victoria's glass and she licked it as it dripped down the side.

"You know, I'm proud of you for the success you've made of yourself, but I agree with your mother that something is missing…actually *a lot* is missing in your life."

Victoria shifted on the couch and untucked her legs from beneath her. So, her life was career focused. But she wouldn't have fought so hard for something she ultimately didn't want. Slumping against the seat, she said, "I'm happy." But she refused to meet her friend's eyes.

"Really? I'm not buying it. I think you were *satisfied* before this trip to Brookhollow, before seeing Luke, your family and all your old friends. But not anymore." Her friend's tone was gentle. "All I'm saying is think about it." She recovered the box of chocolates from under the cushion and, removing the lid, extended the box.

Victoria glared at her then reached forward and took a chocolate. She played with the foil wrapper. "There's nothing to think about. He doesn't want me anymore." He'd signed the papers and let her go. Besides, he had Megan now. Her heart ached at the memory of him flirting with the cute brunette.

"That's crap and you know it. He only signed those papers and let you go because he thought that's what you wanted. Just like he let you leave years ago because it was what you wanted." Heather stood and placed her hands on her hips.

"I've hurt him and I left…again," Victoria said, biting her thumbnail.

"So? Fix it. And get your fingers out of your mouth. Your hands look terrible." Heather smacked her hand.

Victoria shook her head, placing the unopened chocolate back in the box. She set her wineglass on the table. Her depression had to have reached an all-time low if chocolate and wine didn't help. "I can't."

"That's it then? You're giving up on what could be the best thing you've had since… well…the last time you had Luke?" Her friend sounded defeated.

Victoria nodded. She didn't have any other choice. She'd left Brookhollow. Luke would have to be a sucker to take her back now. She swallowed the lump in her throat.

"You're sure?" Heather hesitated, studying her.

No. Victoria nodded.

"Okay then," her friend said, lifting her wineglass. "Let's make a toast."

She didn't feel like toasting anything. "To what?"

"To leaving the past in the past. I'm happy if you're happy." Heather clinked her glass and raised it to her lips.

Victoria hesitated. *Was she happy? Would she ever be truly happy again?* She drained the contents of her glass before she could give herself an honest answer.

LUKE BENT AND TIED his bowling shoes. He took his time, aware of the six pairs of eyes on him. For the first time since joining the league, he wasn't looking forward to bowling. No doubt the guys had heard he'd signed the store papers and let Victoria leave, and no doubt they all had their own opinions about it. Opinions he didn't want to hear. His mother and sisters had already given him an earful that morning. He shook his head. He'd never understand the women in his family. First they warned him against Victoria, offering their unsolicited advice, now they said he was wrong to let her go. People needed to make up their minds. Sighing, he stood. Time to face his teammates.

Russ picked up a beer from the table behind him and handed it to Luke.

"Thanks," Luke said, taking a swig. He looked around at the silent, expectant faces. "What?"

The men glanced at one another.

Derek cleared his throat and stood. He approached Luke and laid a hand on his shoulder. "Luke, you know we all love you like family, and when it comes to business you are the smartest, most successful man we know…" Derek hesitated, turning to the others.

No one jumped in.

"But…" Luke raised an eyebrow.

"But, you're an idiot." Derek's tone was gentle as he broke the news.

"What?" His friend thought he was an idiot? For selling the store? Doing what they'd asked him to? "I thought you all wanted me to sell." He glanced toward the waitress who was listening behind the bar. "Care to back me up here?"

Melody shook her head. Emptying the dishwasher, she restocked the beer glasses.

Russ shined his bowling ball. "We did, but you were supposed to sell the store and *keep* the girl."

Luke scoffed. "It doesn't exactly work that way. A person can't force someone else to do something they don't want to do."

These guys didn't know about it anyway. Not one of them would ever have had the courage to go up against a woman as smart, ambitious or determined as Victoria. The last twenty-four hours had been torture as he'd replayed the previous day's events. She'd given him the opportunity to stop her from leaving and he'd done nothing. Just as he'd done nothing twelve years ago when she tearfully told him about the job with Clarke and Johnson and had waited for him to ask her to stay. He hadn't, and for twelve years he'd lived with the knowledge that his own stubbornness and unwillingness to tell her how he truly felt had cost him the love of his life, and now he'd gone and made the same mistake again.

"Oh, my God, Victoria, you didn't tell me he was so gorgeous," Heather whispered, coming to stand next to Victoria near the bar at Cask Bar and Kitchen. The company Christmas party was under way in the downstairs cellar bar, closed to the public for the private function.

Victoria jumped and her cheeks flushed as she quickly hit the button on her iPhone to hide the image on the screen. "Who?" she asked nervously. Had Heather caught her staring at the picture of Luke?

"Who do you think?" Heather said with a laugh. She turned and leaned her elbows against the bar, nodding across the way to their table. "That hunk of a stockbroker you've been hiding from us for four months now."

Victoria turned. Across the upscale tavern with its brick walls, dark wood tables and dim lighting, Jordan winked at her from where he sat with her big boss, Mel Clarke. "Yeah, he is gorgeous." She forced a smile.

"So things are going well?"

Victoria nodded. "Yeah." She picked an imaginary piece of lint from her short, tight, black dress, avoiding Heather's gaze.

"Great, because Mel absolutely loves him," Heather said excitedly. "Now we can finally do couple things." She ordered another round for herself and Mel and repinned a stray dark curl behind her ear with a bobby pin.

"That would be great." Victoria tried to sound enthusiastic, but no matter how hard she tried to enjoy herself and focus on her date with Jordan, her thoughts returned to Luke. Whenever he smiled, she compared his thin lips to Luke's full mouth. When he gently touched her arm or wrapped his thin, manicured hand around hers, she longed for Luke's big, rough hands and solid, strong arms. Desperate to forget about the man she couldn't shake from her every thought, she drained the contents of her Grey Goose martini and gestured for another one.

The bartender raised an eyebrow, but reached for the bottle of expensive vodka.

"I'm glad you feel that way, because Mel just kind of invited him on the ski trip." Heather bit her lip, a sheepish look on her made-up face.

"He what?" Two weeks ago, the idea would have been great... But now, the thought of spending the romantic, winter getaway with anyone but Luke made her stomach ache. "What did Jordan say?"

"That he would love to, but he wasn't sure you two were there yet." Heather eyed her suspiciously. "Which brings me to my question—why aren't you?"

Victoria shrugged. "Our schedules have been so busy, this is our first real date." They couldn't possibly go from a first real date to a trip away, could they?

"But you talk all the time…"

She nodded.

"And you said yourself things are going great…"

"Mmm-hmm."

"So, what's the problem?"

"I don't know. After four months of communicating, and the lunch dates, I just thought there'd be more of a connection. I was hoping for…" She paused. *Luke.*

Heather released an exasperated sigh. "Brookhollow? Do I need to remind you that you didn't *want* Brookhollow? Have you changed your mind?"

Had she? Did it matter? "No." She shook her head. "I just…"

"Just what? Hoped to find a Luke Dawson among the Wall Street boys? Come on, Victoria. You can't have your cake and eat it, too.

If you want the city, the lights, the noise, the pollution, the career-driven men, you have to embrace all of it, and let go of the fantasy of finding a sweet, thoughtful, family man who wants to marry you, settle down and have babies. Start with a ski trip and let the rest take its course."

Victoria sighed. "I don't know." She took another sip of her martini.

"Here he comes. Invite him," Heather urged, collecting their drinks. "It'll take your mind off Brookhollow and give you something else to do than stare at that picture on your phone."

Victoria's mouth dropped as Heather sauntered back toward the table where their co-workers mingled.

Jordan leaned against the bar stool next to her. "Hey, pretty girl, why do I get the feeling you're avoiding me?" he asked, signaling the bartender for another drink. "Red Bull and vodka, please."

"Not at all," Victoria insisted, staring at the can of Red Bull on the bar. "You know, it says on the can not to mix Red Bull with alcohol."

Jordan laughed, wrapping an arm around her waist. "I work on Wall Street, a heart attack is in my future anyway." He paused, then said, casually, "So, your boss invited me on a ski trip."

Victoria cleared her throat and studied her hands. Looking into his dark eyes, knowing that she was still in love with someone else was torture. He was such a great guy—smart, good-looking, kind… Just not Luke. She suspected no one would ever fill the hole Luke had left, the one that had gone unacknowledged for years, but begged to be filled now. "What did you say?"

Jordan lifted her chin until her eyes met his. "I told him I hadn't been invited…yet."

Victoria swallowed hard. "I…um…"

"Look, it's okay if you're not ready. But just know that I am. I'd love to go, if you want me to. No pressure."

She hesitated.

"I mean, I will be alone for Christmas…" His tone was teasing, but it was clear that he very much wanted her to invite him along.

Luke was her past. In time she'd learn to leave him there as she'd done before. Maybe the quickest way to get over him would be to spend the holidays with Jordan and her friends. She lowered her gaze again. Who was she kidding? Getting over Luke was going to take a Christmas miracle. A ski trip with another man was definitely not going to work. "I've actually decided not to go this year," she said, her mind made up. "Please don't say anything to Heather, I haven't told them yet."

"Oh," Jordan said, clearly disappointed. He gently lifted her chin and she saw the concern in his chiseled features. "Where are you, Vic? I mean, you're standing right here, but your mind has been somewhere else all night."

Victoria struggled to breathe. "I know, I'm sorry."

"Is it me?"

She shook her head. "No," she insisted, touching his hand.

"Am I not what you expected?" He frowned, worried, and she felt so bad for him.

"No," Victoria said sadly, "*I'm* not who I expected."

"I don't understand."

"I wouldn't expect you to. I don't, either." Easing his hand from her chin and his arm from around her waist, she collected her purse. "I'm sorry, Jordan. I have to go." The tears she'd been holding at bay for hours threatened to fall as she made her way to the coat check and she didn't want anyone to see. In time she hoped to regain at least a part of who she was before this acquisitions trip, but it wouldn't be tonight.

CHAPTER THIRTEEN

"VICTORIA, I NEED that paperwork for the new Boston deli mart acquisition on my desk before you leave for the day." Erik stuck his head around her office door and pointed to the stack of papers spread out around her.

She nodded and bit her tongue, fighting the urge to remind him she wasn't even supposed to be in the office that week. "Sure, no problem." Except it was the third project he'd had her finalize the details for that day, each one requiring more work than the previous. Forcing a smile, she reached for the paperwork for the Boston acquisition.

Erik disappeared out into the hall and Victoria sifted through the mess cluttering the desk in search of her coffee cup. Taking a sip, she grimaced. Ice cold. The third one that day that had gone cold before she could drink it. Her head hurt from too much wine the night before. No more drinking alone in a slump of depression with old black-and-white holiday movies, she vowed. Her stomach growled. She couldn't remember the last time she'd eaten. The leftover chocolates the night before were the last thing she remembered consuming.

Having gone on vacation already, Heather had left several messages on her voice mail but she wasn't ready to face her friend's criticism just yet. She knew Heather would be puzzled and slightly annoyed at her behavior—abandoning Jordan at the office party and canceling on the ski trip at the last minute. She hoped by the time Heather returned in the New Year, she'd have gotten her head on straight again. A quick glance at her watch revealed it was 3:45. She blinked. That couldn't be right. She checked the time in the corner of her computer monitor. 3:47. Even worse.

She scanned the ever-growing stack of papers on her desk. How was she going to get through all of this? It was a good thing she hadn't gone skiing, otherwise she'd never catch up once she returned. She reached for her pen among the clutter.

"Victoria."

Her office intercom lit up. She jumped and spilled coffee onto her tan dress pants. Good thing it hadn't been hot.

"Yes, Erik?" She grabbed a tissue and dabbed at the dark stain.

"Just wanted to let you know I'll be leaving at four-thirty, so I'll need the final documents by then."

"Uh…" Victoria raised her hands in defeat. There was still hours of work required on the file and she was supposed to have it to him in less than an hour? "Sure, Erik."

The light disappeared.

She picked up the Boston acquisition paperwork, shoving the rest aside to make room to work.

December was usually a slow month for their department, with a real surge occurring in the early part of the year, as companies went under, not having survived the Christmas season. People were spending less these days. She surveyed the heaps of work on her desk. If she was this busy now, the New Year would be crazy. She frowned.

She was being ridiculous. This is what she wanted. So, she had to work harder. She didn't have a family or husband or even significant other...not even a goldfish to worry about. Overtime was *not* a problem. As always.

The thought depressed her.

Her birthday was in two weeks. Thirty-three years and what did she have to show for it?

A great career, a beautiful apartment...

A demanding, stressful career, an empty apartment... She rotated in her plush, leather chair to face the frosted window. Snow fell in tiny flakes onto the streets below. Families and couples, smiling and laughing, rushed along the busy sidewalks as the lighted pole lamp decorations came to life one by one. *That's* what Christmas was about. What *life* was about. Family, love, being with the people who mattered. Not buried under a pile of paper until New Year's.

Stay for Christmas. Her mother's words echoed from the previous week. But she'd had to get away. Back to her life in the city and away from Brookhollow, her past and Luke. She hadn't expected those things to follow her here.

Maybe she should have stayed. An image of Luke's face as he'd handed her the signed papers flashed into her mind. So hard, emotionless.

She groaned. She couldn't go back. Luke didn't want her. Besides what would she do in Brookhollow?

She turned her attention back to the Boston paperwork. She had less than forty minutes to get it to her boss. She gulped back the cold coffee. Might as well get used to the taste.

"Victoria, I have a call for you on line four." Kim buzzed her office phone a moment later.

"Take a message please, Kim." Whoever it was could wait. She had to learn how to set her phone to do-not-disturb mode. She suspected she would need that feature a lot in the coming months.

"The lady on the line said it was urgent," Kim said.

What wasn't urgent today? Sighing, she said, "Okay, put her through."

Victoria heard the distinct click of the call transfer and plastered a fake smile on her face. A smile, even a fake one, was supposed to elevate your mood. It didn't work. "Hello, this is Victoria."

"Victoria?" an older woman said.

"Yes, Victoria Mason speaking. Can I help you?" Victoria fought to keep the exasperation she felt from creeping into her voice.

"Oh, yes, dear, this is Mrs. Harris. Margaret."

Mrs. Harris? Did I forget something at the bed-and-breakfast? "Hi, Mrs. Harris." The familiar voice made her smile for real. "Is everything okay?" she asked suddenly. Her parents? Luke?

"Everything's fine, dear. I found one of your business cards in the room you stayed in and I hope I'm not bothering you." The woman sounded tired.

Victoria surveyed the work on her desk. There was no possible way to get the Boston acquisition work done by four-thirty. "No bother at all, Mrs. Harris. What can I help you with?"

"Actually, I'm calling about a business matter."

"A business matter?"

"Yes. I've decided to sell the bed-and-breakfast. As I mentioned last week, I'm getting too old to run it and it is in desperate need of repairs…" The woman's voice was sad as it trailed on.

"Selling it? Isn't there a family member who could take over?" Victoria asked, lowering her voice as she stood to close her office door. If anyone heard her try to talk Mrs. Harris out of selling to a chain hotel she'd be fired. But the bed-and-breakfast was like the old sporting goods store; it was a landmark in Brookhollow. The difference was the hotel chain wouldn't add to the community. Mrs. Harris couldn't sell it. She felt a pang of guilt and she hoped things were going well in Brookhollow with the store close-out. Her mother had said the store had shut its doors and the executives from Play Hard Sports had already gathered the stock items.

"There's really no one. My cousin's daughter had planned to, but they are expecting a baby in the spring, so it doesn't look probable."

"And you're sure there's no one else?"

"No. That's why I'm calling. I was hoping your company could help me. A few years ago a big hotel chain…um…the Western something…"

"The Great Western?"

"That's it. They were interested in buying me out, but before Al died, we wouldn't even consider it." Her voice sounded sad at the mention of her late husband. "Do you think they might still be interested in buying it? Could you call them?"

Victoria smiled and shook her head. "I'm sorry, Mrs. Harris, my company doesn't work that way. We just do acquisitions for the bigger companies once they've approached us with an interest to buy."

"Oh…" Mrs. Harris said. "So, you don't know anyone who would be interested in buying?"

"No," Victoria said after a pause. She thought frantically. The last thing she wanted was a hotel chain buying the inn at a ridiculously low rate due to its current state, but the woman sounded desperate to sell it. She drummed her fingers against the side of her coffee cup and tapped her pen against her desk. *Did she know anyone who could help?*

Oh, my God. Actually, she did. Rachel. At least she'd always fantasized about it, and Victoria suspected, given the opportunity, she would do an amazing job breathing life into the old place. The financials would be problematic—Victoria bit her lip—but that's where she came in. She had more than enough in her savings at least to buy the place. The renovations would be a challenge, but once she sold her apartment here in the city… With the right business plan, she didn't doubt the place could do well and the investment gave her a reason to return to Brookhollow. Another one.

"Victoria?"

"Yes, I'm still here." *Could she really do this?* Rachel could, of that she was certain. "Mrs. Harris, I think I do know someone."

The woman let out a sigh of relief. "That's great, dear. Who?"

Victoria stood and tossed her scarf around her neck. If she hurried she could catch the last bus to Brookhollow. "Mrs. Harris, can you keep a secret?"

The woman lowered her voice. "Of course."

Victoria smiled. *No, she couldn't, and that was perfect.* She grabbed her coat and threw it over her arm. Leaving everything scattered across her desk, she hit the light on her way out of the office. "*I'm* buying the bed-and-breakfast. I'll see you tonight."

"VICTORIA, WHAT A SURPRISE." Her mother faked shock as she swung open the front door hours later, her eyes gleaming.

Victoria put her hands on her hips. "No, it isn't. Don't tell me Mrs. Harris didn't call you the moment she hung up from speaking to me."

"So, it's true?" her mother asked, ushering her inside, taking her small suitcase. She frowned. "That's not a very big suitcase for someone moving back home."

Victoria held up a finger. "Mom, I'm moving back to Brookhollow, but not to live *here*." She suspected her mother had already converted the sewing room back into her old bedroom.

Her mother nodded. "Of course, of course."

"I didn't have time to pack more, but I will." A lot of packing and selling the apartment and all her furniture waited for her back in New York, but she could focus on that in the New Year. She needed to figure things out *here* first. One step at a time.

"Oh, I'm so happy," Sheila said, squeezing her tight. "And you'll be here for Christmas?"

Victoria nodded.

Her mother seemed reluctant to let go. She

pulled back and held Victoria at arm's length and studied her face. "Something's wrong." Her mother led her into the kitchen.

"Nothing's wrong. It's just been a crazy afternoon," she said, sitting at the kitchen table and accepting the hot apple cider her mother gave her. *Crazy* was an understatement. She'd quit her job, packed a suitcase and boarded a bus to Brookhollow in less than an hour. Her boss had been too shocked to be angry, but she knew he would be. She'd promised him an official letter of resignation after the holidays. She hoped he wouldn't insist she work out her two weeks' notice.

Her hand shook on her cup. She'd only ever made a decision this important once before, a major one that had changed the course of her life. The decision to leave Brookhollow. And this one had now led her back.

"Does Luke know you're back?" Her mother refused to meet her gaze.

Victoria cocked her head. "I don't know, Mom, does he?"

Her mother shook her head. "I saw Darlene at the old sporting goods store an hour ago and I didn't say a word. She didn't mention it, so I guess Mrs. Harris kept your secret…

as best she could. Darlene and I decided after you left that if you and Luke could move on, so could we. It's nice to have my friend back."

Sheila wore a sheepish grin as she reached across the table for Victoria's hand. "By the way," she added, "the town committee has agreed to turn the store into a sports museum." Her eyes twinkled. "With all the extra space, Mr. Jameson's memorabilia has enough room to be displayed properly. He'd be proud," she said with a smile. "I heard that was your idea." Her eyes misted with tears. "I'm so proud of you, baby doll, and I'm happy you're home." She squeezed Victoria's hand.

A warmth spread through her. "So am I, Mom." For what seemed like the first time in twelve years, her heart swelled with true happiness. Her future was a mystery, but right now it just felt good to be home. "And speaking of secrets, is there anything *you* may have forgotten to mention?" She'd been patient enough. Her mother had to fess up about her business.

Sheila's cheeks flushed and her eyes gleamed. "Actually, yes…"

Victoria's cell phone rang in her purse and

she retrieved it. Erik's cell number flashed on the screen.

"Go ahead. We can talk about this another time," Sheila said, patting her daughter's hand. She stood and collected their empty mugs.

Victoria grabbed her hand. "Nope." She silenced the ring tone. "Sit. I want to talk about it now."

Sheila's face lit up. "Really? You have time? If that call was important…"

Something more important was sitting in front of her. "I'm all ears, Mom."

HAMMERING ON THE ROOF of the bed-and-breakfast two days later startled Victoria awake. She sat up straight and waited.

She heard the noise again. It came from directly above her head in the loft bedroom. *Santa?* What a ridiculous thought. Even Santa didn't work this early, not even two days before Christmas. She held the alarm clock from the bedside table closer to her face. Without her contacts, she couldn't see a thing. 6:24 a.m. She groaned. She hadn't gone to bed until after two. Going over the financials for the bed-and-breakfast had taken a lot longer than she'd anticipated. Rubbing her tired eyes, she yawned.

She pushed back the down duvet on the bed and slid her legs over the side. Instant goose bumps covered her bare flesh in her T-shirt and reindeer shorts. Sliding her feet into her red Ugg slippers, she raked a hand through her disheveled hair. She put her glasses on as she headed downstairs.

The only guest sat at the dining table in front of the big, stone fireplace. A young woman, traveling through town on her way home for Christmas.

"Sorry about the noise. I hope the hammering didn't wake you," Victoria apologized, wishing she'd gotten dressed before coming downstairs, but she'd expected her guest to be sleeping. She'd have to remember in the future that while she may live here, it wasn't just a home, it was also a business. *Her* business. Hers and Rachel's. As she'd suspected, Rachel had jumped at the opportunity to take over the daily operations at the Brookhollow Inn.

"Not at all. You can't hear it over in the guest quarters." The woman held up a muffin. "These are delicious by the way," she said through another big bite.

Thank God Mrs. Harris was still helping out with a few things, to ease the transition. She'd offered to continue baking, as long as she could. Victoria doubted she'd ever learn to bake well enough to fill the role. At some point they would be outsourcing the job to Mrs. Norris's bakery. For now, it was one less thing to worry about.

Grabbing her sweater off the hook by the door, she went outside. Two vehicles were parked in front. She recognized Bob's Jeep. Voices from the backyard confirmed two men talking.

She walked around to the side of the house where Bob was pointing to the awning on the house. "We need to remove that one. A replacement has been ordered and should be here by noon," he told a young man holding a clipboard.

The kid took notes.

"Bob?" Victoria wrapped her arms around her waist, shivering with the cold. It was definitely colder than the forecasted twenty-four. Heavy clouds loomed on the horizon in the otherwise sunny sky, threatening snow.

"Victoria, hi," he said, smiling at her reindeer shorts. "Sorry, if we woke you with the hammering, but we had to get an early start."

Early start? "On what?"

"The roof. It needs to be done by the end of today, otherwise the men are off until January 2," he explained as he moved around her and pointed to a shingle hanging from the roof at the corner of the house. "We should probably start on that side." Bob told the young man.

The roof was being fixed? Mrs. Harris hadn't mentioned she'd already hired contractors for the project and based on the numbers in the expense books, the job wasn't paid for. Victoria had been hoping to put it off until spring, once business picked up and she'd sold her apartment in the city. "Bob, I think there's a mistake. I know the roof needs repairs and it's on my list of things to do…but not quite yet." She danced back and forth in the snow to keep warm.

"The roof needs to be fixed," a deep voice said behind her.

Victoria shut her eyes. *Luke. Of course.* She glanced down at her reindeer shorts, wishing she'd at least put on a pair of jeans. "I know,

Luke, but it's not quite in the budget just yet."
She lowered her voice, as Bob and the young
man left them to continue their inspection of
the work to be done.

"Do you have a budget to repair water damage in most of the house? Because that's what
you can expect if we don't fix this…soon,"
Luke said, putting his hands on his hips.

She bit her lip as she looked at the roof.
Water damage sounded expensive. She sighed.
"How much is the new roof going to cost?"

"It's been taken care of."

"Oh." Maybe Mrs. Harris paid for it in cash
and forgot to note it in her account books.

Bob and the young man returned. Bob
glanced at his watch and cleared his throat.

Luke turned his attention to them. "All
set?"

"Yeah, we just have a few supplies to pick
up and then we can get started if it's okay
with Victoria," Bob said with a glance in her
direction.

"It's…" She started.

"It's fine," Luke said pointedly as he climbed
a ladder leaning against the side of the house
and pulled the loose shingle free.

She wanted to argue, but the roof did need

to be done. "Just let me know if you need anything, Bob."

"Great. We will be back shortly." Bob and the young man disappeared into one of the parked trucks.

"Luke…" Victoria didn't know what to say. Sorry? I'm back? I still love you? She doubted any of that mattered. She shuffled her feet in the snow and glanced toward the second truck parked in front of the bed-and-breakfast. "New truck?"

"Yeah. It was time to let go of the old one. Left me stranded one too many times."

She heard him loud and clear. A lump formed in her throat. *Quit it, it was just a stupid truck.*

"You should go back inside. If the crew needs anything they'll let you know. They're scheduled to be done by six." Luke wiped his hand on his jeans and pulled the collar of his coat around his neck.

Victoria nodded as she walked the pathway to the side door. Pausing, she turned back. "My mom said you decided to turn the store into a museum."

Luke cleared his throat. "Yeah, well, I brought it up at the town meeting and the vote was unanimous. It was a good idea," he admitted. "Thanks."

Victoria opened the screen door. "You're welcome. I can't wait to see it," she said to his back, as he trudged through the slushy sidewalk.

"Stop by anytime," he called over his shoulder.

She fought the urge to run after him. She ached from the mere sight of him. "Thanks, Luke."

He didn't turn, just lifted a hand in a wave. A moment later the truck started with a roar and he drove away.

LUKE STARTED THE ENGINE of his new truck and as she purred to life, he frowned. It sounded too easy. He preferred the sputtering to life of the old one. *Don't be stupid.* This truck was perfect. It didn't break down without warning. The door handle didn't stick. And best of all it didn't haunt him with unwanted memories.

So she *was* home. He hadn't believed it when his mother had casually dropped it into conversation a dozen times the previous morning at their annual Christmas brunch.

He'd had to see it for himself. And now he had. Reindeer shorts, disheveled hair, sleepy eyes and all.

He turned the truck onto Main Street and sighed. She was home. What was he going to do now?

Not a thing.

Twice now, he'd left himself vulnerable to that woman, and she'd trampled over him. Getting over her the first time had been tough. If in fact he could dare claim he *had* gotten over her. A second time would be torture. This time she was so close. He'd see her often. Until she left again…and she would. No doubt about it. He could understand why she'd bought that old, run-down bed-and-breakfast, but he knew Victoria. Within six months, she'd be tired of the slow pace in Brookhollow and craving the lights and noise and fast pace of the city.

Maybe he would spend more time in the city, Boston, not New York. The restaurant in New York was almost complete, but the new housing development he'd designed last month would be breaking ground in early spring. Being away from Brookhollow would be good. Out of sight, out of mind. He groaned inwardly. That certainly hadn't been the case before.

Pulling into the parking lot of the grocery store, he grabbed the shopping list his mother had given him and jogged into the supermarket. The miscellaneous baking items were near impossible to find, but thirty minutes later, arms full, he approached the registers.

"Luke, what a nice surprise," a familiar voice behind him said.

He cringed as he turned. "Hi, Mrs. Mason."

"Shopping for your mom?" she asked, gesturing at the items in his arms.

"Yeah." He shifted the weight. "And you? Getting some last-minute things for dinner tonight?" It seemed like the safer topic of conversation. He was desperate to avoid the one he knew the older woman was bound to approach.

"Yes. I'm making my honey-glazed ham, Victoria's favorite. She's home, you know." The woman beamed.

Ah, there it was. In less than twelve seconds. That had to be some sort of gossip-spreading record, but the woman's smiling face was contagious and Luke's shoulders relaxed as he grinned. "My mom did mention it." *Victoria is home.* Despite his best efforts he liked the sound of it.

"That's right. Victoria called to say your crew was working on the roof of the bed-and-breakfast today. That was very nice of you."

The line moved and Luke let her place her items on the belt before him. "It's nothing. I had already worked it out with Mrs. Harris," he said with a shrug and dropped a can of cranberry sauce. He bent to get it, careful not to drop anything else.

He stood and met Mrs. Mason's direct gaze. "Nice try, Lucas, but I've been around a little longer than that."

He felt his neck turn a deep shade of red along his collar.

The cashier grinned, listening to their exchange.

"The roof needs to be fixed and my men needed the extra hours," Luke explained, setting his produce down on the belt, avoiding the two pairs of eyes staring at him.

Mrs. Mason winked. "Okay, I'll pretend to believe that."

Luke cleared his throat, uncomfortable. "Do you need help carrying your groceries to your car?" He pulled his wallet out of his back pocket.

"No, thank you. I'm okay. Say hi to your family for me. Tell your mom I'm looking forward to Christmas Eve brunch tomorrow," she said with a smile, as she grabbed her bags from the counter. At the Christmas craft fair, the two women had finally agreed to let the silly feud between them end.

"Will do," Luke mumbled. He handed the cashier his debit card.

"Must be nice to have her home, huh?" the cashier asked, surprising him.

He sighed. He may be able to fool himself about his feelings for Victoria, but the rest of the town was too smart. "Yes, it is." Even if it wouldn't do him a bit of good. She was further out of reach now than she'd ever been.

VICTORIA REREAD THE first line in a novel by the fireplace in the sitting room of the inn over and over again. She couldn't concentrate. Tossing the book aside, she pushed back the curtains in the window. Bob's Jeep was the only vehicle out front.

Luke wasn't coming back and hanging around in the hope of seeing him was ridiculous. The hammering on the roof was making her crazy. She had to get out of the house. She had hours before her mother's dinner at six.

In the entrance, she wrapped her tan scarf around her neck and pulled her coat over her shoulders. Sliding her feet into her Ugg boots, she grabbed her gloves and toque. She locked the door behind her and sprinkled more sand onto the stairs and walkway over the thin sheet of ice. By later that evening it could be dangerous if the temperature dropped lower.

"Bob," she called as she walked around the side of the house. They worked fast. In six hours they were almost done. The new shiny shingles on the roof made her smile. One less thing she had to worry about.

"Over here." Bob waved from the back corner of the house.

She stepped over the base of the ladder. "I'm going to head out for a bit. If you need me for anything, just call my cell. I've left the back door open in case you need to go inside and there's fresh coffee and muffins in the kitchen. Help yourself," she said, shading her eyes from the glare reflecting against the white snow draped across the rooftop.

"Thanks. We should be out of here in an

hour. I'll lock up when we leave." He stopped hammering and smiled at her. "Hope we weren't too disruptive."

"Not at all. I guess that's why Mrs. Harris arranged to have this done today. The last guest checked out this morning." It would be quiet until the next guest arrived on January 4 and she was grateful for the time to settle in.

Bob chuckled as he shook his head.

"What?"

"Nothing." A wide grin spread across his face, as he placed another shingle flat on the roof.

"No really, what?" *What did he find so amusing?*

He stopped working and sat on the edge of the roof. "Look, if I tell you, *do not* tell Luke. He's still angry at me for telling you about the store." Bob shook his hammer toward her.

"Okay, I won't mention it." She was dying to know.

"Mrs. Harris didn't arrange this. Luke is funding it," Bob said, opening a new box of shingles.

Victoria felt nothing but pure shock.

"He pulled a couple of us away from the Riverside Drive restaurant remodel today to do the work." He took a sip of his coffee from the travel mug.

"Where is he? I can't let him do that." Luke was funding this renovation for her? She couldn't understand why he would do that. With everything they'd been through, it didn't sound plausible.

"Uh-uh." Bob waved a finger at her. "We had a deal, remember. You said, you wouldn't mention it."

"I know, but this is too much—"

"Victoria, even a daft, unromantic man like me can see Luke Dawson would do a lot more for you. Try not to abuse that power this time. Financially Luke can handle it, but I'm not sure about his emotions."

Her argument died on her lips. Bob was right. Without meaning to, she had used Luke's feelings to her advantage—again. "Fine, I won't say anything to him." She didn't even know when she'd see him again, but when business picked up in the New Year, she'd find a way to repay him.

"Hey, if you're heading into town, you should stop by the arena. The contractors from Play Hard Sports were there last week and they've already started the renovations. Thanks to you the place is looking great."

Victoria nodded. "Yeah, thanks. I think I will stop by." She beamed as she followed the walkway through the front gate onto the sidewalk. She'd done a good thing for the community and the pride she felt far outweighed any she'd felt in the corporate world. The pieces were falling into place.

LUKE REMOVED HIS sunglasses and climbed the ladder to the roof.

Bob and Darren worked at opposite ends and the work was being completed fast. He knew he could count on the men to get the job done. The truth was he needed them back on the restaurant remodel the next day.

"How's it going?" He paused next to Bob and picked up a shingle from the box. The same high-quality shingle he insisted on for all of his major projects. Victoria shouldn't need to replace the roof for twenty…maybe thirty years.

Bob outstretched his hand and took the shingle. "She's not here. Said she had to run out for a while," he told him, not looking up from his work.

Luke frowned. "Who?"

Bob shot him a look. "Victoria. I think she was planning to go by the arena, why don't you check there?"

"I didn't come here to see her." Luke put his sunglasses back on. Bob knew him too well. "I just came by to check on the progress of the roof." He glanced toward Darren and nodded his approval of the job being done.

"Luke, I've worked for you for three years now on bigger projects. This is a simple roofing job. You know we can handle this." Bob laughed, hammering the shingle in place.

"Humph." Luke kicked at a lump of snow melting in the sun beating against the black rooftop. The freezing temperatures of the last few weeks had eased and the weather was mild. One look toward the west however predicted snow...and lots of it.

"Why don't you just call her?" Bob suggested, taking his cell phone from his pocket and extending it to Luke.

"No, thanks. I have a phone." He refused to call her. Things between them were complicated. The feelings they had for each other were crystal clear, yet were never enough. But this time was different. Now she was back home. He dismissed the thought. He wouldn't allow himself any false hope.

"Do you need her number?"

"Forget it. I'm not calling her."

"Thanks for checking in, boss."

Luke descended the ladder and made his way around the side of the house, inspecting the frame and windows. The paint was peeling but other than cosmetic work, the place was in good shape. The windows were another story. The frost trapped between the thin panes of glass suggested they were a source of escaping heat. That was a cost Victoria could do without. He pulled out a notepad and jotted down the various window sizes. He'd place the order for them in the New Year. Victoria would throw a fit over it, but she'd have no choice but to accept it once the work was done.

VICTORIA REMOVED HER gloves and stuffed them in her coat pocket. She unbuttoned the top of her cashmere winter coat and untangled the crocheted scarf from around her neck. She'd walked only three blocks, but as she approached the center of town and the twenty-foot Christmas tree came into view she already felt better. She could feel the tension of the previous weeks melting away.

For years she claimed she'd never return to Brookhollow. The pace in the small town was slow, the opportunities slim and the excitement minimal in comparison to life in a big city. Now it was the only place she wanted to be. The roof being fixed was a blessing she hadn't planned on. And it was all thanks to Luke.

She opened the door to the arena and gasped. The ticket booth and ice rink walls shone with a fresh coat of paint. The deep crevices in the concrete floor were being repaired and the old wooden bleachers had been removed, replaced with tough plastic, stadium chairs. She smiled as her gaze met Jonathan's.

He beamed and stood as she approached. "Hello, again."

"Hi," Victoria said, taking in the improvements behind the ticket counter. A new computer system had been installed and a debit machine sat on the counter. "It looks great in here." A coat of paint could do wonders.

Jonathan nodded. "Yes, and I hear we owe that to you."

She shook her head. "I just put in a request, that's all." The bantam team, newly outfitted, was finishing a practice game and rushing in from the ice.

"Well, I know you met with a lot of resistance when you first came back here, but I don't think anyone could argue against the benefits the new sporting goods store has already provided us."

"I'm glad." She checked the skating schedule on the wall. Public skating was next. "You know, I think I'm going to skate today."

"What size skates do you need?"

"Size six, please."

He turned, gathered the rental skates and slid them through the open window. "Here you are, enjoy." He unlocked the gate to allow her to pass.

"Thanks." She carried the skates down the concrete hallway toward the ice rink.

The sound of a familiar giggle behind her made her pause. *Megan Thompson. Oh, please* do not *be with Luke.*

Fighting the urge to turn to look, she kicked her feet out of her boots and slid them into the skates. She tied the laces with shaky hands.

The last thing she needed right now was to see Luke with another woman.

"Hey, Victoria!" Megan called from a few feet away.

The stomping of skates approached from behind her.

She turned, holding her breath. The brunette was alone. Victoria scanned the area. No Luke in sight. She released a sigh of relief. "Um…Megan, right?"

"Yes." She nodded. "I'm so glad you remember me. I was only twelve when you left Brookhollow."

That's it. Brag about how young you are. Victoria remembered being twenty-four. Thirty seemed old then. "How are you?" Faking a smile was a challenge.

"I'm great. I just wanted to thank you." Megan looked at her feet.

"Thank me?" Victoria was puzzled. For what? Not marrying Luke while the young girl was still in diapers? It was the worst decision of her life. She waited for the girl to explain.

"Well, you see, it's because of you that I decided to go to college."

Because of her? She barely knew the girl. "Me?"

"Yeah." The girl shrugged. "You know how it is around here." She lowered her voice. "Everyone expected me to finish high school, settle down and have babies, but when you didn't do that, I realized I had options. Your mom was always gushing about what a big success you are in New York and...well...it motivated me."

My mother...gushing? Victoria was too stunned to speak.

"Anyway, I just think it's so cool how you've made such a great success of yourself."

Obviously the woman hadn't heard the latest. She'd quit her big successful life to come back here and live the life Megan had just described with disdain. She wasn't sure what to say. "Well, thank you, but I don't think I can take the credit for your ambition."

"I hope you don't mind, but when Luke drove me home the other night, I grilled him for information about you." Megan looked embarrassed by the revelation.

Luke...right. For a moment, through the compliments, she'd almost forgotten that the young woman had set her sights on the man Victoria loved.

"Megan, here's your hot chocolate," a young man said as he approached them and handed the steaming cup to Megan. "Hi, I'm Neil." He extended a hand to Victoria.

"Hi."

"Victoria, this is my boyfriend, Neil." Megan beamed.

"Boyfriend?"

"Well, soon-to-be-husband," Neil corrected, kissing Megan's hand.

"Shh…" The woman giggled. She turned to Victoria. "Neil's not from a small town. He's yet to learn that nothing stays a secret for long around here." She swatted his arm. "Please don't say anything yet. We were planning to tell my folks tonight at dinner." The girl extended her ring finger to Victoria.

A sparkling solitaire diamond lit up her hand.

She was engaged? To Neil? The rumors about her and Luke weren't true? Relief flowed through her. "No. Of course I won't say anything. I know how fast gossip can spread here." Whether it's true or not apparently. She couldn't believe she'd trusted a ten-year-old to be a reliable source.

"Yeah, I heard you and Luke have created quite a buzz yourselves lately," Megan said as she turned to Neil. "If you want to go warm up, I'll be just a second."

He nodded and kissed her cheek. "Nice to meet you, Victoria."

She nodded. "Congratulations."

Megan waited until he was on the ice, then, lowering her voice, she moved closer to Victoria. "Luke still loves you."

Unexpected tears sprang to Victoria's eyes. "Oh, I don't think so, that was forever ago." The truth of the girl's words were too much to hope for. *Maybe someday they could... What?... Be friends?*

"Yes, he does," Megan insisted. "He needed very little prompting the other night to tell me how wonderful you are and how proud he is of you and your success." She squeezed Victoria's hand. "He also said he was happy you were home."

"He said that?" That didn't sound like Luke to confess something like that. The two must be close.

The girl laughed. "Well, not in those words.

We both know Luke is too manly to come right out and say it."

Megan did know him well. All of a sudden she needed to know just how well. "But I thought you two were…" *How could she put it?*

"Luke and I? Gosh, no. Luke's like an older brother to me." She shook her head and shivered as if just the thought disgusted her.

"But I thought you dated last year?" Had her ten-year-old source been wrong about that, too? She felt like an idiot.

"No. We knew everyone thought that, but he was just helping me study for my SATs."

"Oh." Wow, she'd really been misinformed.

"From the look of relief on your face, I think it's a safe assumption that you still love him, too?"

"Yes, I do," Victoria whispered. There was no point denying it.

"There's Neil, so I have to go, but one last thing." Megan started for the ice where her fiancé waited.

"What?"

"Don't you think it's time you two quit being so stubborn and just admit it to each other?"

Victoria sighed. There was nothing she'd rather do, but, well… "It's complicated."

Megan laughed again.

"What?"

"That's the excuse he gave, too."

CHAPTER FOURTEEN

"LUKE, WHAT IS THIS?" Luke's mother asked, removing a package of dry mustard powder from her grocery bag and holding it up for him to see.

He swallowed his eggnog and tore his attention away from the football game he and his father were watching. "The stuff you asked me to pick up." He shrugged, glancing back at the television. "Whoa, what a pass." He smiled as the New York Giants' receiver caught the ball in the New England Patriots' end zone.

"I didn't have mustard powder on my list. The cashier must have put it in your bag by mistake," she said, checking the receipt. "She didn't charge you for it."

Luke was only half listening. "Okay, Mom. Just toss it back into the bag and I'll return it after Christmas." The supermarket would be too busy to stand in line to return something on Christmas Eve or Christmas Day. He refused to venture into the crowded parking lot if he could help it. He leaned forward in his armchair as the quarterback threw the ball toward the opponent's goal line. "Come on…"

The phone in the kitchen rang and Luke could hear his mother answer it as she put her grocery items into the fridge. "Hello? Oh, hi, Sheila."

Luke glanced toward the kitchen. *Mrs. Mason?*

"Oh, yes. We suspected a mix-up at the register…. Sure, no problem. No, don't send Al. I'll get Luke to come over with it right way."

Luke's face fell. His mother couldn't be serious. *What was so important about mustard powder that it couldn't wait?* The football game was in the second quarter and the score was tied.

"Yes, I'm looking forward to brunch tomorrow, too. It has been too long. Talk to you then," Darlene said, replacing the receiver.

The quarterback was tackled by the Patriots' defense and the play was stopped. Luke muttered a curse as the game went to commercial. He stood and stretched. Grabbing the cup on the end table, he drained the contents of his eggnog. "I guess we solved the mystery of the mustard powder?" He opened the fridge and dipped his finger into the icing on the ginger-bread cake.

His mother swiped his hand away and closed the fridge door. "Yes, Sheila's making her ham tonight. I told her you'd take this over to her. She uses it in the honey gaze. She's offered to give me the recipe, so make sure you get that from her, as well," Darlene instructed, handing him the mustard powder.

"Mom, the game's on. Can it wait?" Luke poured more eggnog into his cup.

"Nope, it's almost supper time." She picked up his coat from the back of the couch and tossed it to him.

"But I've been drinking your spiked egg-nog all afternoon, I can't drive." He'd planned to just crash on their couch that evening. The idea of waking up alone on Christmas Eve in the decorated Kingston house depressed him.

The last person he wanted to see that evening was Victoria. Actually, that was a lie—he was dying to see her. He'd gone to the bed-and-breakfast that afternoon *hoping* to see her. But there was no way he could face her without taking her into his arms. If he wouldn't be spending Christmas with her, he didn't want to see her until after the holidays. He just couldn't handle any more disappointment.

"Well, I suggest you start walking. It looks like the snowstorm's going to come anytime now," his mother said, looking out the window.

Small flakes had already begun to fall. Small snow meant lots of it. Luke huffed and took his coat. "I think I liked it better when you two weren't talking to each other," he grumbled, sliding his coat over his sweater and wrapping his checked scarf around his neck. "Dad, text me with the score updates," Luke called.

His father snored in his armchair.

His mother laughed. "The day your father learns to text is the day I fit back into my wedding dress."

"VICTORIA, CAN YOU GET the door?" Sheila Mason called out.

"Sure, Mom." Victoria stood from where she was wrapping Christmas presents on the living room floor and walked backward toward the hallway, her attention glued to the football game on the television. The New York Giants approached the end zone in the last thirteen seconds of the second quarter. "Let's go… Woo-hoo!" Victoria squealed, pumping her arms as her father and uncle high-fived in the living room. The halftime intermission started as she made her way to the front door. A cold breeze gusted in snow as she opened it and a bundled Luke stood in front of her. "Luke."

Surprised, she glanced down at the oversize football jersey she wore over a pair of leggings. He certainly wasn't catching her at her best today. She ran a hand through her hair and tugged at the elastic band, freeing her blond waves from a low ponytail. Luke was the last person she'd been expecting to see.

"Here." He held out a supermarket bag.

"What's this?" Victoria opened it and peered inside.

"Mustard powder. There was a mix-up at the grocery store." Luke pulled the collar of his leather coat up around his red cheeks and rubbed his bare hands together.

The distinct smell of spiked eggnog lingered in the air between them as he spoke.

"Your mom made her famous eggnog?"

He nodded. "That's why I had to walk over here in this crappy weather, missing the end of the second quarter of the game," he said, looking past Victoria to the television inside.

"They just went to second intermission. Giants scored in the last ten seconds to take the lead."

"Of course they did."

"And FYI—mom has a cupboard full of mustard powder already." The sweet aroma of the ham glaze filled the air.

"Of course she does. Well, I'd better get back before the third." He turned to leave.

"You can come in to watch it here…warm up a little." She didn't want him to leave. Fear of his rejection was the only thing preventing her from diving into his arms. Fear *and* his scowl.

"No, thanks." He stopped. "There are more renovations to be done at the bed-and-breakfast in the New Year, so, I'll see you around. Merry Christmas."

"Okay. Merry Christmas." She started to

close the door. "Luke, wait." She couldn't just let him leave.

He stopped but didn't turn.

"Bob told me about the roof." *Oops! Sorry, Bob.*

Luke spun around. "Bob," he muttered.

Sliding her feet into her Uggs, Victoria dashed outside, closing the door behind her. She jogged down the slick, icy path to where Luke stood, hands in his pockets.

"I can't believe he spilled to you…again." He took his phone from his pocket and began to dial.

"What are you doing?"

"Calling him. When it comes to keeping a secret that man is worse than a…a…whatever."

Victoria took the phone.

"Hey!" A deep frown creased his forehead as he reached for it.

She took a step back, moving it out of his reach. "Deal with Bob later. I…uh…need to tell you something." She fiddled nervously with the phone, refusing to meet his gaze. She wanted to tell him she loved him and needed to spend her life with him. Maybe now wasn't the right time. *But when would be the right time?*

Luke glanced pointedly at his watch. "The third quarter is starting in twelve minutes."

Victoria lost her confidence. "Fine, just go." *Why couldn't he just take her into his arms?*

"Okay. See you." He started walking again.

Shivering as a blast of cold rustled the thin football jersey, Victoria said, "No, Luke, wait."

He kept walking.

"I love you."

He paused, then continued walking.

"Didn't you hear me?" she asked, running the few feet to catch up to him and grabbing his arm.

"Yes, I heard you." He removed her hand from his arm.

Her heart sank. "And?" *Did she dare hope he still wanted her, too?*

"That's it?"

"Yes." *That* was huge.

Luke shrugged. "So? I've loved you since the second grade and look where it's gotten us. I wasn't the one who left Brookhollow two weeks before our wedding. I've always loved you enough to put us first. *You* were the one who chose your career—twice."

"If that's true why didn't you fight for us?" Victoria demanded. "I may have left Brookhollow, but you didn't try to stop me." She rubbed her chilled arms for heat.

"Would it have worked?" he challenged her.

She hesitated. "I don't know."

"I do," Luke said, moving toward her. "You see, I've finally learned that there's no point chasing something already gone. Even if you'd stayed, your dream was New York. It still is."

"No, it isn't. I'm home now…to stay. I just bought the Brookhollow Inn."

"Well, we'll see how long that makes you happy. We both know that was Rachel's dream, not yours."

Victoria met his gaze defiantly. "I'm not leaving, Luke."

"Fine, great." He shrugged. "I'm sure your mom will be happy to hear it." He trudged down the sidewalk, head down against the blowing snow.

Again, she chased after him. "So, we're just supposed to go on living in this small town together, seeing each other all the time, doing what? Pretending we don't still love each other? Letting our pride and our past stand in the way of being together?" Tears misted her eyes and she fought to control her overflowing emotions.

He turned to face her. "It's not pride or our past preventing me from taking you in my arms right now, Victoria, the way you want and expect me to. It's *common sense*. Look at us. We push and pull and go hard at each other, expecting the other to give in. How is this—" he gestured between them "—supposed to work?"

"You said yourself—the Kingstons made it work." Her voice was barely more than a whisper. Her throat was tight. He really was saying it was over between them. He didn't even want to try. The realization was hard to take. She'd been foolish to think moving back was enough to convince him they were meant to be together after all they'd been through.

"Well, the Kingstons were tougher and braver than me, because if there's any chance that we try again and it doesn't work…" He stared at the ground at his feet.

"So, you're just going to walk away from

what could be the most fantastic future either of us could have hoped for?" Now the tears welled in her eyes.

Luke put a hand on each of her shoulders. He placed a gentle kiss on her forehead. "I'm sorry, Victoria. I just can't do this anymore."

"WHERE CAN I SET THIS?" Luke asked, struggling under the weight of a heavy box of Mrs. Kingston's belongings he'd found in the attic. The box contained items he thought she'd like to have with her at the seniors' home. Her wedding dress, old family photo albums and a handmade quilt.

"Anywhere is fine, Luke. Thank you for thinking of me. I thought all of this stuff would be long gone by now." She beamed. Her eyes shone the same way they had in her wedding-day photos.

"No problem. I thought your kids might be coming by this evening." He scanned her room. A tiny Christmas tree sat on the edge of her dresser next to the photos of her children and grandchildren. The single bed was dressed with her Christmas quilt and a string of multicolored lights hung in her window.

A cinnamon-scented candle flickered on the tall dresser.

"Not tonight. They're picking me up tomorrow for dinner. Tonight is the Christmas Eve social here at the seniors' complex," she said, gesturing, her head full of curlers. "I'm trying to look pretty."

Luke laughed. "That shouldn't be hard." Mrs. Kingston had aged beautifully and gracefully.

"Well, I'm still looking for a date if you're interested," she said, freeing a lock of hair from the first curler. A silver twirl bounced free, landing on her shoulder.

"As tempting as that is, Mrs. Kingston, I'll have to pass." The woman was adorable.

"You'll be spending the evening with Victoria, I assume?" The older woman's eyes held a hint of mischief.

News of Victoria's move back home had even reached the seniors' complex. "Nah, I don't think so."

Mrs. Kingston frowned. "Why not?" She paused and stared at him in the mirror.

"We're not exactly back together, despite what you may have heard." He bit the inside of his cheek, forcing his voice to sound nonchalant. "You know, just because she's back in Brookhollow doesn't change anything."

"I don't understand." Mrs. Kingston's forehead wrinkled.

Luke squirmed. She wasn't making this easy. Forgetting about Victoria and the fact that it was Christmas Eve and all he wanted was to fall asleep with her in his arms near the fireplace by the tree, this Christmas and every Christmas, would be impossible with everyone talking about her.

"We decided that us—together—just doesn't make sense." Actually *he'd* decided it. Last night. He was desperate to believe he'd done the right thing walking away from her and preserving himself from further damage, but his current torment suggested otherwise.

Mrs. Kingston scoffed. "That doesn't make sense. You two are perfect for each other, always have been." She removed another curler.

Luke shook his head. "No we have very different ideas about what's important in life." Excuses, all excuses.

"So, what you're saying is neither of you are willing to work hard to make it work?" Her disappointment showed in her face.

Wow, she was tough. Almost as tough as Victoria. All he'd wanted was to drop off her things. "It's not as simple as that. We have a history...and we did try."

Mrs. Kingston snorted. "You two were children back then. Of course it didn't work. You're older, wiser now. Or at least you should be." She shook her head. "All my years as a teacher, did I teach you children anything about life?" she asked, sadly.

"Of course you did. We learned a lot from you."

The older woman turned in her chair and studied him. "Why do you think that girl moved back here, after years of showing no interest in Brookhollow? She'd accomplished her goal of acquiring the store...she had her career in the city...she had no reason to come back."

Luke shrugged, avoiding her eyes. "She wanted to buy the bed-and-breakfast," he mumbled.

"That's crap and you know it."

Luke's head whipped up. "Mrs. Kingston!" His eyes widened. Hearing the distinguished older woman speak like that was shocking.

"What? I'm old so I can't call a spade a

spade?" She waved a hand. "It's because I'm old that I can call it as I see it. She came back for you, leaving a very successful career behind. You bought my house, hoping someday she'd live in it with you. You both still love each other…anyone with a grain of sense can see that…and you're both too stubborn to do anything about it."

Guilt washed over him. *He* was the one being stubborn. Victoria was right—he hadn't fought for her, hiding behind the claim that he was doing what he thought she wanted. Stepping aside to allow her to follow her desire without following his own. In truth, he'd been terrified.

"Maybe I should be talking to *her,* if I can't get through to you," she said with a frown, fluffing her curls around her neck.

"Actually, Victoria is willing to try again," he muttered.

"So, it's *your* fear holding you back from what you've wanted for years." She cocked her head to the side.

He nodded. He couldn't argue with the facts. Victoria had confessed her love for him the night before and he'd been the one to walk away from everything he'd ever wanted.

"Look here, Luke. My house...*your* new home...deserves to hear the laughter of children echoing in its halls, to hold the secret passions of a lover's quarrel and to be passed along through generations of strong family ties."

Sitting on the chair near the window, Luke rested his head in his hands. She was right, as usual. "I made a mess of things...again. What do I do to get her back?" He looked expectantly at the older woman.

She smiled and stood. "Didn't you do some renovations for her at the inn yesterday?"

"My crew did, yeah." He stood and held her coat out for her to slide into.

"Well I'm sure someone must have left something behind."

Luke frowned. "No, I doubt it. My guys are pretty good about cleaning up after themselves. I don't think—"

Mrs. Kingston shook her head and interrupted him, "Luke, help me out here—I'm sure there must be a reason you could stop by."

Of course. He nodded. "Yeah, I'm sure

there has to be a tool or box of shingles or something. Thank you, Mrs. Kingston."

"Man, you kids were smarter when you were fifteen."

CHAPTER FIFTEEN

"I STILL CAN'T believe we are really doing this," Rachel said in disbelief as she scanned the paint color swatches Victoria had gathered from the hardware store that morning. The first thing they wanted to tackle on the inside of the bed-and-breakfast was a fresh coat of paint for the guest rooms, dining room and sitting areas.

Victoria carried their steaming cups of peppermint hot chocolate to the table in the sitting room, near the fireplace. The heat radiating from the bright flames and the early-morning sun shining through the large windows created a comfortable and cozy atmosphere, despite the frost crystals gathering on the outside. "I know. I keep waiting to come to my senses," Victoria said with a laugh. "I'm kidding. This was the best decision I've made in a long time." She sat on the couch next to her friend. "So, which of these do you like for the dining room?" she asked, holding the tan and brown color swatches for inspection. "I was thinking more neutral tones for the main, common areas of the house."

Rachel nodded as she studied the walls and took the paint swatches from Victoria. "Yeah, I agree. Um…I like the chestnut brown for the walls and then maybe the pearl for the moldings and trim around the windows and ceiling."

Victoria's face fell.

"What's wrong? Too dark?" Rachel pointed to a different shade on the palette. "If you'd prefer something lighter…"

Victoria shook her head. "No, that's not it. The paint choice is perfect. One of my favorites. It's also the color Luke and I picked out for his bedroom," she explained, touching the deep shade of brown.

Rachel put the swatches aside. "Things aren't going so well between you two?"

"No. I think I may have hurt him one too many times." She stared at her hands on her lap.

Rachel touched her hand and said, "He'll come around. You're home now."

"I don't think that matters."

"It's what he's been waiting for," Rachel insisted, lifting Victoria's chin, forcing her to look at her. "Believe me, Luke isn't still single for any other reason than he's been waiting for you."

"I don't think so." She'd put herself out there for him the night before and he'd walked away.

"Luke is a gorgeous, successful and smart man. The single women around here are dying for him to show them the littlest bit of attention, but he never does. He hasn't been serious about anyone since you, and since having you back, he's been happier than I've ever seen him. He loves you. Just give him time."

"I hope you're right." But she had her doubts. *I can't do this anymore* was pretty final. "Okay, let's get back to the paint colors." She jotted down the chestnut and pearl color numbers on her order slip.

Rachel leaned forward and picked up her hot chocolate. "Ow…" She set the cup back on the glass tabletop and rubbed the side of her stomach.

"Are you okay? That's the third time you've

had a pain since you got here." Maybe the excitement or stress of this whole thing was having an effect on her friend. The last thing she wanted was for Rachel to overexert herself.

"Yeah, I'm fine. Just this nagging dull pain all morning that won't go away, and every now and then, I feel a sharp twisting pain in my side." Resting against the cushions on the couch, she propped her feet on the ottoman. "I'll be okay in a minute. I just need to relax for a bit."

Victoria gathered the paint samples and tucked them into her renovations folder. "Okay, that's enough for the day. It's Christmas Eve after all. By the way, where did Nathan take the kids?" Victoria asked, curling her legs under her on the couch and resting her head against her hand.

Rachel rolled her eyes. "Christmas shopping. I swear that man leaves everything to the last minute, and then they're heading to the parade. It was postponed last week due to the weather."

"Oh, I hope I'm not keeping you from going with them." She'd just been excited to start planning the future of their business. Realizing a new dream seemed surreal after all the years she'd been working in New York.

"No way. Are you kidding? The mall on Christmas Eve will be crazy." She laughed. "You saved me," she insisted, rubbing her stomach. "Wow, that really hurts."

Victoria's eyes widened. "Do you think you may be in labor?"

"No, I'm not due for another two weeks," Rachel said, but she seemed worried as she bit her lip.

"But since this is your third pregnancy, isn't it likelier that you could go early?" She didn't know much about pregnancy, but she did know babies came when they were ready. Early, late, it didn't matter.

"Yeah, but it's Christmas Eve. I can't go into labor today. I'm sure it's nothing. The pain is…" She clutched her stomach and her eyes widened even more. "Uh-oh."

"What?"

"My water just broke." In panic, Rachel pushed herself up from the couch. "Ow, ow…" She bent in pain, as a pool of water collected at her feet on the hardwood.

"Oh, my God. Right now?" Victoria jumped up and moved closer to her friend.

She hadn't expected to be right. *What should she do?*

"Yes. Sorry about the floor." Rachel clutched her arm for support as another contraction buckled her knees.

"Don't worry about the floor," Victoria said, standing in front of her friend, holding her arms. "What do I do?"

Rachel panted through the painful contractions. "Get me to the hospital." She struggled to catch her breath.

"Shouldn't I call Nathan?" She fought to keep the panic from her voice, but she was beginning to sweat. Rachel was in a lot of pain and she had no experience with this sort of thing. But they had time—or she thought they did. Most women complained of long labors, right?

"No, there's no time. This is my third pregnancy, Vic. This baby is just going to slide out and soon."

Victoria's eyes widened. *Oh, crap.* "Okay, sit here. I'll get your shoes." Running to the entry, she grabbed Rachel's running shoes.

Her friend struggled to slide her feet into them. "Forget it. My feet are not going in there. They're too swollen. I'll go barefoot."

"But your feet will freeze." Victoria scanned the sitting area, looking for something else she could give her friend to wear.

"Trust me. I won't even notice." Rachel took Victoria's arm and gave her a pointed look. "Just get me to your car. Quick."

"Okay." Victoria agreed, with a nod. She stopped and her face fell. She cringed. "Problem."

Rachel shot her a look. "You're telling me," she said, supporting her stomach with her hand.

"No, even bigger problem. We don't have a vehicle. I returned my rental this morning and Nathan has your truck, right?" Panic finally reached her voice, despite her best efforts not to lose control. Her friend needed her to keep her cool, but she was freaking out. Rachel could deliver any minute.

Rachel paled. "Oh, no…"

"Hello?" A voice called from the hallway.

Luke. Oh, thank God. "We're in the sitting room!" Victoria helped Rachel limp toward the hallway. Another contraction took hold and they paused.

Luke walked in. "I just came by to pick up some tools I left…" Pausing in the entryway, his gaze fell to the puddle on the floor near the couch and Rachel's hunched frame, clutching her stomach. "Are you okay?"

"She's in labor," Victoria explained, helping Rachel straighten.

"I'll come back for the tools." Luke spun on his heel and disappeared down the hallway.

"No, wait!" Victoria chased after him and grabbed his arm. "We need a ride to the hospital."

"Where's Nathan? Shouldn't he take her?" Luke's terrified expression mirrored her own.

"Yes, but he's not here and there's no time." She lowered her voice. "Her water's broken and the contractions are less than two minutes apart. We have to get to the hospital or the bed-and-breakfast will have its first guest under my management."

"Okay, let's go. Grab her stuff, I'll grab her," he said, rushing into the sitting room and reappearing with a struggling Rachel in his arms.

"Luke, put me down. I can walk." Rachel fought between gasps of air.

"Not without shoes on. Let's go." He tossed his keys to Victoria, and kicked the screen door open.

He was amazing. Thank God he'd arrived when he had. Otherwise she wasn't sure what they would have done. She shuddered as she ran ahead and opened the back door of the new truck.

Easing Rachel into the backseat, Luke wrapped a blanket around her legs. "You okay?"

"I will be. Thanks, Luke." She gave a small smile of relief, then grimaced as a contraction hit. "Just drive fast."

"Got it." Luke jumped into the driver's seat and shoved the key into the ignition. He grabbed his seat belt and glanced at Victoria. "Hang on."

Victoria gripped the handle of the door as the truck peeled out of the driveway and down the side street. Luke glanced in each direction and coasted through the stop sign. Turning the truck onto Main Street, he hit the brakes.

Rachel lurched forward and Victoria shot him a look as her head bounced off of the back of the seat. "Why are you slowing?"

"Look straight ahead."

"What is that?" Huge crowds of people

gathered on both sides of the street. "Oh, no, the rescheduled parade."

"Parade?" Rachel's eyes widened. "We're stuck behind the parade?"

"Is there any way around it?" Victoria asked, scanning the side roads. Most were barricaded to prevent traffic from crossing Main Street. She bit her lip and tapped her fingers on her leg. This wasn't good. If they followed the end of the parade, it would be at least an hour before they reached the end of Main Street. Her friend wouldn't last that long.

Rachel panted in the backseat. Groaning as another contraction made her stomach tighten, she said, "Victoria, I'm not going to make it."

Luke grabbed his cell phone and dialed 911. "I'm calling an ambulance." He lowered his voice and shot Victoria a look. "Why couldn't this have happened in the old truck?"

Victoria hid a nervous giggle.

Luke pulled the truck to the curb. "Yes, I need an ambulance to Main Street…in front of the deli. We have a lady in labor… Great, hurry. New upholstery," he whispered.

Victoria swatted his arm.

"The ambulance will be just a minute. They were in the parade." He turned in his seat and took Rachel's hand. "You're doing great." He wiped a sweaty hank of hair from her forehead.

Victoria's heart melted at the kindness and calming effect the gesture had on her friend. She almost wished she were the one in labor.

Rachel yelped in pain as another contraction took control of her body.

Almost wished.

Wincing in pain as Rachel squeezed his hand, Luke handed Victoria his phone. "Here, why don't you call Nathan now so he can meet her at the hospital."

The sound of sirens wailing in the distance provided a sense of comfort to them all.

Victoria scrolled through his contact list, ignoring the tug of jealousy she felt noticing some unfamiliar female names, and dialed Nathan's cell.

"Hello? Luke?" Nathan yelled above the noise of a marching band, passing in the parade.

"No, it's Victoria. Rachel's in labor. We've called an ambulance, but you better get here quick." The words came out in a hurry.

The ambulance stopped behind the truck. Thank God they had been nearby. Maybe getting stuck behind the parade was a good thing after all. The ambulance was much better equipped to deal with an emergency delivery.

"Where is she? Is she okay?"

"We're with Luke. She's doing great." She gave her friend an encouraging smile as Luke opened the back door for the paramedics.

"I'm on my way," Nathan panted. "I see Luke's truck and the ambulance."

Victoria squinted through the crowded street. There was Nathan, a block away, dragging all three kids down the street toward them. She beamed as she hung up the phone. Getting out of the truck, she raced to the back of the ambulance. "Nathan's coming."

"There's no time," the paramedic said as he reached to close the door.

"Wait, I'm here. I'm here." Nathan caught the door and struggled to catch his breath. He glanced back and forth between his wife and kids.

"Don't worry about the kids. We got them. Jump in." Luke nodded at Nathan. He took Melissa from his arms.

The sight of Luke holding the little girl was

too much. Resisting the urge to kiss him right there among the commotion took all of her strength.

"Thanks, Luke—Victoria," Nathan said as he dove in and reached for Rachel's hand as the doors closed.

All eyes watched the ambulance speed away, lights and sirens wailing, making a path through the parade.

Victoria turned to Luke. "Okay, so...you got this?" she asked, motioning the twins, Jacob and Caleb, who were throwing snowballs at each other on the snowbank, next to the deli.

Luke laughed. "You're kidding, right? You're just going to leave me with three children?" He readjusted Melissa on his hip and picked up the diaper bag Nathan had tossed to the ground at his feet.

"*You* offered to babysit," Victoria pointed out.

"I'd appreciate your help," Luke said, opening the door and helping the children into the backseat.

Victoria bit her lip. She wanted nothing more than to spend the day with Luke, but to what end? He'd made his feelings about their turbulent relationship clear the night before. Being around him would be tough when she loved him as she did. But it wouldn't be fair to abandon him with the kids. Who knew how long Nathan could be at the hospital. She prayed everything went well for her friends. "Um…well…the bed-and-breakfast is under so much construction, it's probably not safe…"

"We can take them back to my place." Luke clasped the girl into the middle seat between the twins and shut the door.

Victoria hesitated. His house. The idea of spending Christmas Eve at the Kingston house hurt. Deeply. She'd been hoping for that chance, but not this way. She sighed. "Okay," she agreed reluctantly, climbing into the truck and fastening her seat belt.

Luke got in the driver's side and put the truck in Reverse. "I'm just going to back up into the back alley and avoid the parade traffic." He glanced into the rearview mirror. "You guys did see Santa go by, right?"

Melissa pouted. "Yeah, but we were in such a hurry, I didn't get to tell him to bring presents for our new brother or sister." She looked close to tears.

Luke's eyes glinted as he turned to Victoria. "Mind if we take a detour?"

She smiled and shook her head "Not at all."

Luke stopped the truck and turned in his seat to face the kids. "Well, it's your lucky day because I happen to know Santa personally. Do you guys want to go meet him?"

The three faces lit up brighter than the decorative lights on the pole lamps, lining the street. "Really? You know Santa?" Jacob's eyes were wide.

"You bet," he said with a wink at Victoria. "How about you, Vic. Do you want to go tell Santa what you'd like for Christmas?" He stroked her hand on the passenger seat and her pulse raced.

Victoria felt a glimmer of hope as her eyes met his. Turning her hand, she grasped his, never wanting to let go. "Very much so."

LUKE COLLAPSED ON the couch next to Victoria and stretched his legs out in front of him. The twinkling white lights on the Christmas tree reflected on the window, mixing with the soft, big snowflakes falling outside. The fireplace radiated heat as the logs blazed, casting a beautiful red-and-orange flame on the brass-rimmed, stone hearth. He let out a loud yawn and checked his watch. "I can't believe it's only nine o'clock. I'm exhausted."

Victoria hid her own yawn behind a hand, tucking her legs up under her on the couch. "Me, too. I don't know how Rachel and Nathan do it. Kids are exhausting. So much energy." She scanned the messy living room. Blankets scattered everywhere and paper-towel-roll forts had been knocked over and littered the hardwood floor. The kids had had a fantastic afternoon, all hyped up on candy canes and hot chocolate. They'd played for hours with Madi in the backyard and had made prebaked chocolate chip cookies to leave for Santa. Luke was amazing with the children and as the day progressed, her heart belonged to him even more.

Luke reached for her legs and lifted them onto his lap. Grabbing a fleece blanket from the floor, he draped it over them and massaged her feet, sticking out one end.

"That feels great." Too great.

His eyes met hers in the flickering light and she struggled to breathe. He moved closer and touched her flushed cheek. "You are beautiful."

"Luke, I…" She swallowed, unsure of what to say. She'd said it all the night before. She'd poured her heart out to him, offered him her soul and he'd confirmed what she'd feared. It was too late for them. Now, here he was, so close, touching her…it was too much. So familiar, yet new and exciting…and unattainable. This hurt so much.

"Shh, let me say—"

The doorbell made her jump, and she swung her legs from Luke's lap.

Luke stood as Nathan entered through the unlocked door. He looked as exhausted as they felt, but he smiled from ear to ear. "Hey, guys," he said, collapsing in a plush leather armchair near the fireplace.

"Hi. How's Rachel?" Victoria asked, folding the blanket and fighting a small tinge of disappointment she felt at the interruption.

"She's great. She was wonderful today… we have beautiful twin girls." Nathan laughed and shook his head.

"Twins?" Victoria's eyes widened. "But I thought the doctor was certain it was just one baby this time?" *Couldn't they tell those things on the ultrasound? Jeez, what if there'd been four in there?*

"Yeah, I saw only one baby on that ultrasound picture you carry around," Luke said as he collected the paper-towel rolls.

Nathan shrugged. "Sometimes, they get it wrong. Apparently one baby was hiding behind the other during the ultrasound and the heart beats were so in sync, the second one just sounded like an echo." He stared into space. "Five children."

"That's the number you two always talked about. Do you think you're done now?" Luke asked, tossing a blanket over his arm.

Nathan grinned. "*She* says we are. But she said that after each labor." He stood and stretched. "Looks like the kids had fun." Glancing around the room, he reached for a half-eaten cookie from a plate on the end table.

"We did, too," Victoria said.

"Well, thanks again for all your help. Are they upstairs?" Nathan headed into the hallway.

"Yeah, third room on the left. I'll help you," Luke offered, glancing toward Victoria as he headed up the stairs.

She smiled, then forced her gaze away from his. Collecting the dishes, she carried them into the kitchen. She set them in the sink and stared through the window into the big, snow-covered yard. The snow angels they'd made were still visible on the ground, illuminated by the back porch light. Five snow angels. Two big, three little. The perfect family. A tear formed in the corner of her eye. Maybe someday. She moved away from the window and gathered her sweater and purse from the closet in the hall. She opened the front door as Luke and Nathan descended the stairs, children still asleep in their arms, warm blankets draped over them. Smiling, she gathered their snowsuits and boots and carried them outside to Nathan's minivan.

Caleb stirred as Nathan fastened his seat belt. "Dad, did we miss Santa?"

Nathan shook his head. "No, buddy. It's still Christmas Eve." He kissed the little boy's forehead, as his eyes flitted closed. He turned to Victoria and Luke. "Thanks again. Stop by over the holidays." Nathan shook Luke's hand and gave Victoria a quick hug. "We're happy you're back," he added.

"Me, too."

Luke rubbed his bare arms in the cold.

"Sorry, I didn't even ask, Victoria, do you need a ride?" Nathan opened the driver's side door and waited.

"Um…" She hesitated, glancing toward Luke.

He remained silent, waiting for her response.

Baby steps. Today had been a good start to trying again…starting over. She would just have to be patient. In time he'd see they were meant for one another.

"Okay, yeah. That way Luke won't have to take me home," she answered, avoiding Luke as she took a step toward Nathan's van.

Luke grabbed her arm and waved Nathan away. "Get out of here," he said with a wink to his friend.

Nathan smiled as he climbed inside the minivan. He waved through the window, as he pulled out of the long drive.

Victoria studied the ground at their feet. "I really should go home, Luke. It's getting late."

Moving closer, Luke drew her into his arms. "You're already home," he said, softly kissing the top of her head and dusting the snowflakes out of her hair.

Victoria held her breath. "But, what about everything you said last night? You weren't wrong." She hated to admit it, but history had it that they just couldn't get this right, but maybe if they took things slowly.

"I was scared. I was stupid," he said, pulling away and his eyes met hers. He caressed her cheek and brushed a stray hair off her forehead.

"Aren't you still scared?" *She* was. In a short time, she'd come to realize how much he meant to her and she hated to think of a life without him. If they tried again and it didn't work, she'd be lost.

"Yeah, I am, but I'd rather be scared of losing you while holding you in my arms every night, than missing you and wanting you every day. I've already lived that way, and I choose us this time and I'm ready to fight... whatever it takes."

Tears froze on Victoria's rosy cheeks as she touched his face. "I love you, Luke."

Luke shivered as a blast of cold snow drifted around them. "I love you, too. Let's get inside. I bought some new mistletoe that I've been dying to try out."

Victoria raised her mouth to his and pressing her body close, she whispered, "Who needs mistletoe?"

* * * * *

The World of Mills & Boon®

There's a Mills & Boon® series that's perfect for you. We publish ten series and, with new titles every month, you never have to wait long for your favourite to come along.

Blaze®

Scorching hot, sexy reads
4 new stories every month

By Request

Relive the romance with the best of the best
9 new stories every month

Cherish™

Romance to melt the heart every time
12 new stories every month

Desire™

Passionate and dramatic love stories
8 new stories every month

What will you treat yourself to next?

*Ignite your imagination,
step into the past...*
6 new stories every month

INTRIGUE...

Breathtaking romantic suspens
Up to 8 new stories every month

Medical Romance

*Captivating medical drama –
with heart*
6 new stories every month

MODERN™

*International affairs,
seduction & passion guarantee*
9 new stories every month

nocturne™

*Deliciously wicked
paranormal romance*
Up to 4 new stories every mont

MODERN tempted™

*Fresh, contemporary
romances to tempt all
lovers of great stories*
4 new stories every month